M000284019

A Rose Blooms Twice

A Prairie Heritage, Book 1

by
Vikki Kestell

www.vikkikestell.com
www.facebook.com/TheWritingOfVikkiKestell

A Prairie Heritage

Book 1: *A Rose Blooms Twice*
Book 2: *Joy on This Mountain*

Scriptures quotations taken from
The King James Version (KJV), Public Domain.

The Amplified® Bible (AMP)
Copyright © 1954, 1958, 1962, 1964, 1965, 1987
by The Lockman Foundation (www.Lockman.org).
Used by permission.

Copyright © 2012 Vikki Kestell
All Rights Reserved.
ISBN-10: 0-9824457-3-3
ISBN-13: 978-0-9824457-3-0

A Rose Blooms Twice
Vikki Kestell

Available in Kindle and Print Format

Rose Brownlee must choose whether she will bow to conventional wisdom or, like Abraham, follow where God leads her ... even to a country she does not know.

Set in the American prairie of the late 1800s, this story of loss, disillusionment, rebirth, and love will inspire, challenge, and encourage you. *A Rose Blooms Twice* is Book 1 in the series, *A Prairie Heritage*.

Joy on This Mountain
Vikki Kestell

Available in Kindle and Print Format

The little town of Corinth, Colorado, lies in the gateway to the majestic Rocky Mountains just west of Denver ... just far enough from the city to avoid close scrutiny, but close enough to be accessible. Few know of the wickedness hidden in the small town, so picturesquely set in the foothills of the mighty mountains.

Joy on This Mountain is the eagerly-awaited sequel to *A Rose Blooms Twice* and is Book 2 in the series *A Prairie Heritage*. The legacy of Jan and Rose has far-reaching and unexpected consequences.

Dedication

Dedicated to my daughter, Maaike, who took a class in Kindle publishing and inspired me to explore the world of ePublishing!

Acknowledgements

Many thanks to my esteemed proofreaders, Cheryl Adkins and Greg McCann. I could not have done this without you! The Lord reward and bless you.

To My Readers

This book is a work of fiction, what I term "faith-filled fiction." The characters within its pages are not based on any known persons, but you may find that they are very real, indeed.

To God be the glory.

Chapter 1

The wilderness and the dry land shall be glad;
the desert shall rejoice and blossom like the rose . . .
(Isaiah 35:1, AMP)

Rose glanced up and saw James watching her. Their eyes met and held, and Rose's world was in that look. While the carriage jounced and swayed, they smiled, tired and content.

James' birthday party had been wonderful. Rose glanced fondly in the fading light from James' relaxed and satisfied face to each of the children. Jeffrey was teasing his younger sister, Glory, her chubby six-year-old cheeks dimpled in laughter, while baby Clara bounced on her daddy's knee singing "Ride a pony! Ride a pony!" softly. Jeff and Glory burst out in strains of "Happy Birthday to You" making James chuckle in appreciation. Clara crowed a late "To Yew!" after every line, and they all laughed.

Rose shivered a little as the temperature outside sank a few more degrees. Bundled in warm clothes nearly to their eyes, the children didn't seem to notice the cold. Only a few minutes ago, while Vincent, their driver, had waited patiently just outside the door, Rose had bustled Glory into her coat and warm hat, making sure she had her mittens. James had held baby Clara until Glory's last button was done.

"Goodbye, Mother. Thank you for the party; it was perfect as usual, just like its hostess," James had declared, winking and grinning rakishly.

Rose's mother had acknowledged the compliment graciously. "You know how much pleasure it gave me, James! And don't be flirting. What will your children think? Well, you had better be going. It will do none of you any good to be out in this miserable cold very long. Goodbye, dears."

She had kissed Rose, her son-in-law, and then each of the children. "My kittens," she liked to call them. Jeffrey, who had often complained to his father that, "if Grandma had to call him a baby name, it should at least be puppy," had been ready and fidgeting some minutes.

As they had crossed from the doorway to the carriage, the wind had whipped them mercilessly until they were tucked safely into the coach and Vincent had the horses pulling them down the drive.

Yes, everything had gone well. Mother had been a lovely hostess, as usual insisting on being allowed to prepare the celebration for James' thirty-eighth birthday party.

How very odd that he can be that age, Rose thought. *He was only twenty-five when we married, and yet he seems no older at all!*

"But *you* are thirty-two," an inner voice whispered, "and no longer a fresh-faced girl." The thought irritated her, and she pushed it aside. Thirteen years of marriage and three children had made a difference, yes, but she was still young. Not willow slender anymore, true, but "round in all the right places" according to James, and his was the only opinion she minded.

Only what looked back in her mirror distressed her. The golden blonde hair that had framed her blushing cheeks as a girl was dull ash now, stylishly coiled and curled around her head, yes, but her cheeks, too, had lost their glow. The overall result was a rather colorless, even sallow, one.

Oh, if only her brows and lashes had darkened, too, but the solemn gray eyes were the only real color in her face. Mercifully, the children all took after their father, each with honey-brown curls and James' gentle hazel eyes and bright cheeks. "Such frivolous concerns," she chided herself. "A good life is too precious for fretting over what cannot be changed—and is inconsequential. No triviality could ever mar the perfect joy of having a wonderful family and a happy home."

Her musings turned back to the party. Even Roger and Julia had been civil, almost pleasant tonight, for a change. That had been nice. James' younger brother had always seemed to resent that James, the older son, had inherited the Brownlee family home some years ago. It would be Jeffrey's one day too, Rose remembered fondly. Altogether, with her brother, Tom, and Abigail, his lovely bride, it had been a memorable evening.

Tom and Abby had made a happy announcement tonight, too. They would be blessed with a baby in late summer! Rose smiled in anticipation. She would be Aunt Rose! That would be sweet. And a cousin for the children! Roger and Julia didn't have children. "They wouldn't much fit our lifestyle," Julia had mockingly mentioned once.

"Mummy, I'm sleepy," Glory whispered.

"Come lay your head on my lap, love," Rose whispered back. Jeffrey and Glory traded sides in the coach; Clara stayed on Daddy's lap but cuddled now rather than bounced. Outside, the frigid January wind blew, and Rose was glad that Vincent was well sheltered in the driver's box. She pulled her own long, heavy cloak tightly about her and stroked a curl of Glory's lovely honey hair peeping out from her bonnet. It really was too inclement to be out, but January 6 only came once a year, and James rarely unbent from his heavy work schedule except for a holiday.

They seemed to be alone on the dark country road. In addition to the freezing temperatures this evening, the bitter wind had driven and beaten the wet snow into icy drifts and glazed the road.

"Only a half-hour more, son," James encouraged Jeffrey. The boy began nodding sleepily in the corner by his father.

They entered their quiet town with its cobbled streets. The river was just ahead, and the Brownlee family home a few miles beyond. The team's hooves rang hollowly as they mounted the bridge. Below, the river was choked with heaving, black ice floes. Only last week an unseasonable thaw, accompanied by a warm wind from the south, had caused the river to break up. Now with the cold settling back in, the rushing water would soon freeze over again.

The carriage was slow going up the bridge's incline because of the unsure footing for the horses, but they labored sturdily. Across the bridge they trotted now, another lone carriage passing them in the other direction.

Rose looked up and saw James watching her again. He smiled, and she warmed to his look.

The horses were going down the other side of the arched bridge now, and Vincent was calling to them, reining them in, for the ice was treacherous on the downside incline.

Without warning a horse screamed and the carriage lurched. One of the horses had fallen on the slick cobbles! James threw open the door just as the back end of the coach began to swing, making a wide, sliding arc across the breadth of the bridge. Vincent was shouting, panic in his voice. The carriage slammed against the stout railing at the bridge's edge with an ominous cracking.

Inside the carriage, unable to see what was happening, the children were shrieking, and Glory fell to the floor. James, holding precariously to the door saw what was now inevitable—the railing was shattered, near to letting go, and the carriage was suspended over the seething torrent, only moments from disaster. Vincent was standing in the box futilely whipping the team, but the one horse still standing had no traction, and the far one was splayed on the ice, thrashing in terrified panic.

Clara was grasping at her daddy's legs, and James stumbled over Glory on the floor. Hoarse with fear, he jerked Rose to her feet and to the doorway. "Jump!" he begged. They were hanging so deceptively near the levy.

Rose was frozen in terror, unable to look away from the pain, pity, and hopelessness on his face. James wrenched himself free from Clara's grasp and, with one extraordinary effort, bodily vaulted Rose from the coach.

As she was falling, falling, she could never later be sure if what she remembered was what she actually saw or if the horrible sounds printed their own pictures forever in her mind.

The railing gave way abruptly, and the carriage slid over the bridge's edge, pulling with it the screaming team. She landed on the ice-strewn rocks of the levee at the water's edge. Rose heard something inside herself snap and felt the painful stabs of icy water soaking her through as the current sucked and pulled.

Then she heard and felt nothing at all.

Chapter 2

Out of the black cave she fought her way. Surely daylight was ahead? But it kept moving away. Every time she thought she was at the opening it was farther beyond. Tired, so tired of trying.

Sleep instead.

It hurt to move. Her whole body was on fire, her head too heavy to lift. No, not fire, ice. Ice! No, no, no, they were falling in the river, freezing, numb . . . How can it be so hot in the river! Is the water burning? No, no . . . so cold . . .

She was in her room. Yes, this was her bed . . . no . . . yes! But . . . her room at home . . .that is, at Mother's where she grew up . . . silly, you're not grown up; you're just a girl. You had a bad dream. A dream about James and being married and . . . falling? So tired still . . .

"Mrs. Brownlee. Mrs. Brownlee, do you hear me? It's Doctor Cray. Please try to open your eyes for me, Mrs. Brownlee?"

"I'm sorry, Mrs. Blake, not yet, I'm afraid. But we'll know soon at any rate. If the fever has done . . . damage . . . well, we'll just hope for the best, shall we?"

"Rosie, don't leave us . . . please try to come back! You don't know how much we love you . . . I love you, Sis . . . oh, Rose, it's Tom! Do you hear me?"

Tom . . . so tired, so heavy . . . rest in the darkness.

Rose forced open her eyes. The light in the room was dim, either early morning or twilight, she couldn't tell. No one was in the room with her, it seemed; no, someone's regular breathing was coming from . . . the chair by the fireplace? She tried to turn to see but was too weak to do more than raise a few inches and fall back exhausted. All around her chest ached horridly.

"Mother?" she whispered weakly.

Well, later maybe.

The next time she awoke it was daylight. She lifted a hand feebly and groaned.

"Ma'am, she's awake. Ma'am!"

Several sets of footsteps hurried to the bed. Anxious faces peered down at her. Mother. Tom. Who was that man? Dr. Somebody she thought she remembered, and someone else standing away from the bed.

"Mother?"

"Yes! Yes dear, I'm right here!"

"Rosie, I'm here too—it's Tom, y'know!"

"Oh. . . . What? I'm sorry . . . I don't understand."

"Mrs. Blake, Mr. Blake, be so kind as to move back and let me examine our patient. Yes, madam, don't be alarmed. I believe you are going to be all right, but see here, you've been ill. Do you understand what I am saying?"

Rose nodded, and the doctor went on.

"You've been ill, and you've had a great shock. We must be quite careful of you right now or bear the consequences. Now, I am Doctor Cray—do you remember me?"

"Yes."

"Very good. Your mother and brother and a nurse are here with you also. It is enough that they are here—do not talk to them today for you must rest. I will come again this evening, and then we will see how you are. Do you understand me?"

"Yes," she answered again, because "no" was too heavy, and she was so tired.

"That is good; now sleep again. You are safe, and in time will be sound also, thank God."

"Yes, thank God!" Rose's mother added earnestly. Tom sat by Rose's bed and held her hand until sleep overcame her again.

Four days later they judged it wise to speak the truth to her. Her waking periods were closer to normal now, but reality was still a faint dream just beyond grasping, a truth that needed to be confronted. Mrs. Blake called Pastor Greenstreet to be with them. Tom and Dr. Cray completed the group, and together they stood around the bed. Tom felt it his duty to do the speaking, to help her the best he could through this ordeal.

"Sis? Rose, we want . . . need to tell you about your illness."

"Yes, Tom," she replied softly. "I can't seem to get it right in my mind. I'm so confused—tell me, what am I so afraid of?"

12

Tom began cautiously. "They found you, Sis, lying on the rocks at the bottom of the levee."

Rose looked bewildered.

"Well, you'd fallen there, see, and, well, Dr. Cray says you'd broken your ribs and hit your head mostly. The blow to your head made a bad cut, but anyway you were unconscious and then, see, you'd been lying half in, half out of the cold water and all, so you became ill with fever. We thought we were losing you, Rose! But you've gotten better, bit by bit; now you'll be able to get up soon."

A small frown puckered her forehead. "How long have I been sick, Tommy?" Her voice was almost childlike in its dreamy confusion.

Tom glanced at Dr. Cray for guidance. He nodded.

"It's been about three weeks, Sis. Since January 6?"

Puzzlement replaced the frown. Something nagged at the back of her mind. What?

"Rocks, Tommy? I don't understand where."

He took a deep breath and his voice quavered, "The rocks on the levee . . . by the river. By the . . . by the bridge. Close to your house?"

"My house? Bridge?"

Tom rushed on, looking down at the counterpane. "You see, Vincent crawled up to the road, and some folks saw him. He was nearly frozen because he was soaking wet, but we would never have found you in time if he hadn't gotten out. Of the river . . . Rose, do you remember falling in the river?"

Tears were streaming down his honest face, and Rose stared at him bewildered. River? What would anyone be doing in a river in January? January 6. Oh! James' birthday, of course! His birthday party and . . . the river . . .

Tom held her through the storm. Over again and again she saw the carriage sliding and falling, sliding and falling, James throwing her out . . . sliding . . . falling . . . Clara! Glory! Oh, God! My little boy! Oh, mercy, please God!

James, don't be dead . . .

Chapter 3

Over the weeks of her recovery, her memory became sharper—jagged tearing edges that wounded her with each recollection. Vincent had leapt from his box as the carriage struck the water and struggled in the ice-strewn water the few feet to shore. Bleeding and freezing, he'd climbed to the road atop the levee and flagged down a passing coach. They'd found Rose, as Tom had said, crumpled on the river-washed rocks. No trace of the carriage was found. Next day the river had frozen over again, and hope of finding James or the children died cruelly under the ice. No compassionate way existed to explain that sometime in the spring, when the water warmed, the bodies would surface, possibly far downstream, if at all.

Rose had been brought to her mother's home to be cared for, and when they began to hope for a speedy recovery from her injuries, fever had set in. For days the battle had raged: delirium, alternating chills, and periods of unbearable heat that devoured her strength.

That was when Roger Brownlee had presented himself to Mrs. Blake and Tom "to carry out a simple bit of business," he said by way of explanation. His attorney accompanied him, and they waited on Rose's mother and brother in the parlor.

"I realize how serious Rose's condition is—that she may very well not recover even. And we are deeply concerned for her of course, being my poor brother's wife—"

"My sister will recover, I assure you, sir!" interrupted Tom fiercely, "and I would have expected you to show proper consideration to us all at this time. What possible bit of business is so urgent that it cannot wait for a more propitious moment?" Tom's blue eyes sparked angrily at the man's effrontery. Tom had never cared for James Brownlee's younger brother. Tom had judged Roger Brownlee as lacking in moral character and natural affection the first moment they'd met.

Roger coughed politely. "Believe me; I have just lost my only family in this tragic affair. I feel, and my dear wife, Julia, feels, deeply, deeply, about Rose's condition. It is precisely the unsure state of things that brings me here—but may I introduce Mr. T.H. Carton of Carton, Simmons, and Northbrooke, our family and Rose's attorney. He has some timely information that will concern us all. Mr. Carton?"

Mr. Carton was a mild, honest man whose family's law firm had served the Brownlees for three generations. His father before him was counsel to the Brownlees. Mr. Carton disliked this sprig of the family tree and his task this evening, but he began gamely.

"Mrs. Blake, Mr. Blake, I offer my condolences on your losses and my sincere hope for Mrs. Brownlee's complete recovery." He stroked his short, brown beard nervously. "However, hmm, as you know, when the former, that is the *elder* Mr. Brownlee passed on, the Brownlee estate home was entailed to his older son, James. This included the grounds and furnishings. Some business holdings were attached also. The estate was to pass in time to young Master Brownlee, er, Jeffrey?"

Tom's jaw tightened and Mr. Carton became visibly uncomfortable, shifting his portly figure in his chair. However, he continued.

"Both Mr. James and Master Jeffrey being deceased, the will stipulates that the estate and estate holdings will revert back to the second son of the elder Mr. Brownlee, that is Mr. Roger Brownlee, here."

He stopped, smiling tentatively as if hoping that all were perfectly clear and he might be dismissed.

"Go on, Mr. Carton," Roger prodded tightly, "as we discussed on our way here."

"Ah yes, sir, of course, sir." Mr. Carton was perspiring in discomfort. "What we need to clarify tonight, of course, is that at the death of Mr. Brownlee (that is, James) and his son, Jeffrey, the Brownlee home and accompanying holdings (he swallowed here) became the property of Mr. Roger Brownlee, and—"

Tom's roar of indignation quenched Mr. Carton. "Do you mean to come here and tell me that my sister is now turned out of her home? That she is left with nothing?" Tom was on his feet. "This is outrageous! —Now, Mother, dear, don't cry, please, dear, we'll not put up with this, naturally!" Silent tears were sliding down the lady's cheeks, and Tom's hand reached down to cover her quavering one. "Mr. Carton, I cannot believe the effrontery of your coming here at this time and on such a mission! Why—"

"Now, Tom, don't jump to conclusions." Roger's voice and manner were smooth and conciliatory. "Do sit down and hear old

Carton out. There's a very pressing reason for this right now, and you'll feel better, I'm sure, when you understand our concerns. Now, Mr. Carton, please continue."

"Yes, sir. I do apologize, madam, for distressing you—please do forgive me and allow me a few more minutes. Just a few explanations will suffice. As I was saying, the estate reverts to Mr. Roger here. There is, however, a goodly sum belonging to Mr. James which becomes his wife's. Also his personal business holdings separate from the estate. Oh, no, she'll not be in any financial difficulty, I assure you, and we can see to the details of her property at your convenience, certainly. Which brings me to the primary, ah, purpose of this evening, which concerns the various business holdings I've mentioned."

Mr. Carton used his already moist silk kerchief on his upper lip again. "You see, for these past few weeks, the businesses have had no active supervision, and we feel this must be remedied immediately. For that reason and ah, personal considerations, Mr. Roger moved to take possession of the estate as of today. This of course includes the house and grounds. Because the future ability of Mrs. Rose to manage her affairs is in question, Mr. Roger suggests it would be prudent for him to oversee her finances and investments at this time, also. At any rate, Mrs. Brownlee's personal effects, those of her family, and the furnishings and household items separate from the estate will be packed and shipped to you for their care in the next few days." Mr. Carton wiped his gleaming face and hands with his kerchief and concluded hopefully, "Does that cover everything, Mr. Brownlee?"

"Yes, thank you, Mr. Carton. Let me say, Tom, that you are young and perhaps think I am callous in my handling of your sister's affairs, but business waits for no man, and we mustn't let sentiment keep us from doing what will ensure her future wellbeing, must we? In any event, that concludes our visit. I bid you both good day, and extend my sincere hope for Rose's rapid recovery." He smiled obligingly again and ushered Mr. Carton to the door.

"Mr. Brownlee!" Tom's voice held a measure of dignity beyond his experience. "The Blake attorneys will be in touch with you at the first possible moment. No doubt we cannot curtail the transfer of the estate, even in this indecorous and most irreverent manner. But my sister's inheritance from her husband will never be administered by you. We will take the proper steps to secure that immediately. And I will take this opportunity to say that your brother would be ashamed to see how you treat his wife today. Good day. Good day, Mr. Carton."

Rose's clothing had arrived next day, the first in a long line of boxes and dray loads of her belongings. Tom, accompanied by two attorneys from their own firm, had toured the Brownlee house (under Roger's close scrutiny) to ensure that Rose's interests were protected. The two law offices had consulted the provisions of the will concerning the estate and reviewed James' personal assets and holdings, transferring temporary control of them to Tom until Rose was able to make her wishes known. In all of this, Tom had stood in the gap for her, shedding much of the happy-go-lucky attitude of a young man and growing wiser under the responsibility.

Rose's physical recovery was rapid after the shock of the tragic disclosures, so Dr. Cray encouraged her to sit up in a chair whenever awake and to begin walking on a regular basis, increasing the length of the walks each successive day. Friends and neighbors called, expressing love and sympathy. Rose received them calmly and graciously, but remained somewhat detached. She made no effort to respond to callers or return visits. Emotionally she seemed to still be just semiconscious. She kept to her rooms except for meals and to receive visitors. Most of her grieving was done in private, but she could not altogether hide the vestiges of secret tears and the fact that her cheeks grew thinner. Those watching ached for the hurting heart she hid.

February drew to a close, and the cold remained unabated. Often Rose stood at the windows gazing in the direction of the river. On such a day Pastor Greenstreet called. The two sat in the parlor exchanging trivialities the way people do. Then for a time the conversation lagged, and Rose walked to the view of the river, gazing out with troubled, tear-filled eyes.

"Reverend," she burst out, "why did God allow this to happen to James, to my children—to me?" Anger broke the surface now and words, bitter words, came out in torrents. "How can I believe in a God who drowns little children! He's supposed to be all-powerful, so why did he do this? I don't think we were terrible people—Clara, my baby, never even had the chance to be a sinner. She didn't deserve—Oh, God! Did I do something wrong, and that's why I am still alive? For it's far greater punishment to be left alive, left alone, than to be dead—oh! I am so alone! Can I hate God for this, Pastor? I feel that I must, for he is become my worst enemy . . . Oh, why?"

"Dear, dear child," the old man murmured, putting a gentle hand on her heaving shoulders. Her head was bowed in her hands, desolation pouring from her broken spirit. Pastor Greenstreet felt quite inadequate at that moment as most do in tragedy. He was, besides, a quiet, reserved man of the cloth. He'd attended his seminary, worked hard at earning his superiors' approval, and earnestly tried to please and serve his congregation, as he wanted to help now. He was ashamed to admit in his heart to have no answer that really satisfied. Why, indeed? But feeling duty bound to repeat the answers he'd been taught, he attempted to put a good face on it.

"Mrs. Brownlee, my dear, we can't know what purpose this loss serves in God's plan. Surely he has a reason for allowing this and, if we are willing to say 'Thy will be done,' why, someday, in God's time, we will understand. In the meantime, you must ask God for patience to help bear this sorrow and to accept the changes in your circumstances."

"No! I will not accept it!" Rose's anger burst out again, her voice harsh and strained. "I've always been taught that God loves us. This is not love—I would never do this to my child!" Rose pushed back the distressed gentleman. "No! Either there is a real answer that shows me God truly does care or . . ." At this Rose recognized the seriousness of all she said but finished firmly, "or I will never believe in him again."

The door closed with a jolt as she quitted the room.

Later that night, winter winds beat at the house, shaking shutters and hurling frozen snow through the dark sky. Rose tossed in her bed trying to harden her heart against God. The rage was spent temporarily, and over and over her mind cried out, "Why? Oh, God, why?"

A conversation she'd once had with James came to mind. They'd often talked early in their marriage of their hopes and dreams. To Rose's naive thinking, James could only succeed at what he tried. His business was going through a difficult time just then, however, and he surprised her by confessing unexpectedly that evening, "I know that if I do my part—to the best of my ability—God will do his part."

She had questioned eagerly, "What do you mean by 'God's part'? What will he do?"

Now James was surprised. "Why, Rose! I thought you knew. Whatever he says in his book, of course." He took her soft hand in his, gazing with his steady hazel eyes into hers. "And my part is there, too, darling. Everything the Lord wants of me. That includes taking care of you and loving you truly all my life. I know that from the Bible, because my mother raised me to live by it, to live to please God. 'The Bible has all the answers to life,' she always said when I was young. She's been gone so long; I believe I'd forgotten much of what she told me. But I remember now. I'm trying to live that way, and if we have any question too big for us, why, surely we can find our solution there, too."

It wasn't "acceptable" to talk about God in such an open way in the society they moved in. Rose had grown up never even thinking seriously about eternal consequences. She had been raised to understand that if she lived a "good" life, was a proper wife and mother, and attended church faithfully, that heaven was her due. This other side of James affected her deeply, but they had never opened up to each other like that again. Instead, faithful to church and to charity, and single-minded to each other in marriage, they had gone on—until that January night.

Now, lying alone in the dark, Rose rethought, *The Bible has all the answers to life . . .*

Surely if it did, it would be easy to understand God. Why, everyone could. Rose stumbled out of her bed in her haste and fumbled to light her lamp. All her things were in boxes, in several rooms in the house. How would she ever find a Bible? Instead, Rose fled silently downstairs to the library. On a shelf she found several Bibles, none of them used or worn. *Perhaps no one knows because they've never really read it?* she wondered. But Pastor Greenstreet would have read it, wouldn't he? Creeping back to bed, she drew the covers up and expectantly opened the book. Page after page she scanned, recalling names and books from Sunday school days, but it didn't take long to discover, in frustration, that finding the exact piece of information she was looking for would not be easy.

"Begin at the beginning," she scolded herself. Genesis 1:1 was familiar, and she kept reading, forcing her eyes to stay open through the long hours of night and keeping watch for the answer she needed. Somewhere after Moses went up on the mount to meet with God, Rose's eyes closed, and the book slipped slowly from her fingers to her chest. Slumber was heavy on her in the dawn hours.

Too many restless, tormented nights had cheated her of deep, recuperative sleep. The human body will bypass emotion when neglected too long though, so when breakfast time came and Rose did not appear, kind Mrs. Blake crept into her daughter's bedroom and, finding the sleeper in peace, left her so for her own good.

Strong sunlight falling on her finally aroused Rose. The storm of the night had blown the sky free of clouds and, although the temperature outside remained cold, glorious sunshine warmed her room.

It was past lunchtime, so Rose hurried to climb out of bed. In her haste she threw back the covers, and the Bible, tossed by her impatient tug, fell to the floor where Rose stood. It lay open, and she quickly retrieved it, smoothing the bent pages back.

Her glance fell on the text. Tears started to her eyes. What did it say? Eagerly she scanned it again—and again! Oh, blessed hope! Was this a message to her? The passage read:

> *But if from thence thou shalt seek the Lord thy God,*
> *thou shalt find him,*
> *if thou seek him with all thy heart and with all thy soul.*

All her heart and soul! Is that what was required to find God? Amazed, she read on:

> *When thou art in tribulation,*
> *and all these things are come upon thee,*
> *even in the latter days;*
> *If thou turn to the Lord thy God,*
> *and shalt be obedient unto his voice;*
> *(for the Lord thy God is a merciful God)*
> *He will not forsake thee, neither destroy thee,*
> *nor forget the covenant of thy fathers*
> *which he sware unto them.*

Rose stood full in the sunshine, far away in her thoughts. Half of what she read made no sense at all, but those few words had kindled a small hope inside.

"O God," she prayed, "I want to know and understand you. I don't know how, but your Bible says to seek you with all my heart and soul. How do I do that? If I try, do you mean that you won't hide from me or hurt me? Is that what it means? Please help me, for I've been blaming you, and I don't know what to feel about that."

Over and over she read the three verses until they were committed to memory. Carefully she wrote down the reference, Deuteronomy 4:29–31.

Pacing the distance of her room, still deep in thought, she reached a decision. By her bed, on her knees, she made a pledge. "Lord, I will seek you. I only know to read the Bible and go to church. Somehow I don't know if church will help me find you. I've gone there all my life and it never did. But I do promise that I will seek you with all my heart and soul."

Rising quickly, she went down to find something to eat.

Chapter 4

Next Sunday Rose attended church for the first time since the accident. Many people greeted her warmly, but some avoided her. Maybe they were afraid to come too close to death or sorrow. Rose could only assume. Their behavior made her suddenly realize how wasted she must appear, but she was oddly unconcerned about it herself. Today she had more important things on her mind.

During the singing she listened studiously to the words, trying to draw upon them for help. All were lovely to be heard, but Rose couldn't grasp any meaningful message in them. A woman soloist stood behind a screen during communion and delivered a technically perfect song. Rose listened with her eyes closed—yet nothing touched her on the inside. Almost in tears of discouragement, she repeated "her" three verses under her breath. Instantly a feeling of hope welled up within. "Thank you, Lord," she breathed. "I haven't forgotten. All my heart and soul."

At last Pastor Greenstreet stood to deliver his sermon. For his text he chose St. John, chapter 10. Rose fumbled in her Bible to find it, turning pages back and forth in haste. Her mother glanced at her curiously and Rose, having at that moment found the right book, decorously turned to the tenth chapter as Pastor Greenstreet commenced reading:

Verily, verily, I say unto you,
he that entereth not by the door into the sheepfold,
but climbeth up some other way,
the same is a thief and a robber.
But he that entereth in by the door
is the shepherd of the sheep.
To him the porter openeth; and the sheep hear his voice:
and he calleth his own sheep by name, and leadeth them out.
And when he putteth forth his own sheep,
he goeth before them,
and the sheep follow him: for they know his voice.
And a stranger they will not follow, but will flee from him:
for they know not the voice of strangers.

"Let us pray! Our gracious heavenly Father, we thank you for this opportunity to join together as fellow pilgrims on this earth, looking to the time we may see you, if in your kindness we are counted worthy to be called one of your sheep. We ask that you make us truly worthy, in the name of your Son, amen."

"Today's scripture reading reminds us that each of us must come into the sheepfold to be received by God. The sheepfold represents the church today, and there is a door to enter that sheepfold, which, of course, is Holy Baptism. Those who have been born into Christian homes have been given a blessing indeed by the example of their parents and families. In America today, the church flourishes as fathers and mothers train their little boys and girls in the rudiments of church membership. Not all peoples have such benefits, as those who labor abroad in foreign fields can so ably tell us."

"Many, many, are like those who climb up another way—like a thief and a robber. They worship strange gods and participate in idolatrous ceremonies not even realizing how far from the fold they are. And yet the passage reads, *And the sheep hear his voice: and he calleth his own sheep by name, and leadeth them out.* Today, although many preach in those Godless lands, few are led out— because few know his voice. I can only conclude that few are his own sheep. Therefore we ought to give great thanks to God Almighty who has chosen us, yea, ordained us, that we should be called 'the sheep of his pasture; the work of his hand.' Let us stand and close with hymn number 319."

Rose stood with the congregation and sang along with the choir, but something in her heart was dismayed by the message. For so long she had never heard God's voice—and she had been a "church member" all her life! Surely there was more to being a Christian than being born into or joining a Christian church?

More dismayed, she wondered if she really had heard his voice.

"But if from thence thou shalt seek the Lord thy God, thou shalt find him," she whispered. She *would* find him, if there were any way!

Was there a way for the lost heathen of the pastor's sermon? Couldn't they find him if they sought him with all their hearts, too? It was all very confusing.

In the rear of the church members either lined up to shake the pastor's hand or went out the other door. Rose deliberately stepped into line.

"Why, Rose, what are you doing?" her mother asked, surprised.

"I'm going to say 'hello' to Pastor Greenstreet, Mother."

"But you saw him only this week when he visited—surely he will overlook our passing out the other door? You know how very fussy cook is when we dine late and her half-day is shortened."

"I'm sorry, Mother. I have something to say to him, and it's important to me. Would you wait in the carriage for me, please?"

Mrs. Blake made her way to a group of old friends, all members of the church from far back. Their bonneted and plumed heads bobbed together as she approached, and they were discussing how very ill Rose Brownlee looked. But what could be expected under the circumstances?

As soon as Mrs. Blake joined them they began to insist with one voice that Rose was appearing far better than they had believed possible.

Rose made no small talk when she shook the good parson's hand. She delivered her message to the point: "Pastor, the last time we spoke, I told you I would never believe in God anymore. I'm afraid I must have upset you terribly. I just wanted you to know that is all changed now. From now on, I am going to seek God with all my heart and soul. Then I will find him."

Pastor Greenstreet, a bit nonplussed by her succinct announcement, managed to provide a friendly "Well, well!" to cover the gap.

Rose believed he understood perfectly and went home happy. How blessed are the ignorant! And Rose was at peace for the present and willing to let the questions wait a time, not realizing that her decision was also the first step in getting her health back. Her greatest strength was the time now spent seriously pursuing her Bible reading.

Mrs. Blake expressed her curiosity about this distraction and began to feel it took too much of Rose's attention and concern, for the dear lady cherished hopes that Rose would become her companion in her various clubs, societies, and civic functions. Being a wise woman, she dropped her hints but tried not to push or pry.

About the preemptive loss of her home Rose was reconciled. Without James and the children what did it matter? Her feelings about Roger and Julia Brownlee were harder to deal with, so she pushed them down, burying them under the other grief. Roger and Julia, in turn, seemed to have forgotten she existed, but Tom insisted that their shame and greed kept them away. He also took time to explain her finances in detail and amazed, Rose responded,

"But it begins to sound as if I am a wealthy woman, Tom!"

"Certainly you have more than enough to be independent all your life, Sis. And bless James for such care as he took to make sure you would never want for anything should he be gone one day."

"Yes," Rose murmured softly.

"So to be sure you understand," Tom went on, "his life insurance, savings, and Jeffrey's college fund are cash in the bank. You needn't touch them though, because the investments I am handling will bring you enough income to maintain yourself—even in your own house if you like—quite comfortably. If you decide to buy a home or travel, the savings are there. Do you want me to continue taking care of your holdings? We can hire a broker if you like."

"Oh, no, Tom. I am quite satisfied with you, of course. And you shall draw a percentage from the income because you and Abby will have so many things to buy in preparation for the baby. In any case, I would pay a broker, and I would rather pay you—please?"

Tom acquiesced, secretly vowing not to take a penny.

"Rose, do you have any plans right now? It's almost spring, and Abigail and I have both thought that a short trip—perhaps somewhere warm—would benefit you. Fatten you up, you know," he smiled. "If you like, we could go with you. Be good for Abby, too."

She glanced ruefully at her ill-fitting dress and smiled too. "That is so kind of both of you, Tom. I can't even thank you and Abby enough or ever repay all you have done, have meant to me through . . .during these last two months. I . . . I love you, Tom, and a better brother could never be found."

They embraced. Their feelings of mutual affection had matured through this crisis, bonding their hearts together.

The suggestion of a trip planted a seed in Rose's mind, as time hung so heavily on her. With the absence of James and the children to do and care for, Rose wandered aimlessly about the house. At last she gave in to her mother and started to make the rounds of her favorite clubs and functions. Without fail Rose returned home empty and depressed. Most of the women were her mother's age or older yet, and any younger women were sad objects of pity—Mrs. So-and-So's maiden sister or poor Mrs. Nobody, a widow with five children and no money. Perhaps she might attend a dinner and if we invite Mr. Widower or old Bachelor, well, who knows what might happen?

The raw edge of Rose's grief made such maneuverings demeaning and repulsive. Thinly veiled pity hurt her even more and sank her in a classless caste of nonpersons. Women without husbands were misfits to be treated with kindness but not as complete persons. The whole sub-culture of women's aid groups and lunch clubs filled her with fear—fear of years to come consumed by joyless, meaningless work. Traveling, even for a brief time, became the inspiration for escape.

Where would she go?

"Where would I like to go?" she pondered.

It occurred to her slowly that nothing and no one prevented her from doing exactly as she pleased.

This novel idea, first unnerving, almost set her quivering with excitement. The next minute the very lack of restriction made her desperate with anxiety.

"I won't go flying off just anywhere. I should plan and have a definite itinerary, with places to visit and things to see and view. Not out of the country, though." The thought of getting on a boat and being surrounded by water nearly made her ill in her stomach.

Rose took immediate steps; she visited the train ticket office and returned home with a neat packet of schedules. The next day she found a travel coordinator and brought home colorful brochures touting resort hotels and seaside cottages. She found maps in the library and spread them out in her room.

With schedules and brochures in hand she explored one possibility after another, discarding some ideas and jotting down others in a little notebook she had purchased. For days she was caught up in the excitement of planning and, with a start, realized that spring was close at hand.

What she was considering was a real prospect—and the time was approaching when these "fantasies" could actually be implemented. Still, she was undecided. She could visit New York—New York had much more to see there than she would ever be able to take in! Savannah was a possibility—Savannah had wonderful hotels and beaches.

A combination tour of several cities suggested itself. Yes, New York would be fashionable (or Boston for that matter); Savannah would be restful and promised good food. For sheer busyness she could travel the trains up and down the seaboard and see and eat the best of everything! After all, Tom and Abby needn't go and be worn out. She didn't envision them with her anyway. No, this was going to be a solitary trip, without others to take into consideration. She wanted the independence almost as much as she was afraid of it! Oh, yes, they'd raise a fuss ("they" meaning Mother), but what could they do?

Rose laughed aloud. "I have my own money and may do as I please! Well! I may as well be pleased by what I do."

Dinner that night was pleasant; Tom and Abigail joined them and the meal was served in a congenial, even festive atmosphere.

At one point, Tom, with grinning hilarity, announced, "I say, the most remarkable thing was in the paper today! Do you remember Raymond VanBourne? Well, it appears he has sold his business, his home—virtually everything!—to take his family out west! Something about cattle ranching in Montana or Dakota Territory. I really couldn't envision it, but Sam Toole, (do you recall him, Rose?) was in the Post Office today and insists it's true. Well! I can just see Marie VanBourne in a clapboard contraption—she must be in sorry straits at this point. Anyway, Sam says VanBourne's family raised dairy cows for several generations, and he figures raising cattle is the next best thing to getting back to the family business and will be a whole lot more profitable—if he doesn't lose his shirt (I beg your pardon, Mother) in the process." He chuckled and shook his head.

"Surely he has weighed the possibilities, dear," Abigail interposed gently, "and must feel he will have more than a measure of success. As for Marie, she is a strong, cultured woman and will make a great contribution to the civilizing of that country. Someone must be brave enough to do it, although I am not sure I could be."

Tom grinned. "Why, Abby! You never cease to surprise me. Imagine, a pioneer spirit right in my own home! I'll go out first thing tomorrow to buy a covered wagon."

"Oh, Tom!"

Rose had listened silently, her interest held. West! What a novel thought. Later that night she scanned her maps and schedules where she hadn't before considered. Illinois, Minnesota, Iowa, Kansas, Nebraska, Dakotas, Montana, Colorado, all with railway connections. Indians, too, she shuddered. Her mind was turning these new possibilities over as she readied for bed. At last, pulling the covers up and getting her Bible from the lamp table by the bed, she began her nightly reading. The page before her couldn't keep her attention, though. She kept visualizing maps, schedules, and the western states—and a whole frontier beyond that!

Rose shivered. "I might consider riding a train somewhere, but I'm no real pioneer. I'm too much of a coward!"

Since she couldn't concentrate on her reading, she turned back to "her" verses, Deuteronomy 4:29–31. A phrase she hadn't noticed before caught her eye:

> *. . . If thou turn to the Lord thy God*
> *and shalt be obedient unto his voice . . .*

Obedient to his voice?

"How can I be obedient to his voice, if I can't hear it, if I don't even know what his voice sounds like?" Rose was irritated. "This isn't fair, and I don't know what to do now. If I take this trip—any trip—I don't know if I'm obeying him if I do, or for that matter, if I don't!"

She slammed the book closed. Immediately she was contrite and whispered, "Lord, I'm sorry, please forgive me. Do you want to speak to me? I'm listening."

For a while Rose waited expectantly; then sighing, she opened her Bible again. It opened to Genesis 12, and she read,

> *Now the Lord had said to Abram,*
> *get thee out of thy country,*
> *and from thy kindred, and from thy father's house,*
> *unto a land that I will shew thee.*

The hair pricked on Rose's neck. This wasn't the way one heard God's voice! She quickly turned elsewhere to escape the eerie coincidence. The verse at the top of the page read,

> *Fear thou not; for I am with thee:*
> *be not dismayed; for I am thy God:*
> *I will strengthen thee; yea I will help thee;*
> *yea, I will uphold thee with the right hand*
> *of my righteousness.*

Rose jumped from her bed, sending the Bible flying. In a chair by the fire she sat, all scrunched up and shaking.

"I'm not going to look at any more maps or train schedules," she vowed. "This is too much. I'll turn into a fanatic if I go on like this!"

About an hour later she went back to her bed, having convinced herself to go to the ocean in May. Bending over and retrieving the open Bible on the floor these words stared up at her:

By faith Abraham, when he was called
to go out into a place
which he should after receive for an inheritance, obeyed;
and he went out, not knowing whither he went.

Obeyed. Rose began to weep, her tears spilling on the pages.

. . .obeyed . . . not knowing whither he went.

Chapter 5

For two days she kept her maps and schedules hidden in a drawer. The immensity of what she was considering . . . what would she tell her mother? What would Tom say?

Sunday she again stood in line to shake Pastor Greenstreet's hand. He looked a trifle embarrassed when she asked him aloud, "Pastor, does God talk to people today? If he does, how do you hear his voice?"

Several heads swiveled their direction immediately, and he coughed and smiled. "Well, God may not speak in an audible voice today, say, as he did with Moses, but certainly we may feel he is always telling us to do good and help others?" This last was a little weak and evasive, but Rose didn't notice, and went on innocently,

"Yes, but when he talks to *you*, Pastor, how do you know it's really him?"

Now the attentions of more than a few were firmly fixed on their conversation, and poor Reverend Greenstreet hemmed and hawed before responding, "Mrs. Brownlee, one can always trust the Bible, I say. One will never get into trouble following the Bible example."

Rose beamed her thanks, the poor man breathed a sigh of relief, Rose was shuffled off with no further ado, and the next hand was shaken with real fervor.

Rose wandered slowly to the carriage, pondering this happy information. Later she read the whole passage in Hebrews 11 from verse one to forty over again and again. Parts were understandable, others referred to characters and events she was unfamiliar with. But the message was clear. God expected you to have "faith" in him.

Exactly what faith *is* was the mystery. Yet all those people had done something that God approved of, and he called it "faith." The maps and schedules came out of the drawer and Rose utilized her notebook again. She had to decide what to carry on the train in her bag, what to pack in her trunk.

What to say to her family! Ignoring that, she renewed her planning.

A note was penned to Tom:

> *Dear Tom,*
>
> *I've decided to take your advice and go on a trip. Be a dear, please, and take a few hours off this afternoon to discuss details with me?*
>
> *Your loving sister,*
>
> *Rose.*

Tom's ring at the door came at four. "Sorry it's so late, Sis!" he called merrily. "Couldn't get away, and then got caught at the door and pulled back. I hope I didn't offend that last client when I rushed him out. Now, where are we going?"

Rose had two chairs pulled in front of the fireplace, and they sat together cozily. "I've been thinking about a trip—like you suggested—but I don't want to trouble you and Abby to accompany me right now. You're busy at the office, and Abby is expecting and, well, you don't need to come. I'll just go by myself."

"By yourself? Where do you have in mind? The seashore? That might be all right, but why don't we come along? You know, just for company, hey? I can get away—hang the office anyway."

"Oh, Tom! You've worked too hard building your clientele. You don't fool me, you know. Besides, dear brother, I want to go alone. No, listen, please. I've quite made up my mind—and I have my reasons, too."

Tom was looking at her a trifle puzzled and a little hurt. Rose took his hand and squeezed it in reassurance.

"Tom, all I can say is it's . . . it's a kind of pilgrimage. Can you understand?"

"Pilgrimage? Like a religious trip?"

"Well, yes, something like that."

"Can't you tell me where you're going?" He pulled at his collar a bit. "I'm sorry, Rose; I don't wish to see you do anything hurtful or foolish."

"Thank you, dearest of brothers. I won't be foolish, I promise. My trip is on a train . . . west."

"And where west? Just "west" isn't enough, you know!" His face folded into a concerned frown.

"Well, call it a sight-seeing tour. When I buy my ticket here you'll know where I'm headed, and if I change direction I can wire you. Really, Tom, if I stay with the trains, what harm could I come to? I'll be perfectly fine." She said this with a little more conviction than she felt and smiled to compensate.

"I never noticed before how you can look like Father when you have your mind made up. Something in the chin perhaps." Tom stared at her earnestly. "And I cannot talk you out of this?"

Rose's smile grew. "I think you know you can't, dear heart."

Tom stood up and ran his hand through his hair distractedly. "I hope you know how Mother will receive this. Lord! Why couldn't you have gone to the seashore?" His humor was reasserting itself. "So when do you cry 'wagons ho'?"

"That's more like you, Tom! I knew I could count on you. My birthday is next week. I think Mother would be hurt if I left before that. So, tentatively, in ten days' time."

"So soon?"

"Yes; I have my reasons."

"So you said, little pilgrim."

"Thank you, Tom. Will you help with Mother?"

"Sure thing. As Abigail said, someone has to civilize the frontier." He leaned down to kiss her cheek before letting himself out.

Rose's birthday was the happiest day she'd had since January 6. Her mother, Tom, and Abby worked hard to make the celebration a memorable one, and Rose couldn't help but feel the love that motivated them. Mrs. Blake's gift to Rose was a crocheted shawl of deep spring green edged in beige. "For your brown traveling suit, Rose dear." It was Mother's way of conceding her reluctant acceptance of Rose's journey after vigorous disapproval. Tom and Abigail presented her with a roomy, dark red carpetbag. Inside were new slippers, wrapper, and night gown.

"How perfect, how very perfect!" Rose was delighted. "Now, I have gifts for you!" She had managed to surprise them all and dismissed it lightly as a whim.

"Mother, here is yours, and Tom and Abby, here are yours." They opened identical envelopes and found tickets and prepaid reservations at the beach for late June. Even Mrs. Blake chuckled delightedly.

"How thoughtful of you, dear! Mrs. North will be perfectly envious. And Tom and Abby for company! Why, Abby, what a blessing getting out of the city will be at that stage of your development. Two cool weeks at the ocean."

"But you will be back by then, won't you, Rose?" Tom asked intently. "You will go with us?"

Rose brushed his questions aside. "In any event, I'll probably have other obligations in June, but don't worry about it. It could work out."

Cook brought the lovely pink-frosted cake into the dining room followed by the staff, who joined in singing "Happy birthday to you!" She thanked them all with tears in her eyes. When would this family circle be together again?

The echoes of their singing came back to her that night as she lay in bed, and in her mind Rose imagined she heard a baby voice piping "to yew!"

Chapter 6

Rose lifted her cheek to Tom's goodbye kiss while he held her hands in his. He grinned his "little brother" grin but spoke soberly.

"Sis, I know this change of scenery will be good for you, so don't be worried about Mother's fussiness. I'll see she has company and doesn't get too lonely—but you mind your 'Ps' and 'Qs' and see we have nothing to worry about, right?"

The look of manly concern on his face made her proud and caused tears to prick her eyes. He stared down for a moment and then continued, still keeping her gloved fingers in his.

"Only don't be gone too long, Rosie. What I mean is . . . You will be coming back, won't you?"

Good Tom! Her loyal champion, proven and true. Rose disliked distressing him. And yet she mustn't fool herself into believing her future was bound up in his. Tom had Abigail and a child coming soon.

"Tom, dear, I promise I'll do what I believe is best for me. Will that please you?"

His curly head nodded mutely. Rose stretched up to plant her kiss on his cheek.

"Give my love to all. I will write soon."

She turned and the porter took her traveling bag in hand and assisted her to mount the steel steps into the train. A few minutes sufficed to settle in the car he led her to but she was on the wrong side of the train to see Tom. The cars lurched backwards as the conductor strode through shouting, "Allll abooooard!"

One unoccupied seat remained on the other side of the car, and she hurried to its window. Tom was searching anxiously for her. His face cleared when he saw her waving.

What am I doing? Rose wondered. Fear surged up into her throat and her mouth went dry. The train moved forward sluggishly, great puffs of black smoke belching from its engine. In panic she thought, *I can still get off! I should go back!* But she stayed, waving until Tom's blonde hair was blocked from view.

Cautiously she returned to her seat, inwardly cringing from every stranger around her. She sat still in the seat and watched the station as they passed through and beyond, faster and faster. Brushing the unwanted tears away, she pressed her lips tightly together in resolve.

"If God has spoken to me, then I will be led by him. I'll find the right place because he will show it to me, and everything will be all right. At the very least I will have obeyed him."

She drew a measure of strength from the thought, and out of her bag she pulled her notebook. With pencil in hand she began to make plans. When no one appeared to harass or intimidate her, she relaxed and the day passed quickly. In and out of busy stations, rolling south for now through bare fields and smoky cities they steamed. New faces arrived and familiar ones departed. The car wasn't overly crowded, and no one came to claim the seat next to her.

Rose had never traveled alone before, but as long as no one made familiar, she was happy to be left singular with a warm glow of *this is it!* running around in her heart. Her scribbling continued until the porter surprised her by announcing dinner. Even alone in the dining car her serene mood remained. She lingered over her coffee until the porter showed her to her sleeping compartment. The swaying of the train was soothing, and her thoughts wandered.

"I am thirty-three years old now. And for the first time in my life I am doing something on my own." The newness of the experience was satisfying, and she recalled a similar one from when she was thirteen years old. She and Tom were returning from town in their family's carriage when Tom pointed out Pastor and Mrs. Greenstreet walking. Rose took it into her mind to stop the coachman and invite them to ride up. They were happy to and expressed their thanks to such a degree that Rose was inspired to invite them to dinner.

Such an invitation was proper, and the circumstances did warrant it, but she knew full well Father's particular aversion to mixing socially with preachers, even their own. He went to church on Sundays, and that was duty fulfilled. One didn't have to see the minister outside of church, after all! Rose chatted pleasantly with the Greenstreets, quenching every other consideration and ignoring Tom's goggling stare, and soon handed them neatly, with grace as befitted a young lady, into her mother's keeping.

Such an afternoon! Everything was of course properly gone through and the Reverend and his wife enjoyed their dinners immensely. But Rose had never seen such struggles for composure in her parents.

"Whatever possessed you to do such a thing, Rose?" her mother remonstrated fruitlessly that evening. Mr. Blake had merely retired to his study in tight-lipped silence and had not reappeared for supper.

"Why, Mother, did I do something wrong?" Rose had inquired sweetly.

"No child, of course not." Her harried mother left the room, defeated, to speak placations to an indignant cook.

Rose laughed aloud at the reminiscence and smothered her face in the pillow of her rocking sleeper car. Yes, she was stepping out like that again. This time looking for . . . *a place . . . a place to dream,* she thought sleepily. *I can always go back,* were her last conscious thoughts. *Trains run both directions.*

The train carrying Rose on her venture in faith stopped early the next morning, and she was required to transfer to another one. This new vehicle was pointed due west and began its chugging progress through heavily populated communities and small patches of country and past landscapes the likes of which were new to her experience. Rose stared transfixed for hours at the unfolding miles.

They stopped often, sometimes only for an hour or a few hours to take on coal, water, or other passengers. Twice they stopped overnight, and Rose would enjoy a hot bath and a "real" bed in a hotel—taking care to return in plenty of time for the train's departure. One day began to blend with another, and all the while she kept her Bible close by, waiting for some indication, some direction.

The passing scenery was more open as the days sped by. Farms abounded now, newly plowed. Any cities were mostly smaller and farther apart. Miles to the north were the Great Lakes, she was informed, the inland fresh water seas of America. Rose had no real desire to see large bodies of water, and they had already crossed more rivers than she could count. Still she paid her fare and rode on.

Every other day she wrote a letter to her mother, Tom, and Abigail combined. She knew they would all read each other's letters from her so she just wrote the one, filling it full of colorful descriptions and observations.

Her most meaningful comment was how the whole land was coming alive right under her watching window. To Rose, it was like seeing a flower unfold before her eyes, and she always remembered the sweet joy of it in years to come.

Some days she was forced into company. Most was pleasant; with other companions she remained silent and aloof. Once a drunken young man presumed to talk to her but a gentleman passenger alerted the conductor, and the two of them removed the offending individual. Then in Illinois, she faced a swiftly approaching choice: Would she go north, south, or across the Mississippi? Mainly because it was the most daring thing to do she continued straight west.

The day they crossed the wide river a spasm of trepidation came on her, and haunting memories of the icy tragedy besieged her. However, seeing the broad expanse of water flowing calmly in the warm April sunshine banished the ice-choked images. This river wasn't the frozen deathtrap of her imagination! It could be gotten over.

Into the homestead and frontier country they went. Rose had already seen more of "real life" on this trip than she'd ever seen in her sheltered existence; now she began to experience it too.

The nicer trains with new upholstery and sleeping cars were gone. She found it difficult to sleep in the same seat she also spent the day in and harder still to keep up her standards of grooming. Often she would walk up and down the aisles of the car to get relief from aching bones and cramped muscles.

More than once she put her head slightly out of an open window, risking soot or cinders to briefly escape the smell of soiled babies, greasy food, and unwashed bodies. Finally, one evening, the train slid into a small town, and the conductor announced a layover of several hours.

Instantly Rose was on her feet. She questioned the conductor at length and then returned to her seat and pulled her bag out. She was going to take a rest from riding trains! Stepping down from the car without assistance (no fancy porters out west!), she made her way to the ticket office, spoke to the man about her trunk, and turned to the town's main street. A clean hotel was her desperate concern—and there it was!

Chapter 7

The next morning Rose felt like a new woman. She had gotten a room from a Mrs. Owens who managed a genteel boarding house and had even finagled a long, hot soak. Rose had washed her wheat-colored hair twice, rinsing it in lavender water. Finally, with a clean gown on and the smell of smoke, food, and other unmentionable odors cleansed from her senses, she'd slept long and soundly. The sun was far up and breakfast past when she opened her eyes. But what did it matter? She was off that moving train, and would not get back on until she was good and ready to.

The town was certainly primitive by city standards, but somehow on this morning it was quaintly pleasant—and besides, it was standing still and the breeze offered a delightful mixture of fresh, natural scents. She looked around curiously. There were so many strange sights, sounds, and people. And here it was spring, wonderful, wild, western spring. Even the wide prairie views all around the town were green and alive. From what she'd heard and read, prairies were dreary and dry, but these weren't! Somehow she must find a means to get out from town a distance to really see it.

The people in the streets were dressed far more casually than she was. Rose turned right and found a "general store," a sort of mercantile/dry goods and grocery combined. Shyly she entered to the rustic clerk's cordial greeting in an accent unfamiliar to her. Thus encouraged, she fingered some of the yard goods and notions while trying to surreptitiously see everything else in the store. Her clothes were definitely out of place here with their sweeping skirts and yards of ruffles. Most of the women made their own clothes, she surmised by what she saw, and made them more for service than style.

Other people were looking too, Rose finally noticed. At her. A faint flush crept up her neck, but she bore their scrutiny well. The discreet appraisals from the other customers were friendly and frankly admiring.

Back out in the warm sunshine, she strolled the remainder of the street and found a very respectable-looking establishment with a prominent sign that read "RiverBend Savings and Loan: Real Estate, Bonds, Investments."

Rose let herself into the tidy front office and was ushered into the presence of a young "Mr. Robert Lewis Morton, Loan Executive," complete with suit, vest, and ascot. A definite transplant.

"Hmm! I shall get on very well here!" she smiled to herself and Mr. Morton as he rose to make introductions. His quick brown eyes summed her up, and he self-consciously adjusted his tie while seating her opposite his desk.

Yes, she'd just arrived last evening while traveling and sightseeing. A short layover to recover from the rigors of the train, she responded to his questions. No, she was traveling alone. His eyebrows went up slightly in what Rose took to be disapproval.

"This is a charming little town, Mr. Morton," she went on, ignoring his look. "Tell me something about the area and the people living here. I'm particularly interested in the lovely countryside."

"Ah, Mrs. Brownlee, RiverBend is a humble but hard-working community. It is a small part of a larger, mainly agricultural area. Many families have farms acquired by homesteading, (an extremely demanding way to earn a farm, I assure you!) and are now successful in their endeavors. We have a variety of nationalities represented 'round about: German, Irish, Swedish, and your plain, garden-variety American."

"All good quality mostly. Even have a small Norwegian group. Not much different from the Swedes as far as I can tell, but they'll tell you how different. Do a little dairying too, although we don't foresee dairying as a major growth here—too far west, at least right now. Still, they're prosperous folk. Very determined and industrious. Do almost everything. Have to way out here! Well, we're also proud have a little church, three schools (one in town, and two in the country), and socials often enough to keep everybody happy."

"And we're growing! Why, our town has doubled in population in the last three years. My goodness, yes, many folk from back east, down south, and even from foreign countries have found a good life here. I myself am finding great success in my business."

He paused to let that impress her while he drew a breath. Running his eyes over her fashionable attire once more, he suggested brightly, "Perhaps you would care to see some of the country? I have a buggy, the weather is fine, and there is a business property I must examine. Would you be available to accompany me on a day excursion tomorrow? We could, say breakfast at seven-thirty at Mrs.

Owens' and leave around eight-thirty while it is still cool, take a basket lunch, and return in the early evening?"

Secretly, Rose was delighted at the prospect of being shown the countryside, but she was not particularly impressed by the forwardness of Mr. Morton, so she replied with a studied politeness, "Perhaps we can meet around nine o'clock, Mr. Morton, and tour as you graciously offered. I will have Mrs. Owens prepare a lunch and let her know I will be back by tea time."

"Of course, of course, madam, just as you say! Nine o'clock sharp will be fine," he smiled ingratiatingly.

"Well, then, Mr. Morton, I thank you for your time and hospitality."

She stood, keeping her manner indifferent and civil. It wouldn't do to have Mr. Morton or any man attaching significance to her behavior. She would be doubly careful from now on.

A chain of thoughts unfolded as she made her way back to the boarding house. How very much her life had altered since that night in January! That a gentleman saw her as an object of possibility was both surprising and hurtful. She still found it difficult to accept her single status.

That she was a woman of independent means made her more vulnerable to those whose interests in her money might be of first consideration. Mr. Morton struck her as just such a man. She had to be at least six years older than him.

"I am still Mrs. James Jeffrey Brownlee. No one can take that from me!" she muttered defiantly. Somehow the pleasure of the day had waned, and she retired to her room. With a disciplined determination, she pulled her Bible from her bag and settled in a chair by the window to read. Her passage was in I Corinthians, chapter four. Verse 7 spoke to her strongly:

> *For who maketh thee to differ from another?*
> *And what hast thou that thou dids't not receive?*

"Yes," she reflected, "I have a portion of security, even wealth to some, and yet it was all given to me. I never worked a day for such abundance. It is God who has blessed me."

Rose stopped and bowed her head and sincerely thanked him for what she had. She acknowledged, too, that her many questions remained unanswered and lifted them up to the Lord again. But now with a newly found gratitude she felt a closeness to him that she'd lacked before.

Reading on, she was moved to tears over Paul's hardships and persecutions. No one had inflicted pain on her out of meanness or spite as they had Paul. Everyone had tried to comfort her. How alone he must have often felt and yet, at the end of the chapter, a verse stood out like a beacon:

For the kingdom of God is not in word, but in power.

Rose marched around the room in her excitement. Now she began to understand why Pastor Greenstreet's words held no conviction or comfort—they had no power! Where did one get the power Paul was talking about? For a long while she stood, lost in reflection.

A knock on her door brought her out of her meditation. Mrs. Owens, the owner of the boarding house, was standing there, warmly polite.

"Your trunk was delivered this morn'. Are you wanting it sent up, Ma'am?"

"Oh, yes, thank you!" Ah, the man at the depot was as good as his word. Now she would have a selection to choose from for her excursion tomorrow. The freight man had promised to call for her trunk any day she chose to continue her journey, but right now it would be good to have her things available. Trains running west arrived and departed Tuesdays and Thursdays, barring delays.

After the man brought her trunk to her room, Rose opened it and gently unfolded the tissue surrounding a deep blue skirt and jacket. She began working the creases out with her hands and found some hooks to hang the clothes on. Both of her traveling suits, as fashionable as they might be, were stained and road weary, while this ensemble was fresh and "springy." The dark suit would also convey the measure of decorum needed in a lady still in mourning. Against the inside of the trunk was another box, and she managed to extricate it without disturbing the rest of her careful packing. A brimmed straw hat of natural color, trimmed with royal and white ribbons and a simple nosegay at the crown was snugly fitted inside.

"I'll need this if I don't want to burn myself red," Rose muttered to herself. She found a lovely, clean shirtwaist and fresh stockings too. Putting the outfit in order, she closed the trunk and went to work sponging and brushing the two suits worn on her trip, rinsing out stockings, gloves, and lingerie, feeling generally useful and self-sufficient as she toiled.

"My friends at home would be speechless could they see me at this moment. And wouldn't Mother fuss about my hands?" Rose smiled as she worked.

Dinner was served soon. Later, Rose finished refitting her wardrobe by brushing and blacking her shoes and retiring early. Tomorrow promised to be a new experience, and she was looking forward to it. Before she fell asleep, she thought of James. Would he have approved of her "therapy"? What would he have done if he had been the one left alone?

Buried himself in work, no doubt. But I have no work. No place in society other than attending endless ladies aid meetings with other widows whose lives have no purpose, except possibly to remarry. Surely God will guide me, as he guided Abram, as he led Moses? Or is that only for great men of the Bible?

Rose threw off the troubling new thoughts by once more reminding herself, *I can always go back.*

But she hoped, somehow, that she wouldn't.

Chapter 8

Rose was seated in the dining room promptly at eight the following morning. A young girl she'd not seen before laid the cloth and asked if she would like some coffee.

"Yes, please. That would be nice."

The girl had a lithe figure clad in brown and white gingham under a stiff, white apron. Her hair was a wonderful auburn, two sleek braids coiled at the nape of her neck and pinned. Her complexion was deeply glowing; in all she was the picture of a healthy, lovely girl. She answered Rose's smile with a bright one of her own, so Rose spoke to her when she brought her cup.

"I'm visiting here a few days; my name is Rose Brownlee."

"Yes'm, I'm knowin' that. My name is Meg McKennie—that is, Margaret; I'm just bein' called Meg."

"That's a sweet name, Meg," *and your brogue is enchanting*, she added silently. "I didn't see you yesterday when I had my meals. Were you gone somewhere?"

"Yes'm. I went to me folks to see me new brother just born three day ago. They live about six miles out, and I was wanted to be helping some, so Mrs. Owens said I might have a day. Most days I'm helping serve here, 'cept Sundays."

"A baby brother! Why, you are almost grown yourself! Have you a large family, Meg?"

"This is makin' six. But there haven't been any babies for a while. The next 'un is eight years. That's Martha. I'm eldest and sixteen. Beggin' your pardon for a wee moment, Mrs. Brownlee."

Meg poured coffee at two other tables in the dining room, then disappeared into the kitchen. When she returned she placed Rose's breakfast in front of her. A luscious piece of ham, two biscuits covered with gravy, and a dollop of spicy-looking applesauce filled the plate.

"This looks very appetizing, Meg," Rose said. "By the way, I'm riding out to see some of the countryside today with Mr. Morton from the bank. Do you believe I'll be quite safe in his company?"

"Oh, surely, a lady will be right with Mr. Morton. 'Round here folks be worrying more 'bout their money wi' him!"

"Do you mean he's not honest?" Rose asked, shocked.

"Nae, he's honest enow, but me mother says if he could figure how, he'd be charging a spider rent for spinnin' a web on his property."

She laughed at Rose's shocked expression, then Rose joined her, because Meg's description was not only humorous, it also fit Rose's first impression of the man.

"Some folk who borrowed money of him find he 'lows no slack in t' payin' back, even when times be hard. But that's not drivin' now, is it, I'm thinkin'? And 'tis bein' a foine day fer it, too!"

"I should be back by tea time, Meg. Do you have any time of your own today?"

"Yes'm. Three-thirty to four-thirty I may call me own afore I must be helpin' with th' dinner. An' we're not in the custom of servin' tea, I'm that sorry of."

"That's all right, Meg. I'll be sure to be back by three-thirty and, if you like, we can have tea in my room. I have my own little packet of tea, and we'll have some cookies from the store and talk together. Would you like that?"

"To be sure! Thank ye most kindly, Mrs. Brownlee."

"Good. Then you'd better give that gentleman over there his other cup of coffee, and I'll see you this afternoon, all right?"

Meg flashed her glowing smile and hurried off to get the coffeepot. Rose ate her breakfast heartily, surprising herself. If she continued eating like this, her clothes might begin to fit again rather than slide around like they belonged to someone else. Perhaps it wasn't obvious to a stranger that she'd been ill and grieving; still, she couldn't help contrasting young Meg's vivid, apple-red cheeks to her own thin, sallow ones. Mr. Morton would do well to not appear too interested. Aside from her money, Rose laughed wryly to herself, she had few attractions.

The morning coolness slipped away on a warm breeze. Meadowlark and killdeer practiced their warbles in the brush along the single-lane dirt track. Rose sniffed the air appreciatively. Was that sage? The endless vista was soothing—how wonderful it was to be alive today!

Mr. Morton was enjoying the drive, too. Here and there they saw a house or a farm; some were close to the road, others were off in the distance. He commented on most: who the owners were, what kind of people they were and where they came from, bits and details about their families, and what they grew. The name McKennie caught her attention. Mr. Morton was saying, " . . . good Irish family; lots of kids, of course . . . helps on a farm. Their piece goes straight back from here. See the house over there? Homesteaded it about nine, ten years ago . . . held out during the really bad years. Had to be tough folk to make it. The people who've been here ten years or better got the best land and the hardest 'row to hoe' in order to 'prove up.' Drought, blizzards, grasshoppers."

"But I believe they think it's worth it now. Own their own land, free and clear. Better than land farther west of here. I foresee that part of the state coming of age in cattle, not farming, anyway. When a piece of really good corn land comes open around here now, it generally will sell well. Got a piece I'll show you today that I'm holding sale on. Some folk from Pennsylvania will be out in a few weeks to look it over, so I need to see the house and outbuildings for value. The owners did real well 'til about four, five years ago. Had it proved up and paying, then the man's health broke."

"Well, they held out hoping he'd get better, the wife and kids working it themselves best they could. Finally, her family made a place for them to come back to, and they left. The man wouldn't sell then, though. I figure he hoped he'd recover and they'd come back. But he died this last winter. Now they'll get a fair amount for the place, but it's hard to put a price on ten years of your life."

All of what he talked of interested Rose. She began to feel that she knew some of the people, and what they were like. The few times Mr. Morton attempted to turn the conversation to herself, asking leading questions, she frustrated him by bringing the subject back immediately to the spring prairie they were driving through and the people settled nearby.

It fascinated Rose to hear about folk who laid their futures on the line in order to carve 160 acres of farm land out of unplowed prairie sod in a bet with the government that they could hold out five years. Five years! Five years of back-breaking, heart-rending labor to earn your own land.

"Over there is the river," he waved his hand to the right. "It bends around a bit, which is how the town was named, and there's a creek that joins it . . . right back that way. Other side of the creek are the Thoresens." He pronounced it *Torasens*.

"Actually it's two farms, because the two brothers homesteaded it. They're Norwegian people. I don't rightly know where that Norwegian place is, myself. They don't hardly speak English even now. Well, all the kids do since they've all grown up here and been to school." He coughed politely as though deciding to concede a point. "Thoresens do real well, though. And they're very respectable folk. Now the piece we're going to see is just this side of the creek."

Rose strained to see the little creek ahead. They turned down the rutted trail alongside of it and started up a low rise. Spring runoff made the stream rush by energetically, and soon they were gazing down on it from the top of a small bluff.

The bluff they drove on leveled out, dropped away toward the creek, and they found the deserted farm in the wide hollow between the rise and the streambed. Actually, it was picturesque from the road; only two cottonwood trees and a few low shrubs relieved the vast landscape, but everything was green all around, and the farm seemed sheltered, set apart from the prairie where it nestled in the broad hollow with its face to the creek.

This little hill must be the only 'bump' for miles around, Rose thought.

Across the creek in a stand of trees in the distance was a cluster of buildings: a large house, a much larger barn, sheds, and fences. An expanse of new green spread out in all directions from the house, even near to the opposite creek bank. The Thoresen homestead.

"Here we are!" Mr. Morton gestured enthusiastically. "Why don't you stretch your legs while I examine the buildings?"

He helped her down and excused himself, so Rose walked around, glad to have her liberty. Even to her untrained eye she could see how "let go" the place was. What must have once been chicken coops were scraps of wood blown flat; a small "barn" stood off behind the house, but its doors were missing as were parts of the walls and roof. Everything was wind-worn and scoured to a dismal gray.

Still, the roll of the hill, the creek ahead, and green fields in the distance across the creek all appealed to her. She wandered the breadth of the hollow, wondering if she would ruin her shoes if she walked the fifty yards to the creek bank. Mr. Morton called to her and she reluctantly returned.

"Well, the house is nothing much to speak of, but you can see it's a very pretty place." Rose could almost hear money changing hands as he said the words. "The fields are prime—up over the rise, back of the house. Looks like they had a large green garden right over there."

"Yes, it's lovely," Rose murmured. "How much do you think the people will pay for it?"

"Oh, enough. If they don't care for this one, I've another south of town with better buildings. Not as nice a piece of land, but less cost to them initially. Yes, it would take some work and a little cash to fix this place up—but it would be worth it in my estimation. Good crop land and an excellent location."

They undid the hamper under one of the trees, spreading the food out on a checked cloth. The sun riding high overhead made Rose glad for the leafy branches sheltering them, and she took her straw hat off to feel the breeze on her head.

Mr. Morton was delighted with the lunch—cold chicken and fresh buns, pickles, hard-cooked eggs, a small jar of preserves, and two slices of apple pie. While Rose nibbled, he made vast inroads into it, all the while carrying the conversation. Rose nodded and responded at the appropriate junctures; her preoccupation was missed by him.

"And the railroad built line some 200 miles south of here to connect with—"

"Mr. Morton, may I ask you something?"

"Certainly, whatever you like!"

Rose cupped her chin in her hand and inquired speculatively, "Do men hire out in this neighborhood for, say, carpentry or small farm labor?"

Mr. Morton's puzzlement was evident. "I . . . Well, I'm sure . . . that is, for cash money, I know of several skilled carpenters. And most any of the young men trying to get started will do most any odd job for wages. It makes me curious why you would ask."

"Oh, never mind me. I have peculiar flights of fancy."

Mr. Morton looked like he agreed. They packed the remnants of the meal and prepared to leave, but Rose delayed, saying, "I feel the need to stretch my legs just a bit before we ride back. Would that be a problem?"

"No, certainly. I'd be happy to walk about with you, Mrs. Brownlee."

"Oh, please don't trouble yourself, sir. Just a few minutes will suffice, and I will return."

Neatly done, Rose congratulated herself. This time she did walk to the creek bank, feeling the lively, little brook soothe her spirit. A few minutes were indeed all she needed, and they drove away, hot sun beating on their heads, Mr. Morton loquacious as ever.

Everything was ready. "Perfect!" admired Rose, standing back and examining her handiwork. She had pulled together this little tea party with as much care as she would have used for the Bishop's wife. Of course, the Bishop's wife would have been astonished at her improvisations, but Rose was flushed and proud.

The two straight-backed chairs were each adorned with shawls for color. The night table sat between them disguised with an unhemmed square of muslin and set with borrowed crockery. The "tea table" also boasted a pert flowery bouquet while her straw hat wondered where its had gone.

"This is actually my first real step back into society," Rose remarked reflectively.

Soon the tea was steeping in its little pot and plain gingerbread was arranged on a patterned plate in an inviting way. Rose glanced in the mirror over the washstand, twitched her collar into place, and smoothed her thick, dark blonde coil of hair.

"Oh, no! I believe I've burned my nose!" she giggled. That would never do back home!

There was a timid knock at the door, and Rose flew to answer it. Meg shyly hesitated on the threshold.

"You are my honored guest today!" Rose encouraged gaily. "No shrinking violets here! This is not how we began at breakfast."

Meg took her offered hand and her reticence slipped away.

"I'm thanking ye, Mrs. Brownlee, for th' kind invitation. 'Tis a bright spot in my day, to be sure!"

Rose replied warmly, "You are very welcome, Meg. I've had no companionship these last two weeks. We shall enjoy our tea and get to know one another, shall we? And please call me Rose, so we can be friendly."

"Sure an' I 'preciate the liberty, ma'am, but in our family 'tis not done so. Could I be callin' ye Miss Rose? 'Tis a grand name!"

Rose liked that and seated her guest with decorum. Meg was delighted with everything so the conversation flowed merrily with the sipped tea and nibbled cakes. A veritable fount of information was Meg! Not only did she know something about everyone, (or everything about some!) but it was also always a good and honest report made even more appealing by her fanciful ways of speech and lilting brogue.

Rose speculated that only near-perfect people lived in and near RiverBend, for Meg was careful only to have cheerful things to say about each one. Finally Meg began regretfully to excuse herself to return to work.

Rose was reluctant to let her go. "This has been so much fun, Meg. Will you come again? Maybe tomorrow?"

"I'm bein' more than pleased to come again, ma'am," Meg returned. Her eyes were shining with pleasure at the thought. "But tomorrow bein' Sunday, I'll be goin' home tonight. We go to service and spend the day family-like. I'm wishin' to see the baby, too, and be helpin' me mother a bit."

"Will ye be comin' t' church, Miss Rose? Our minister is grand at preachin'. There's no church of our own kind here—two priests have come and had to leave when times were too bad—but me mother says: 'Tho' 'tis a shame for children to grow up wi' out the church, 'tis a *sin* to grow up wi' out God!' So we go to service with everyone else."

"Even th' other preacher left three year ago, but this new one (he's been here just seven months, an' his sweet wife) is so foine at tellin' th' Bible. If ye'll be comin', I'd be that proud to introduce ye to him and me father and mother. Will ye come, Miss Rose?"

"Yes, Meg, I'll come. It would be my pleasure to meet your family, too."

Chapter 9

Dressing with care and feeling a trifle nervous, Rose set out to church. It wasn't a far walk, but it was out of the regular circumference of RiverBend. Set in an acre of wild spring grass, the whitewashed boards and single spire reminded her of pictures she'd seen of the west.

"Silly! This is the West! . . . and it is so lovely . . . so free."

Unencumbered by streets, buildings, traffic, and smoke, the vista stretched out seemingly beyond the horizon.

Others were walking through the tall grass to church, too. Rose waved to the grocer's wife. She was in her Sunday best with scrubbed, wet-haired children strung out behind her. The grocer didn't seem to be with them. A few wagons appeared and a fairly new buggy. The young man driving it was blond. That is to say his hair was a white-blonde, but his face and hands were brown—no, bronzed. It was a beautiful combination for the eye. He carefully handed down a plump, pleasant looking woman looking to be in her mid-forties. She, too, was blonde and tanned, but her hair was a darker blonde, and her face was work-worn. Still, both of them were in good spirits, and Rose was startled when a wagon pulled up beside them and a horde of children clambered down, some calling "Mamma" to the woman.

"Really," Rose chided herself, counting again, "There are only seven. No, just six; that girl is at least seventeen or eighteen—not really a child anymore."

The man handling the wagon good-naturedly swung the smallest child, a girl of about seven or eight, to the ground as she scrambled over the wheel. He was older than the woman, probably in his early fifties, and sun and wind burned like the boy.

A whole family, thought Rose. *And it took two vehicles to get them all to church.*

There was Meg! Rose realized with a start how much of an impact this girl's friendship had made on her. Meg was flushed and beaming; her whole family stood waiting to welcome Rose, and she felt a tightness in her throat.

"How very . . . cordial of them," she murmured to herself.

> *There is a fountain filled with blood,*
> *Drawn from Immanuel's veins*
> *And sinners plunged beneath that flood,*
> *Lose all their guilty stains!*

The man leading songs closed his eyes and sang with fervor:

> *Lose all their guilty stains,*
> *Lose all their guilty stains,*
> *And sinners plunged beneath that flood,*
> *Lose all their guilty stains.*

A tear glistened on his cheek.

Why, Rose wondered, *is he sad?* They launched into the second verse and a great smile lit his face. *He's not sad,* she marveled. He's *happy!*

> *Wash all my sins away,*
> *Wash all my sins away,*
> *And there may I, though vile as he,*
> *Wash all my sins away.*

She felt a stirring in her heart, a yearning to feel what he felt. Soon hands began clapping and toes tapping as the next hymn was picked up.

> *'Tis the grandest theme thro' the ages rung,*
> *'Tis the grandest theme for a mortal tongue,*
> *'Tis the grandest theme that the world e'er sung,*
> *Our God is able to deliver thee!*
> *He is able to deliver thee, he is able to deliver thee,*
> *Tho' by sin oppressed, go to him for rest,*
> *Our God is able to deliver thee!*

The room was alive with joy and song. Rose had never experienced anything like it. Was this like the "revival meetings" she'd heard about? Her foot kept time with the music and she hummed softly to pick up the tune. Too soon they were through and it was offering time. Rose dug generously into her purse. It seemed right to give abundantly of what she had, and not just a token amount. Wryly she noted that what remained in her purse at the moment didn't amount to much more than a token amount. She would have to fix that tomorrow.

The preacher stood up after the offering. He was very young, she thought, and not at all what a minister should look like either. He smiled at the congregation, and Rose noticed how everyone settled down; a quietness came over the room. He opened his Bible and began to read:

Now the Lord had said unto Abram,
Get thee out of thy country, and from thy kindred,
and from thy father's house,
unto a land that I will show thee;

Rose shivered and felt goose bumps on her arms. In breathless anticipation she waited for him to continue.

And I will make of thee a great nation, and I will bless thee,
and make thy name great; and thou shalt be a blessing:
And I will bless them that bless thee:
and in thee shall all families of the earth be blessed.
So Abram departed, as the LORD had spoken unto him;
and Lot went with him:
and Abram was seventy-five years old
when he departed out of Haran.

The preacher closed his Bible and scanned the room, nodding at several, and smiling a greeting at Rose. Her face flushed, but she felt accepted.

He continued. "Most of you," he spoke looking around at the faces in the room again, "have come from far off to this land. You left your fathers and mothers, your brothers and sisters, just like Abram. And just like him, you didn't know what you would find. Some of you sailed or steamed to this continent across the vast, cold ocean before you traveled west to this place, of all the places on earth. You came looking for a better life, perhaps, than the one you left behind. What you found for sure was work. Hard, unrelenting work."

"Along the way or over the years you may have lost loved ones in the pursuit of your dream. I cannot say what motivated you all individually, and I do not know the circumstances in your particular case, but let me tell you this: God has a plan for your life, and bringing you clear around the world or half across a continent was not too hard for him to do so that you could find him and fulfill that plan."

A smile played over Rose's face.

"Let me tell you about a woman in the Bible named Esther. Esther was taken as a slave far from her home in Israel to the pagan kingdom of Babylon. She was beautiful and became, of all the beautiful women in the land, the Queen, the wife of the King. After she had been Queen for a time, a terrible threat to all of her people arose. Every Jew was to be killed by his non-Jewish neighbors on a certain day in a certain month. But because God had placed Esther in the palace, for just that purpose, she was able to speak to the King and save her people."

"You may not ever be called on to save your people or nation. You may never do anything bold or dramatic. But if you have God living inside of you, the people in your life will see how God loves them too. In this way you become his instrument just as Esther was, to save someone or ones from being eternally lost."

"How important are you to God? He has no one else he can use to do what he has planned for you. Yes, God has brought you here—not just to work hard, raise a crop and a family and grow old, or to fail in spite of your efforts, but to bring the message of real life, life that remains because of Jesus, to the frontiers of America."

Several resounding "amens" from the congregation took Rose unawares. This too was unusual to her. They stood to their feet now as the minister prayed a benediction, then filed out. The mood was cheerful and friendly as they moved toward the door. Several strangers said "hello" and shook her hand as they passed to the McKennies' wagon.

"Mrs. Brownlee! I say, hello there!" Mr. Morton was just arriving in his buggy and jumped down to prevent her from leaving.

"Good morning, Mr. Morton," Rose replied coolly. She didn't know if shouting to a lady was considered good manners in RiverBend, but it wasn't where she came from. "You are late if you came for church; we've just let out."

He laughed unashamedly. "I'm not the church-going type, you can be sure, Mrs. Brownlee, and certainly not the loud, Bible-happy kind like this. No, I've other things on my mind on a fair day such as today. Which brings me to why I'm here. You're alone in town, so this time *I* purchased a picnic lunch, and came to take you to the river for the afternoon."

Rose lifted her eyebrows. "I'm very sorry you went to so much trouble on my account, Mr. Morton, without consulting my plans first. I'm afraid I already have an engagement this afternoon. Do you know Mr. and Mrs. McKennie?"

By reminding him of their presence he was forced to quit ignoring them. He greeted them civilly but without warmth.

"Oh, yes. How do you do today?" he turned back to Rose and, taking her elbow, pulled her a few feet away. "I'm certain that they would not object to your postponing with them in light of my preparations."

"Oh, but I would, Mr. Morton. It would be very rude of me to cancel after accepting their hospitable invitation. And besides, I am quite looking forward to it." She smiled calmly.

"Very well, then. Perhaps another time." Deservedly embarrassed, he excused himself and Rose rejoined the McKennies.

All crowded together in the wagon, children laughing and whispering, adults trying to converse, they meandered to the McKennie homestead. The road was familiar to her, as she had gone the same way only yesterday with Mr. Morton. A happy family rode in the wagon, and Rose, charmed by the whole experience, drank deeply of its overflow.

She held newborn baby Sean part of the way home, delighted by the thick black fuzz covering his tiny head and caressing his miniscule clenched fists. An ache in her chest threatened to overwhelm her more than once, but under cover of Fiona's and Meg's good-natured dialogue she mastered and put aside the welling tears.

Brian McKennie drove studiously while chewing a piece of straw and smiling. His contribution to the general melee was an occasional "yis" or "nae, surely" but it sufficed. Rose didn't think she would ever sort the children out. Try as she did, the three boys between Meg and Martha were interchangeable or identical; she couldn't decide which.

When they finally drove into the McKennies' yard, a large female dog and her two half-grown pups ran out to greet them. Suspicious growls and sniffs met Rose when she stepped out of the wagon, and fearfully she paused.

"Oh, shame! Get back wi' ye!" Meg rebuked. The three dogs circled cautiously and relaxed their guard.

"Bit protective-like but nae a mean bone in them t' be sure," Brian apologized. "Better watchdog canna be found. Connie had six pups an' four are goon t' families needin' a good dog. Sure an' they're not foine to be lookin' at, for a fair mix o' three kin' o' hound they be. Now Connie! Come here. Yis, good girl, meet Miss Rose, an' you an' yours treat her wi' respect or I'll be takin' t' switch t' ye, sure!"

All three dogs sniffed at Rose's timidly extended hand. At last satisfied, Connie lost interest and led her gangly pups off.

Rose sighed. Big dogs frightened her.

"Now off wi' ye all," Brian commanded, and the commotion melted away. On a farm each child had his or her chores to do, Sunday or no Sunday, and Brian McKennie tolerated no slackness. Fiona led Rose inside, put her in a chair by the window to hold the baby, and busied herself with the dinner.

The whole room fascinated Rose. It was clean and neat as a pin, but its contents were a contradiction. The walls themselves were bare board, well sanded and oiled, but bare board the same.

Most of the furniture—table, chairs, and cupboards—were homemade and rough. But on shelves over the table and on either side of the stove was one of the loveliest displays of china and plate she had ever seen, each piece scrupulously cleaned and the silver shining. On the table, too, lay as fine a linen cloth as ever laid on her own table at home.

Then again, the floor was strewn with rag rugs, those colorful creations made by braiding strips of fabric scraps together and sewing the braid into a winding, enlarging circle or oblong. Obviously the McKennies lived off the land and, by Rose's standards would be considered "poor," yet they possessed a valuable collection of dishes and linen.

One by one, the children filed in to dinner. Hands and faces scrubbed, hair combed, they sat down to eat. All was quiet while Brian McKennie prayed in Gaelic before they ate. The meal Fiona passed around that day was plain and simple: strips of beef dredged in seasoned flour and fried, boiled potatoes with gravy, bread, and green beans. There was plenty for everyone to eat their fill.

At the end, Fiona brought a plate of steaming scones, a saucer of butter, and a dish of raspberry preserves. Something in the appreciative "ahhs" from the children made Rose believe this treat was in her honor. The flaky, piping-hot pastries melted in her mouth. They certainly disappeared from the platter!

After dinner, Meg and Martha cleared off the table and set about washing up. Fiona finished nursing the baby and handed him to Brian, then offered her arm to Rose.

"Would ye be takin' a walk about t' place wi' me, Miss Rose? The grass is still green an' the breeze is makin' it a pure pleasure to be outside on such a day."

Companionably they wandered about the McKennie homestead. Rose saw baby chicks scurrying among the mother hens, a sow with her seven piglets wallowing in a puddle near their shed, and the two milk cows out in the pasture, one nursing a wondering-eyed calf. Each sight was such a new adventure for Rose that she exclaimed like a child over them. And the prairie was indeed green, beckoning them to wander, wildflowers splashing the distance with color.

Brian's plowed fields took such a small part out of the vastness that Rose considered if it would ever be "used up," farmed or built up like back east. Proudly, Fiona walked her through the "green garden," too. Brian's fields would supply corn for feed and food, wheat, oats, and hay, but Fiona's plot fed them on good things the year round. Although much wasn't showing yet to point out, Fiona listed off carrots, turnips, beets, onions, radishes, tomatoes, leaf lettuce, peas, green and dry beans, lima beans, several kinds of squash, pumpkin, and (to the McKennies) the all-important potatoes. A raspberry patch removed to the other side of the yard was their only fruit. Rose was so impressed by Fiona's knowledge of growing things that her tongue tripped over the questions that tumbled out.

Fiona laughed at her zeal. "'Tis sounding like you're born to love the growin' of things."

"Mrs. McKennie, do you think I could learn to garden like this? I mean vegetables and food things. I know about flowers, for we had a fine gardener at home, and I learned to cultivate beautiful roses, but I mean do you think I could plant and care for a garden like this?"

Fiona looked skeptically at Rose's lovely clothes and soft hands. Carefully she replied, "'tis sure I am you could be learnin' how, but 'tis mean, hard workin' and not fit for a lady's hands, I'm thinkin'. An' hot! Yis, in summer th' sun is wiltin' th' greens fast as ye can water them. So, bein' considerin' of your fair skin, it moight not be t' thing for ye. An' I'm thinkin' ye have naught to do so."

"But . . . if I put my mind to it, and not thinking of my hands, do you think I could learn?"

Somehow Fiona couldn't resist the earnestness in Rose's question, so responded rather placatingly, "To be sure, to be sure. One can be learnin' onything if 'tis fittin' one's purpose."

Back at the house Meg had carefully laid out tea. Some of the delicate things from the shelves on the wall were used including a magnificent silver teapot and china tea service. Rose complimented Fiona over and over and examined the teacup at her place with care.

"Mrs. McKennie, this is about the finest china I have ever seen. Such art it took to make it—and it's very old, isn't it?"

"Yis," Fiona replied proudly. "These are bein' me dowry, an' me mother's before me an' hers before her, for about one hundred year, I'm thinkin'. We buried every piece in good Irish peat when we come to America. Not one piece broken nor lost, neither. That an' t' linens and napkins I saved up for me weddin' when just a girl. To be sure, 'tis also bein' Meg's one day."

Meg blushed becomingly as she said this but tossed her auburn head and answered saucily,

"An' not for a long while yet, Mother. First I'll be finishin' school, an' God willin', goin' to teacher's college, for I mean to teach an' ye know well."

"Is that why you work in town all week, Meg?" Rose inquired with interest.

Meg suddenly turned shy again, but ducked her head. "Yes."

"That's very admirable, Meg," Rose insisted. "And I believe you will make a fine teacher. Teachers are needed, especially out here in the west, aren't they?"

"Oh, yes!" Meg burst out. "Why, they are needin' at least one new teacher for our three schools every year. Either one is longin' to go back to her home and family or the maiden teachers are findin' husbands an' are marryin' an' no longer wantin' to teach. I am goin' to teach a long time though. For it's makin' good, cash money I can be doin'."

"An' that is all foine an' good—if your heart is not lovin' the money," Fiona said meaningfully.

"Yes, ma'am." Meg was chastened.

The four ladies, for little Martha begged to be included, had their tea, and as the time for Meg and Rose to go back to town grew near, Brian called the family together and brought the big Bible from their bedroom.

First they prayed. Brian spoke at some length, remembering each one in the room and including "Miss Rose, Father, that ye be givin' her of your peace an' t' joy of salvation an' she be blessed in her travels." Then each one in the circle lifted their personal thanks and requests. Rose nearly panicked as she realized she was expected to pray, too.

When her turn came she stammered, "Lord, I thank you for today; I've had a precious day. And I thank you for leading me— please let me know what you wish me to do. Amen."

Brian opened the Bible and pausing momentarily, asked with hesitation, "I'm wonderin', Miss Rose, if ye'd be readin' for us today. 'Twould be pleasin' us."

Rose nodded and took the large book. It was open to Isaiah. Rose hadn't read that far in her own Bible yet. Brian pointed out chapter forty-three. "This is where we be."

Rose nodded again and began in her clear, cultured voice:

But now thus saith the Lord that created thee, O Jacob,
and he that formed thee, O Israel,
Fear not: for I have redeemed thee,
I have called thee by thy name; thou art mine.
When thou passeth through the waters,
I will be with thee; and through the rivers,
they shall not overflow thee;

Her voice stuck on the words "overflow thee." The children looked curiously and Fiona's face showed concern. Coughing and politely murmuring "excuse me!" Rose went on.

When thou walkest through the fire,
thou shalt not be burned;
neither shall the flame kindle upon thee.
For I am the Lord thy God,
the Holy One of Israel, thy Saviour:
I gave Egypt for thy ransom,
Ethiopia and Seba for thee . . .
I, even I am the Lord;
and beside me there is no Saviour.

Brian signed for her to stop and collected the Bible from her.

"Thank ye, Miss Rose. That passage is bein' just t' one that was givin' us courage t' not be quittin' t' year hail ruint t' most of our crop. An' he is blessin' us again, for we be doin' fine now. So! Ian,

Patrick, be gettin' t' team; 'tis time t' be takin' Meg an' Miss Rose back t' town."

Since Brian McKennie was the only one with them on the road back to RiverBend, Rose cautiously asked him a few questions. "Is the land around town particularly good for farming, Mr. McKennie?"

"Particular? Nae, boot it's bein' better than much. Better to be sure than farther west aboot hundred mile or so. Then ye are in plain country—good for wheat I'm hearin' an' maybe to be raisin' cattle. Not rain enow for real farmin'."

"Does land here bring a good price?"

"Oh, good, yis. T' best was 'steaded up years ago, boot some as is changin' hands be gettin' a fair price."

Rose paused for a moment. "And what does a 'fair price' amount to, Mr. McKennie? What do folks pay for land here?"

Brian looked at Rose and laughed. "Ain't ye t' one for knowin' details? Well, I'm thinkin' two and a half is being near fair, boot I've heard as high as four."

"Four dollars an acre?"

"Aye. A homestead w' a good house and water'd be bringin' $640 at that price."

Rose nodded thoughtfully, then she asked Meg to tell her more about college and her hopes of teaching. Meg eagerly explained her plans while Rose listened and offered encouragement. They arrived at Mrs. Owens' soon, and Rose thanked Brian.

"I've had a wonderful visit with your family, Mr. McKennie. You made me feel right at home."

"Aye. That we were meanin' to. 'Twas a right pleasure for my Fiona to be havin' your company today, an' we'll be hopin' t' see ye again afore ye be goin'. Dinna ye be leavin' w'out sayin' 'goodbye'."

"No, I won't, I promise," Rose answered.

Chapter 10

Rose saw Meg in the dining room the next morning. She was bright-eyed and ready to leave for school as soon as she finished serving the boarders. Her brown gingham dress was clean and fresh, her thick hair neatly braided around her head. They smiled familiarly as Meg passed by bearing plates of pancakes.

Later Meg waved goodbye from the door. Savoring the fresh coffee, Rose lingered over her meal. She had decided to spend the day in her room undistracted, but first she ate well and took a short walk around the yard to enjoy the sweet air.

Up in her room again Rose closed the door and latched it. She walked to the window and surveyed the little town, then seated herself with her Bible and notebook at the small desk. For several hours she read and prayed, occasionally stopping to make a memo or jot down a few thoughts. At one point she knelt down at her bed and prayed earnestly for a long while, laying out her plans and desires, waiting for direction. When lunchtime arrived, Mrs. Owens delivered a pot of tea and a sandwich to her room, but Rose did not leave. All afternoon she stayed alone, closeted in her studies and prayer. By four she was satisfied, put her Bible and notes away, and went out into the late afternoon sunshine.

Past the end of town, beyond the livery she walked, out onto the prairie. The shadows cast by the sinking sun gave the miles of undisturbed vista a surreal appearance, a bright two-dimensional effect. The warm breeze, scented with wild onions and sage, filled her with joy, and little creatures (prairie dogs?) scampered into their holes as she wandered by. They whistled and chattered, birds twittered and called, but mostly it was quiet, the peace of the wide-open ranges, and Rose loved it. She roamed until dusk, treasuring each minute, each change as the sun dropped lower and lower on the horizon.

Tuesday morning began much the same. Rose returned to her room to write letters, one to her mother, Tom, and Abby that she was staying in a small town by the name of RiverBend, another to her bank. She sighed in satisfaction and put her writing materials away. Then kneeling by the window she prayed for those dear at home and those she knew in RiverBend, feeling especially to pray for Mr.

Morton and the grocer. At the close she remained kneeling and silent.

A short while later, straw hat in place, Rose went out. She made one short stop before marching down the street to "RiverBend Savings and Loan" and into the tiny office.

"Good morning, Mr. Morton," she announced cheerfully.

"Mrs. Brownlee! Good morning to you also, I'm sure. What can I do to assist your stay in RiverBend?" His manner was ever-so-slightly stiff.

"First, Mr. Morton, I would like to open an account at your bank." She smiled sweetly.

"An account, Mrs. Brownlee?" Mr. Morton didn't "get" it.

"Why, yes! That's right. I am transferring funds from my bank back east into my new account here. That is possible, isn't it?"

"Well, certainly, Mrs. Brownlee, but you should understand that, as a visitor to our community, if you are in need of funds to continue your trip, we would be happy to cash your personal check—with confirmation by wire from your bank, of course." He was all benevolence and condescension.

"The point is, Mr. Morton, that there is no continuance to my journey. In short, I have reached my destination."

His eyebrows lifted slightly. "You intend to remain in RiverBend, Mrs. Brownlee?"

Rose adopted a business-like attitude. "Let us get back to my request, Mr. Morton, and open my account, please. The name of my bank and the amount to be transferred is written on this card. Before I came here today I sent a wire to the bank officer personally acquainted with my finances. His response confirming the transfer of funds will arrive and be delivered to you this noon. When you receive it, I will return and discuss a few disbursements. Will that suit your plans, Mr. Morton?"

He had slid the card off his desk and glanced at the bank name and amount. Seeing the prestigious heading and unexpected amount, he sat up and unconsciously adjusted his tie. Rose remained smiling demurely, but Mr. Morton's demeanor was transformed. He stood to his feet and extended his hand to her.

"I'd be delighted to handle your account, Mrs. Brownlee. And may I be the first to say 'welcome to RiverBend'?"

She returned his handshake graciously. "Let us keep my plans on a confidential basis, Mr. Morton, for the time being. But thank you for your kind welcome."

Rose swept out of the bank on a wave of exhilaration.

"The sky is blue, the prairie is green, the sun is golden! What sentimental nonsense you are babbling," she laughed at herself. But she wanted to run, throw up her hands, and shout. What a day! And it was just beginning.

Almost skipping, she ran across the street to the mercantile, jingling the bell merrily as she pushed the door open.

"Good morning, sir, and your wife too. I'm Mrs. Rose Brownlee. You have seen me before in your store, but I wished to introduce myself to you."

They nodded, so she went on. "I'm going to make some selections, pay for them this afternoon, and I am hoping you can hold them for me until arrangements can be made to move them. You can? How wonderful, Mr. er, Schmidt, is it? I'll just look around and let you know what I decide on."

Rose fumbled in her bag and pulled out her notebook. Dear little friend! Some of her dreams were jotted on its pages.

"Ah, here is the list," she murmured.

Mrs. Schmidt was shyly cordial, answering her questions as she moved about the store, and Rose saw her valiantly restrain her curiosity.

"I'm sure she will be driven to distraction soon," Rose sympathized, "but I need to keep my own counsel for now."

She handed the finished list over to Mrs. Schmidt who consulted with Mr. Schmidt, their heads bobbing and nodding together until it was tallied. The amount was written in Rose's notebook, which she tucked in her purse when she got ready to leave.

"Oh, yes! I almost forgot," Rose reminded herself. "Mr. Schmidt, is there an establishment here in town where I might hire a horse and buggy?"

Mr. Schmidt scratched his jaw, and Mrs. Schmidt looked doubtful. "Vell, I don't know, Frau Brünlee, if der ist ein 'establishment' as you say, but the preacher hast ein gud horse und fair buggy. I am thinking he would not be opposed to making the cash money, since there is not much come his vay. Ve hear it is hard for him to feed the horse, anyvay." Mrs. Schmidt looked shamed by what he said, Rose noticed, but she nodded agreement.

"Fine. I'll speak to him about it. And I'll be back this afternoon to pay for my purchases."

Rose knew from Meg that the preacher and his wife boarded with the elderly couple who did tailoring and dressmaking. She hadn't been in their store and didn't know exactly where their living quarters might be, so she went into the tiny shop and introduced herself there too.

The old lady hand-basting a shirt didn't answer after Rose gave her little speech. Instead, her eyes checked every seam, dart, tuck, and hem of Rose's brown suit. After what seemed forever under her intense inspection, she merely hollered, "Preacher! Sum'uns come ta see ya. I say! Preacher!"

Pastor Medford appeared almost immediately, and Rose felt sorry for his embarrassment over his summons. He was wearing working pants, shirt, and suspenders much like most of the men in town, and everything was clean and pressed.

"It's Mrs. Brownlee, isn't it? Won't you come in? —That is, follow me, please." Through the narrow door to the back of the building (right through the tailor's kitchen and bedroom, with the tailor snoring in his bed!) and up a flight of stairs they went. One large room was inside the door at the top, containing a bed, table, two chairs, a chest of drawers, and some cupboards hung with curtains.

"My dear," he announced proudly, "we have a visitor. Mrs. Brownlee, may I introduce my wife, Mrs. Medford?"

Rose shook hands warmly with the very tall, slender, girl-woman who stood up to greet her.

"How delightful to meet you, Mrs. Brownlee. May I offer you some tea? We saw you at service Sunday, of course, but missed making your acquaintance. Please sit right here. Dear, kindly get the stool so we can all sit together."

Rose felt comfortable right away. Jacob and Vera Medford were from New Jersey and were as new to the west as she was. They were newly married, too, Rose found out.

"How sweet they are to each other," Rose observed. "So young and in love!"

They all sipped tea companionably, sharing a tiny saucer of cream, until Rose declared she must go. "I came especially because Mr. Schmidt tells me you have a horse and buggy, Reverend Medford. I would like to hire them tomorrow if you are willing."

"Hire them, Mrs. Brownlee? They are yours to use without charge. We'd be blessed to loan them to you. I have a spirited saddle horse for my visiting, but the buggy horse, Prince, is a gentle old boy and will give you no trouble."

"You are most kind, and I appreciate your generosity, but I insist on paying for their use. Horses need their hay and oats. Prince will earn his tomorrow."

The Medfords glanced at each other and smiled.

Yes, Rose thought, *I will certainly pay for their use.*

Rose went her way to Mrs. Owens' where she had an early lunch and re-checked her notes. Satisfied, she took her coffee out onto the porch and sat in the warm sunshine, sipping it until her watch indicated the time was close to being one o'clock. With rising anticipation she returned her cup to Mrs. Owens and climbed to her room to freshen up.

"Here goes nothing!" Rose pronounced to her mirror. Two bright spots lit her cheeks with unusual color. She made herself walk downstairs and through the parlor with restraint, but outside Rose swung down the sidewalk like a schoolgirl.

At the door of RiverBend Savings and Loan, Rose paused. She adjusted her collar and cuffs, smoothed her coiled hair, and giggled. She was so excited she nearly walked away.

"It won't do for you to be giddy when you go in, Rose. Get yourself under control," she counseled.

Assuming a business-like attitude, she coolly let herself into Mr. Morton's office.

"Ah, Mrs. Brownlee! I have received the wire from your bank and everything is in order."

"So, the amount I requested is now on deposit with your bank, and I may make withdrawals?"

"Yes, indeed. I've made up your passbook and a pad of checks. You may now feel free to use your account."

"Wonderful, Mr. Morton! In that case, I wish to do some business with you."

"With me, Mrs. Brownlee? You are thinking perhaps of bonds or stocks?"

"Oh, no, Mr. Morton. Real estate."

"I beg your pardon?"

"I'm going to purchase the homestead piece you showed me last week. Across the creek from the Norwegian family?"

Mr. Morton frowned. "You wish to make an investment, madam?"

"No, Mr. Morton, I wish to purchase a home site."

His frown deepened. "Oh, Mrs. Brownlee. But that's not possible, you know. Or even judicious. Please reconsider: in the first place I have prospective buyers arriving in a week or two and," (Mr. Morton's feelings of propriety were being strained) "well, a lady of your refinement would have, that is, should have no reason to . . . to . . . take up residence on a 'homestead'. No, I must deny your request. My duty as a gentleman, my position as your financial advisor—"

"I'm very sorry you feel that way," Rose politely interrupted. "However, the property is for sale, is it not?"

He leaned forward on his desk patronizingly. "Yes, of course, but—"

"What is the asking price, please?"

"Mrs. Brownlee, I will not sell you the land. It would be against my principles to assist a lady into an untenable position."

"But dear Mr. Morton, *you* are not selling the land. Your bank and its owners are, I believe. I am willing to pay for it today. If it is for sale, I am entitled to purchase it. I'm sure the officers of your institution would wonder at your turning down a cash offer. And isn't there another property you thought your buyers would like better?"

He paused and tried another angle. "Perhaps you are not aware of how severe our winters are, madam. Why, during some blizzards no one can leave their house for days at a time. Out there you could be stranded, and you would be alone. It certainly isn't a wise choice, and I know when you give it proper consideration you will agree with my decision." His emphasis on the word 'proper' showed Rose how little he esteemed the women homesteaders. Well, she would be sinking in his regard too, most likely.

"How much is the land, please, Mr. Morton?"

His face flushed an angry red.

She added gently, "I am aware of the going price on farm land. Would you please do me the favor of quoting the bank's figure for this particular section?"

Licking his lips and mastering his temper, he named the price. Without comment Rose made out the check and laid it on the desk between them. He stared at it for several moments before sighing in defeat. Then from his top drawer he withdrew the necessary forms and papers. Twenty minutes later Rose stood outside the bank's doors triumphant. In her hand she held title to the homestead.

"Now," she added, "for the first time in my life I am really going to have to work, and work hard."

All the activity of the day, coupled with the excitement, made her weary, although it was only nearing two o'clock. She laughed at herself and put a spring in her step. Down at the Schmidt's store she called 'hello' familiarly. They greeted her with anticipation. Writing their check was nearly as much fun as the other for her land. Hers was probably the largest cash order they had filled in quite a while, and both of the Schmidts shook her hand enthusiastically. Mr. Schmidt couldn't do enough to accommodate her needs. Recalling that she would require someone to transport her new belongings, he hastened to recommend the station officer who owned a large wagon for hauling freight.

"But you'd need another man to load und drive. The officer cannot be gone during vork hours for he vatches und listens for the telegraph too."

"That's all right, Mr. Schmidt. I believe I know someone who can do the job."

Rose gladly let her feet take her back to Mrs. Owens' then. Inside her room she removed her hat and gloves and sank down on the bed. What a day! Now she was committed to her scheme. Scanning the title to her new home, she gloried in her name, printed with big, bold strokes by the word 'owner,' the seal and stamp of the bank, even Mr. Morton's signature!

Chapter 11

In the morning Rose dressed in her oldest, most worn cotton skirt and shirtwaist. That was not to say they were old and worn, but she didn't really own clothes for what she was doing today. The sun warmed her as she walked to the end of town and around the corner. There was the feed store with its barn and stable. Pastor Medford was standing in the fenced yard and buckling Prince into his harness. Rose approached the gray horse confidently and scratched his forehead. Ears forward, his liquid brown eyes looked her over with interest, then closed and enjoyed the pleasure. The preacher was right. Prince was an old pussycat. Rose thought he was regal.

"Oh, hello!" Pastor Medford called to her. "Just have to hook him up and you are all set." He chuckled when he saw Prince 'lean' into Rose's scratching. "Looks like you've made a friend for life. Believe me, a better mannered horse you'll never drive. Only don't let him make the decisions! He'll take you into a plowed field and show you the best grazing. Folks 'round here take a short view of that."

Rose laughed too. "You wouldn't do that, would you, old man?" she asked, shaking Prince's harness.

Prince opened one eye and shook his head up and down until the tack rattled.

"Oh, my!" she returned and patted him firmly on the withers. She was wearing leather gloves to drive with today.

Thanking Pastor Medford for his help, she chirruped to Prince, and he pulled with a will. In front of Schmidt's mercantile Rose stopped and climbed down.

"Won't be but a few minutes, fella," she whispered, "but the brake is set, so don't think you can go anywhere!"

Mrs. Schmidt bustled out from behind the counter, anxious to help Rose, who explained about the items she wished to take today: broom, rake, hatchet, buckets, rags, tea kettle, and soap. Next she picked out a few groceries and paid for them out of her purse. Into a wooden box Mrs. Schmidt packed tea, a small sack of biscuits, an apple and a quarter pound of mild cheese.

"Would you add a little paper of sugar too, please—oh, and a teaspoon and a paring knife and that little cup and plate." The last items were of the plainest serviceable tin.

Mrs. Schmidt nodded mutely, but her kindly eyes were eager to ask questions. Her friend, Gertrude Grünbaum, would never forgive her for not being able to tell her what the wealthy eastern lady was up to. Still, Mrs. Schmidt experienced an uncommon reticence with Rose. Most of her life she'd worked hard and been poor; around this lady and her nice dress she became shy.

Rose thanked Mrs. Schmidt graciously as she counted out her money. Casually she remarked, "I'm driving Pastor Medford's buggy today. You see, I bought the Anderson's homestead yesterday, and mean to settle down in RiverBend, so we'll be neighbors now. Won't that be nice?"

Mrs. Schmidt's mouth made a little "o" and she moved her head up and down.

"When I am finished putting things to rights you may come and visit, and we'll get to know each other, all right?"

Mrs. Schmidt nodded again.

Rose caught movement outside the front window. Four small faces peeped in at them.

"Are those your children, Mrs. Schmidt?"

Another nod.

Rose looked over the candy jars atop the counter. "May I please have a packet of lemon drops?"

She paid and walked to the door, leaving her other purchases leaned against or on top of the counter. When she opened the door, the children stared silently at her. The youngest, a tiny boy of three or so with a grubby hand in his mouth, hid behind his sister's skirts. The girl was ten, Rose judged, and another brother and sister looked about six and seven.

"Hello!" Rose offered. No one as much as flicked an eyelid back, but the little boy's hand "smacked" between his lips.

Hiding a smile she continued, "I have some lemon drops here. I like lemon drops, don't you? If someone were willing to help me put my things into this buggy I would love to give that someone my lemon drops."

The older boy's eyebrows went up, and he glanced to his sister. The hand even came out of the little boy's mouth, and he whispered, "I vant dem."

The four moved as a unit, and Rose chuckled inside to see how they worked with a will, obeying the unspoken commands of the elder girl. Even the little one helped, carrying Rose's buckets. Rose took the items one by one and carefully set them on the floor of the buggy. The rake and broom had to be leaned out the back, but she managed it.

"Thank you all very much. You did well." Rose handed the packet of candy to the older sister, who received it solemnly.

"Well, goodbye." She turned to get in the buggy.

A gentle tug at her skirt held her. The younger girl said softly, "Danke Schoen, Frau Brünlee."

"You're very welcome, sweetheart." Rose hurried to drive away before the tears came. So even the children knew her name. Well, soon everyone would know she was here to stay, too. Mrs. Schmidt would surely take care of that.

Prince was as happy as Rose was to be out where the fields stretched far and wide. There wasn't another soul to be seen and Rose began to hum softly, then sing,

> *When we walk with the Lord, In the light of his Word,*
> *What a glory he sheds on our way.*
> *While we do his good will, he abides with us still,*
> *And with all who will trust and obey.*

In full voice she let the chorus out:

> *Trust and obey, For there's no other way,*
> *To be happy in Jesus, Than to trust and obey.*

Prince put his ears back and snorted, jumping ahead and giving the buggy a little jerk.

"Oho! Don't you like my singing? I'll sing it again, thank you!"

Soon the McKennie farm came into sight, and Rose turned down the long track past their front fields. Brian McKennie was plowing, putting his shoulder to the plow to help his mule. He waved when he saw her, and Rose gaily waved back. Chickens scattered and dogs barked and howled as she drove up to the house. Prince examined the hound and her two pups regally—just before he ignored them altogether.

Striding out the door and wiping her floured hands on her apron, Fiona spontaneously hugged Rose the minute she stepped down, and Rose surprised herself by hugging her back with enthusiasm.

"Lor' an' I was believin' t' preacher was coomin' to visit, when behold, 'tis Miss Rose I'm seein'! An' 'tis welcome ye air, too. That is bein' t' preacher's rig?" She was curiously taking stock of the rake and broom handles sticking out the back.

"Yes it is, Mrs. McKennie," Rose answered. "He was kind enough to let me use it today."

Fiona gave her attention back to her visitor. "Miss Rose, I'd be fair honored to have ye be callin, me by me Christian name. Would ye be doin' so?"

"I'm the honored one, Fiona. Thank you."

"Well then, be coomin' inside for a cup o' tea and set doon a spell."

"Only for a bit. I've come to tell you some news, and then I must go again."

They were in the kitchen, and Fiona put the kettle on the stove.

"So. Time's coom already to be a leavin'?"

A tiny smile pulled at the corner of Rose's mouth. "Well, I can't be living forever in a boarding house."

"Aye, that's so, I'm sure." Fiona's enthusiasm faded a bit but she kept putting muffins on a lovely pale blue plate. Just at that moment Brian McKennie tramped in the door.

"Sure an' 'tis Miz Rose Brownlee coom to call!" He shook her hand vigorously and "smacked" Fiona's cheek.

"Aw Brian, what a way t' be behavin'! An' Miss Rose just sayin' as how she's going away."

Brian clucked his tongue disapprovingly.

Rose turned red and interjected immediately, "No, no, Fiona, I didn't finish. That is, what I said *exactly* was 'I couldn't live forever in a boarding house,' and that's because . . ."

Brian and Fiona were waiting, blankly.

"Because I . . . yesterday I bought the farm down the road!"

Brian looked at Fiona.

"The Anderson's old place? You know it, don't you?" Rose added hopefully.

"Bless the Lord!" Fiona uttered softly. "An' just what air ye plannin' t' be doin' with it, ye ignorant, wee city lass?"

"Why, I'm going to live there," she stated brightly.

"Air ye now?" Brian began to guffaw and turned to Fiona. "T' grand lady 'tis havin' more spunk than we credit her for, love. 'Tis good we're bein' her close neighbors so as t' be pointin' out to her which way t' creek be runnin'."

"I know which way the creek runs," Rose responded, her face reddening further. "And I'm not *entirely* ignorant. I'm willing to work and learn. As a matter of fact, that's why I came today. I . . . I had hoped you would come with me and look it over and tell me what needs fixing first and what you think and . . .Well, I guess you *did* tell me what you think . . . "

Rose suddenly had a vivid picture of how foolish she must appear to these people, people she really didn't know all that well. Almost as quickly, her "guidance" from the Lord shriveled into silly imaginings with wicked speed and clarity. She was so embarrassed and crushed that she made to stand up and leave. Brian McKennie's hand on her shoulder kept her in her chair.

"Nae, lass. Ye don' be mindin' us. Ye are havin' your reasons, I'm thinkin', and it's certain we'll be helpin' ye what we can, and ye can be sure o' that. When ye are carin' for someone, ye dinna like t' be seein' them hurt. But ye must ken this, Miss Rose; 'tis harder work than ye have ever been knowin', livin' on t' prairie." He sighed a soft sigh. "Boot, aye, we'll be helpin' ye."

Rose's tears trickled down her face and she wiped them away, ashamed. They cared? Brian worked studiously on a chain he was whittling, and Fiona finished making the tea while Rose regained her composure. The three of them drank the hot brew together and, through Brian and Fiona's questioning, Rose gradually unfolded her plans, her hopes. When they finished, Brian was ready to take a look.

"I'll be gettin' t' team and unhitchin' t' mule. Fiona, me love, be fixin' our lunch t' take and readyin' th' wee un, if ye will."

Brian drove his wagon behind Rose as she led the way back down the road. Rose's tools were in his wagon now, and Fiona sat beside her, nursing the baby. They drove in companionable quiet, their eyes following the movement of the prairie grass undulating like waves on the ocean under a light breeze, while baby Sean made little sucking and mewing noises.

"Fiona, may I ask you how old you are?" Rose queried.

"I? 'Tis being thirty-eight this year I am. Is't because o' t' bairn ye be askin'?"

"I suppose so. I had always assumed that having babies would be over at your age, at my age now for that matter. Did you mind?"

"Mind t' baby? Nae. 'Tis makin' ye young when a wee one cooms. 'Sides, 'tis t' grandest gift a man is givin' a woman and a woman is givin' her man, even now." She cuddled little Sean as if to assure him of her love and his importance.

The creek glistened in the sun ahead. Excitement began to well in Rose's heart when they turned up the little rise. Across the stream and fields she saw the Thoresens' barn, the cows grazing, the house and other fields as she remembered them.

"I'll have to meet them soon," she made a mental note to herself.

Then, Oh, yes! There it was, nestled by the slope below them. Prince took them into the yard and stopped in front of the house.

Rose didn't wait, but jumped down as soon as he stopped and ran to the door.

"My door, my house," she whispered. Inside, she began an imaginary cleaning, nodding her head as she looked about. The sound of Brian's wagon in the yard had her running back to unload her things. Fiona helped her and they mapped out a plan of attack that would commence as soon as they had the buckets, soap, and rags ready.

Brian examined the stable, the outhouse, and lean-to. Pulling the wagon up to the house he used it to climb up on the roof and came back down shaking his head.

Meanwhile, Rose and Fiona, after bedding down baby Sean on the floor of the carriage, were sweeping and wiping the walls and ceiling free of dust, dirt, and cobwebs. A fat spider gave Rose a turn, but she pressed her lips together and vowed to overcome spiders *and* blizzards. Right then Fiona lifted the lid to the stove and dropped it in haste.

"Brian! Brian—Oh, L-Lord!" she stuttered.

"What is it, Fiona?" Rose begged.

"Naught but a nest o' snakes, Miss Rose!" Fiona gasped while backing toward the door.

"Snakes!" Somehow Rose had never dreamed of snakes. Had not even considered snakes. Snakes had never entered her mind.

In her stove!

Concern was on Brian's face as he rushed in. "What is't, Fiona?"

"There be a nest o' the Divil's offspring a-livin' in t' stove, Brian McKennie!" Fiona's tone implied "And it's your fault; do something about it!"

"Oh?" Gingerly he raised the lid and received a warning rattle.

Backing off to a safe distance he muttered, "We've got t' kill 'em, sure, or they'll be tryin' t' coom back inside." He thought a moment. "First t' be pluggin' their way in so's they canna be goin' out, eh?"

Rose just nodded, but she was cold and shivering.

They collected her rags, bits of wood chunks, paper and anything small that would burn. The plan, Brian decided, was to trap them in the stove, open the flue and rain fire down on them from the stove pipe on the roof. Any snakes that managed to get out must be killed. They would either be asphyxiated, burned, or hacked to pieces if they managed to crawl out. For that last, Rose lifted her hatchet with a questioning look. Brian approved and fetched a hoe from his wagon, too.

Rose thought she would be ill from fear. Poisonous snakes! Finally Brian chose her to be the one to drop the burning debris on them from the roof, and secretly she sighed in relief. The tricky part was plugging the holes in the stove. Circling at a discreet distance, they examined the stove from all sides, looking for openings, when Rose exclaimed,

"The pipe! It's off the back of the stove!"

Brian maneuvered to where he could see and "hmm'ed." "T' be puttin' t' pipe on is needed, sure. An' I'm hopin' t' snakes will nae be wantin' oot t' same time!"

"Aw, Brian, use yer head an' dinna be takin' chances," Fiona entreated from several feet away.

"Nae." He took a deep breath and in one movement put the piece of pipe on the stove back, where it promptly fell off again. A symphony of rattling began. Brian paled and they all stepped back.

"It dinna fit tight," he muttered.

Rose bolted and ran outside. Her heart was pounding, and she found it hard to catch her breath. She stumbled and looked down. A long, twisted length of baling wire was snagged on her shoe.

"Brian! Can you make the pipe stay on with this?"

Brian picked up the strand and untangled it, then bent it in half.

"If I can be gettin' t' pipe on again, I must be holdin' it whilst some'un else fits t' wire an' twists it tight."

Fiona and Rose looked at each other.

"I-I'll do it," Rose stammered. "It's my stove."

And your snakes, too, she sneered at herself. Her stomach pitched uneasily.

Brian helped Fiona onto the roof and handed her a bucket with paper, rags, and kindling in it and two matches. He climbed up after her, pulled the roof off the stove chimney, and explained what she must do.

"Ye mu' be certain t' catch the rags on fire; t' soap on 'em will be burnin' well. When t' paper and sticks are doon t' pipe, drop t' rags ont' 'em an' be puttin' the lid back on t' pipe quick like."

Brian dropped to the ground, and he and Rose went back inside.

"Dinna ye lose yer nerve, lass. When t' pipe is on, I'll be holdin' it there. T' snakes canna coom out if I am holdin' it. Only be makin' the wire tight an' twist t' ends well. D' ye ken?"

Rose swallowed and nodded again. Together they approached the now-quiet stove. That was when they saw the large snake slither from the back of it. Rose shrieked, but Brian calmly got his hoe and standing between the door and the snake, waited until he had a clean shot. In one blow the snake lay twisting and dying—its head severed about four inches from its blunt nose.

"Now, if we dinna want t' fight 'em all," Brian urged. "An' the wee ones can be killin' ye same's the great 'uns—so ye canna be takin' chances wi' 'em."

Rose clenched her teeth to keep them from chattering while her hands shook badly. They approached the stove again, Brian poised to fit the pipe and Rose with her double strand of wire. In a flash Brian fit the pipe; the snakes began their warnings, and Rose, trembling all over, fumbled to loop the strands around the pipe. She pulled the ends together and, following Brian's hissed instructions, twisted the ends until they tightened about the pipe and made it secure. Brian gave it a few more turns to be sure before opening the flue and calling to Fiona,

"Now, Love!"

Bits of twigs, shredded paper, and other flammable materials fell down on the hapless reptiles. Inside the stove they were angry, rattling and slithering convulsively against the walls of their prison. Both Brian and Rose stood back, weapons ready. The pipe echoed with the thump of the snakes' heavy bodies as they attempted to use their former exit. Atop the roof, Fiona lit her rags in the bucket to shelter them from the wind. When they were full aflame she dumped them into the chimney and threw down the remaining fuel.

As the flames caught, the snakes went crazy, bumping and turning, trying vainly to escape. The sounds of their death struggles made Rose's skin crawl. She and Fiona linked arms while they waited outside, and it comforted Rose to feel Fiona trembling, too.

Brian gathered more sticks and a few larger chunks of wood. When he judged it safe, he lifted the stove lid and fed them in. The snakes' bodies sizzled and crackled as they burned. Brian used the hoe to pick up the decapitated remains of the other snake and added them to the pyre of his departed brother snakes.

"'Tis time t' be joinin' hands and thankin' the Lord for protecting us all," Brian declared. They stood close as Brian prayed fervently,

"Dear Lord, we're thankin' ye for savin' us from a horrible experience. An' I'm thankin' ye especially that Fiona and I was hearin' ye right to be helpin' Miss Rose today. Your Word is sayin' that we have power over serpents—well, it's glad we are for it! We be asking ye, too, to please be blessin' her workin' an' her dreams for a happy home here; we're givin' this house an' this land to You, for glorifyin' You, in Jesus' name. Amen."

After that point the day went quickly. Rose and Fiona gave the house a respectable cleaning, while Brian fixed the outhouse door, removed a pile of brush and debris from the yard to burn, and gathered the small amount of sticks, dry "chips," and wood available for use in the stove.

Since their children would be home from school around four o'clock, they needed to leave before then, but Brian blessed Rose with one more favor before going by cleaning out the remains in the stove and dumping them far from the house. After checking every rock, bush, and outbuilding (including under the house) he declared the area free of further snakes. Then he gave his assessment of the house to Rose too.

"'Tis knowin' the Anderson's to have been hard put t' keep things goin' that is lettin' me to understand how the house is so run doon. First, ye are needin' a new roof, certain. There be places where I could have been puttin' me foot through today easy. Second, some'uns got t' be makin' the whole thing snug afore winter or we'll find ye coom spring next year a thawin' out. Nae, there be a fair piece o' workin' t' be doon, an' me with three fields waitin' t' plow right now."

"But Brian, I don't expect you to do my work. Mr. Morton told me there were men whom I could hire as carpenters. Do you know who those might be?"

"Sure an' I'm knowin' two or three. 'Tis findin' some as not too busy plantin' right now 'tis t' trick. But be lettin' me ask Jan," (he pronounced it 'Yahn'), "Thoresen first, for he's the finest worker as I know wi' buildin' anything. An' besides he an' his son bein' ahead o' the crowd for gettin' their peas an' corn in first this year."

"I would really appreciate your asking him, Brian."

"Right ye are. We'll be goin' now, an' ye too, eh?"

"Yes," Rose answered ruefully. Her whole body was tired. But looking back once more from the buggy she was satisfied. "This time tomorrow, Lord willing and 'the creek don't rise,' I will be back, and this will be my home."

Prince was anxious to get back to his stall, and they trotted down the roads, Rose letting the breeze ruffle her hair and cool her contented face.

Chapter 12

"Pastor! Pastor Medford! May I talk with you a moment?" Rose was breathless from hurrying to catch up with him and not appear unladylike.

"Mrs. Brownlee! How was your drive yesterday? The liveryman tells me you paid for a measure of oats for Prince when he unhitched and groomed him. I thank you very much; I'm sure Prince thanks you too!"

"Oh, he is a lovely animal and deserved a treat. That is mostly what I wanted to talk to you about also. Can we sit down for a minute?"

They seated themselves on a bench in front of Schmidt's store.

"How is Mrs. Medford today?" Rose began.

"She's fine, fine. Doing the wash and general housekeeping chores this morning. It doesn't take much to keep our little home tidy but she does it all faithfully."

"Well, I have a few things to tell you, Pastor, first being that I bought the old Anderson homestead day before last." Her face was shining as she told him.

"You mean you are going to live in RiverBend? That is marvelous! Won't Vera be pleased—why, I can't tell you how happy that will make both of us. Really."

Her eyes twinkled. "You don't think I'm a foolish, ignorant city woman doing such a thing?"

Nodding sagely he replied, "Oh, you will find out how hard it can be, but you'll also find it rewarding. Besides, where God leads us, he will take care of us—don't you agree?"

"Yes! Yes, I do! But how did you know God led me here?" Rose inquired, amazed.

"Any Christian can be led by the Holy Spirit," he answered smiling. "In fact although God uses various ways to speak to us, he wants to guide in everything we do, if we'll listen. You'll find that in Romans chapter eight."

Rose repeated the reference, storing it up to be read later. "I really knew it was him when I heard your sermon Sunday about Abraham. Someday, maybe I can share with you the whole story. But today, Pastor, I have a business proposition for you. Actually, two. First, I have a load of things to be moved out to my house. The stationmaster will rent his freight wagon to me, but I need a man to load, drive, and unload. Will you take the job?"

"I'd be very happy to help you, Mrs. Brownlee."

"It's a paying job."

"That's not necessary between friends, I assure you."

"It's the only kind of job I have."

"But I won't accept payment, Ma'am."

Rose studied the man sitting beside her. He was very young, thin, and sunburned, and his work clothes, though clean and neat, were worn. Still, he had an air of total peace and assurance about him.

"Fine, then! It goes in the offering!"

This bold statement startled him, and he began to chuckle, then laugh. Rose smiled. Pastor Greenstreet and this man were so unlike. This man had such . . . joy! She really liked it.

"Well, (ha ha!) you said you had two propositions, Mrs. Brownlee. I'm anxious (ha, ho, ho!) to hear if the other will be as humorous. Ha! I beg your pardon!" He held his sides, still chuckling.

Rose flushed. "This is a bit bold rather than humorous, I'm afraid, but . . . well, I'll just say it straight out. I would like to buy Prince and your buggy, if you will part with them." She named a price.

Unexpectedly, tears came to his eyes. Rose was totally unprepared for this and began to apologize in confusion.

"No, no. No, Mrs. Brownlee, no apology is needed. You see, God is so good and so faithful. How could you know that a week ago Sunday my dear wife and I asked God together to please find us a buyer for our horse and buggy?"

He paused and cleared his throat. "How could you know we needed just the amount you offered?"

Rose felt a pricking on her neck and recalled the night God had spoken to her.

"Oh!" she breathed. "Is it like that every time? Does God always answer like that?"

"Not every time like that, but when he does it's so special . . . so very personal." He shook his head and began to grin. "Now *I* know God led you here."

Pastor Medford went to get the wagon while Rose went to get Prince. He nickered a greeting when he saw her and she stroked his neck lovingly.

"Good old boy! You're going to live at my house now and be my horse. I'm so glad, Prince!"

His dapple-gray coat rippled as he pawed the flooring with his right front hoof. Rose called to the liveryman.

"I'm buying Pastor Medford's horse today and taking him out of your stable. I'd like to buy some hay and oats from you and also, would you be so kind as to show me how to harness him to the buggy?"

The liveryman stared at her suspiciously and spat on the barn floor.

"Who gonna pay fer the bill he's behind on?" he demanded rudely.

With dignity Rose asked, "How much is it?"

"Ten dollar, count t'day."

"I'll pay it. And the hay and oats. Pastor Medford will be by for them later this afternoon." She took out her purse and carefully counted out the money. "Now, about the harnessing?"

Rose felt like she was just getting the hang of it when her wagonload of store goods arrived. Pastor Medford jumped down and showed her to untwist one of the lines.

"Be a reel homestider yit, Miz. Brownlee, Ma'am," he drawled. "Say, Vera would love to drive out with us. Would you like a little more help?"

"Would I? How marvelous! And here is your check for Prince. I thank you so much for him."

"My pleasure, Ma'am. Now, shall I get Mrs. Medford and be on our way?"

"By all means! I will be right ahead of you."

They worked together unloading the wagon. Mrs. Medford (Vera now) was as excited as Rose over every item. A wash tub, blankets, feather bed, muslin sheets, towels, pots and pans, two lamps with lamp oil, and groceries were stacked on the floor. Next, a small table and two chairs were brought in, her trunk, a wide board and a dozen or so brick blocks. Vera looked quizzically at the board and bricks.

"Do those come in here, Rose?"

"Don't you recognize my bed?" Rose teased. "I'm going to stack the bricks and use the board for a bed frame. Just temporarily though."

"Oh." Uncertainly.

"Well, I should get these groceries put away, but first we should unload my bag from the buggy and send Pastor back to town for another load."

"What next, madam boss?" he asked, sticking his head in the door.

"Well, for starters, what do folks burn to keep warm? There aren't many trees."

"A lot of folk have burned 'buffalo chips' for years, but I recommend coal for you, and you buy that and lumber from the company at the depot."

"I guess I can do with what I have for a few days, but Prince needs his feed and hay today."

"I'll go get it. Be back in a few hours. By the way, do you have a pitchfork?"

"Pitchfork?"

"Yes, for . . . for cleaning out Prince's stall." He was trying not to laugh as he read her face finally draw the right conclusion.

"Er, no. Would Schmidt's have one?"

"I'll pick one up for you—I'm sure they'll trust you for it."

"Oh, Jacob," interjected Mrs. Medford. "Rose has no pillow. She's just forgotten to get one, I'm sure, but we have an extra. Would you get it for her?"

With all his instructions he was finally leaving when Rose said to Vera, "Its lunch time! He'll never get anything to eat if it isn't now."

Waving and "yoo-hooing" they brought him back. Lunch was spread out under the tree again: bread and butter, sweet cucumber chips, cheese and gingerbread. Jacob pumped a pail of cold water from the well near the back porch.

Then, once satisfied, it was hard to get moving again; the creek babbled, cows from the far pastures could be heard faintly, and in the afternoon's warmth, drowsiness settled on them all. At last Pastor Medford got up with a sigh and patted his stomach.

"If a man shall not work, he shall not eat," he quoted. "And a man who eats too much may not get back to work!"

They smiled, friendly, familiar smiles. Pastor Medford left in the wagon, and the ladies went back to their unpacking. Seeing Prince grazing contentedly in his small pasture made Rose think of where he would sleep that night. She walked out to the barn and with the rake cleaned out the old straw and swept away the dirt. She would have to have the stall worked on too. Cleaning it didn't take long. Now to "make" her bed.

Rose positioned the bricks at the four corners of the bed, stacking them two high. Two more stacks were placed halfway down the middle of each long side. Then Vera helped her lift the awkward board onto the bricks. By moving the brick stacks a bit here and there, they got it right. Next came the feather mattress, which was like a thick, overstuffed feather quilt. They laid it on top of the board and then covered it with a muslin sheet, tucking it in all around, and another sheet tucked in at the foot. The blankets went on top of that.

"There! See, now it's a bed," Rose proclaimed proudly.

"Yes, it is," Vera agreed. "Where would you like your trunk?"

"One on either side, I think, will give it a nice effect. The flat-topped one will be my lamp table at night when I am in bed reading or writing to my family."

"Do you have a family, Rose?" Vera asked cautiously.

"I have a dear mother and a brother Tom. He and his wife Abigail will give me a niece or nephew in August."

"It must have been hard to leave them?"

"No, in a way it's been a great help. I do miss them though. I will go back to visit next year."

They pulled and pushed the trunk into place, shouting with laughter like girls over their puny efforts. Rose laid her birthday carpetbag in the corner by the smaller trunk. They set the table near the tiny window, and seeing the chairs drawn up like they had always been there, they sat down.

"I will have to get bigger windows," Rose stated to Vera. "I want sunshine and to be able to see the creek. Isn't the view lovely?"

Vera bent, sweeping her gaze across the trees, the creek, and the fields and pastures of Thoresens' to the distant horizon.

"Worth every penny!" That made them both laugh again.

"Thank you so much for all your help today, Vera."

"Well, we're not finished yet, are we? Where do I put this washtub?"

"I don't know. What do you use it for?"

They shouted until the tears ran. At last Vera pointed, gasping to the back door. "I think you could hang it outside."

Rose looked and found a nail in the wall.

"Not an original idea—there's a nail already here!" She giggled.

The washtub was hung with ceremony. Next the pots and pans were put into a box by the stove and covered by a clean towel, and Rose began to sort through the food items. The little house had only three shelves about two feet long to use, but it was plenty of room for today. Coffee, tea, sugar, baking powder, salt, little papers of assorted spices, several tins of peaches and tomatoes, a few jars of pickles and vegetables, two colorful glasses of crabapple jelly, small sacks of potatoes, beans, dry peas, and lentils were lined up on the shelves. In addition, a piece of bacon, some eggs and cheese and a dish of butter needed to be kept somewhere cool.

"There must be a root cellar," Vera insisted.

Outside they searched the ground all around the house, but didn't find anything.

"Maybe they just didn't have one?" Rose suggested.

"Not likely. Folks can't eat all winter without a place to keep their potatoes and carrots."

Through the overgrown yard they searched, farther from the house as they kept looking. On the other side of Prince's barn and back against the hill was a grassy mound that puzzled Rose.

"What is this, Vera?" she called.

Vera trampled through the tall grass to her side.

"It's an old soddy!"

"What is that?"

"Simply put, it's a dirt and grass house. Prairie grass grows deep roots. When folks first homesteaded a place, they plowed their fields and picked up the chunks of sod to make a house. They stacked them like bricks, sort of, and they actually lived in them. Some people still do. You see, the sod would keep growing and grow the pieces together. In the winter with a stove it was warm, in the summer it was cool. Later when the trains came there was lumber to be bought, and people built regular frame houses."

"What do you think is in there?" Rose wanted to know.

"I don't know, but let's not find out ourselves. Jacob will be here soon; maybe he will open it. Since there isn't a cellar, most likely this is where they kept things cool, but it would have been terribly inconvenient so far from the house."

"Mr. Anderson may have become ill when he wanted to dig his," Rose conjectured.

When Pastor Medford arrived back with the hay and feed, the sun was making the last of its golden sweep across the sky. In the haste to unload and get the wagon back to town, both ladies forgot to mention the soddy to him.

For a long time after they were gone Rose sat on the single front step gazing at the shadows thrown far over the fields and prairie by the sun setting behind her. She knew the moment it dropped behind her hill, when everything for a mile from her creek eastward was quickly thrown into shadow. In the distance sunlight still played on the grassy land.

Tomorrow she would wake up in her own home. Tomorrow it would be one week since she stepped off the train just to spend a day or two in a clean hotel and yet she had found so much more. Tomorrow she would really settle in and, yes, write her family a long letter.

"God, you can help me say it all in just the right way," she whispered. "Let them see through my pen the prairie, the freedom, the place of rest I'm finding in you."

Rose didn't even fill the lamps that night. She ate a biscuit with her tea, washed her face and hands and, in her new nightgown, crawled exhausted into her new bed, glad to have Vera's pillow under her head. As she closed her eyes she remembered that the door had neither a latch nor a lock.

" . . . Whoso hearkeneth unto me shall dwell safely," she murmured.

Chapter 13

"Hello! Miss Rose, air ye there?"

Rose's sleep was filled with vague, lighthearted dreams. Gradually the "halloo-ing" crept in, pushing sleep away. She stared around the room confused and dewy-eyed with slumber until someone knocked at the door.

"Miss Rose! Air ye in there? 'Tis Fiona!"

Fiona! Daylight peeped through the little glass panes of the one small window.

"Oh, my!" Rose climbed stiffly out of bed toward the door. "Fiona, hello! I'm sorry—I've just awakened, and I'm a sight." She opened the door a crack. The bright sunlight hurt her eyes and she smiled sheepishly.

"I must have overslept. Come in. It's so quiet out here that I didn't wake up early."

Fiona walked in and glanced around approvingly. "Ye've been workin' hard, an' it's showin', too."

"Thank you. Why don't you sit down, Fiona? I'll make coffee—no, let me fix my hair first—"

"I'll be makin' t' coffee. Ye can be doin' yoursel' up whilst I poomp t' water."

Rose dressed quickly and combed out her long hair, twisting and winding it until it was in its normal "do." Using the last of the sticks she got a respectable fire going and soon had the chill off the room. Fiona returned with the water bucket full of icy water and set it on the stove.

"I heard a noise in t' stall and what air I findin? T' preacher's horse lookin' at me wi' those big, brown eyes o' his'n."

"Yes! I bought him! Oh, Fiona, isn't he sweet?"

Fiona laughed. "Sweet! Sure an' a cow is a darlin' too. Well, onyway I rode one o' t' team to fetch ye t' news an' I canna stay more'n a minute, for the baby is nappin' an' Brian is in t' field, boot Jan Thoresen an' his son will be doin' yer work for ye—if ye air willin'—an' coomin' tomorra t' start. They have their first plantin' in an' can spare most o' two weeks afore goin' back t' field. That is, after mornin' chores an' milkin', an' home for same in t' evenin'."

"Tomorrow! But that's wonderful. I'll need to go to town today then to make the arrangements for lumber, and I need a load of coal."

She got the coffee for them and they sipped it in companionable silence. Fiona looked around the room again.

"Many a homesteader was startin' with far less than this."

Rose nodded. "Yes. I have quite an advantage. Thank you, Fiona, for coming all the way to tell me about the Thoresens. That's another advantage I have—good friends."

She took Fiona's cup when she stood. Impulsively she hugged her.

"Neighbors. I'm going to like it, Fiona," she grinned.

Fiona laughed, her red-apple cheeks shining. "Aye. 'Twill be grand."

After Fiona rode away, Rose said a "good morning" to Prince. He stomped his feet in appreciation of her company. He wasn't used to being alone! She measured out his feed and pumped a bucket of water before going back in, then made a thorough toilet, banked the fire, and stepped back out.

"Here's hoping I remember how to harness you!" she whispered to Prince.

Twenty minutes later she was just getting it right. Perspiration stood out on her brow when the last piece was buckled. Prince turned his head as if to say, "Well? Can we get started now?"

At this point Rose was feeling very familiar with the road to town and the families owning farms along the way. She hoped she might meet more of them soon.

In town, the stationmaster, Mr. Bailey, greeted her with neighborly friendliness.

"Well, it seems I'm going to need a load of coal today," she began.

"Sure thing, Miz Brownlee. How's it going out there? Gettin' settled in an' all?"

"Oh, yes! But I've been so busy with one thing or another, in and out of town, I don't really *feel* settled yet. But soon, I'm certain. The men are going to start work on my house tomorrow, too, so I would like to make it as simple as possible for them to get materials for me. How would you suggest I do that?"

"Shucks, Miz Brownlee, I know yer good fer it. Why, ever'body knows thet yer—" (He caught himself before the fatal blunder.) "Ah, thet you, ah, always pay yer bills. Yes, that's it. Sure."

"That is very kind of you. Perhaps if you don't mind being paid by check, I will pay my account every month. Just to start off right, here is a payment toward tomorrow's purchase. Mr. Thoresen will pick out what he needs and sign for it."

"Got ol' Thor'sen, hey? He's a great carpenter—know it certain. Couldn't hardly do better. Say, I'll load up the coal. Will the preacher be haulin' it?"

"I think so. I'm going that way now. Thank you very much."

"Sure thing, Miz Brownlee."

This time Rose went through the tailor shop to the flight of stairs, under the rude appraisal of the dressmaker, unannounced. She rapped on the door to Medfords' apartment, and Vera answered. Her delicate face beamed.

"Rose! We thought we wouldn't see you again until Sunday! Come in."

"Hello! How are you today, Pastor Medford?"

The young man stood when Rose entered. His Bible, notebook, and another large volume lay open on the table before him.

"Just fine; doing a little studying this morning. Won't you please sit down? What can we help you with?"

"If you're busy, I can find someone else; it's not important enough to—"

"Whatever it is, I will be happy to do it. Now tell me."

"It's a load of coal. But you drove out there twice already yesterday."

"And today will make three. I'll get my hat and work gloves." He carefully closed and put away his study things while Vera showed Rose a quilt she was making.

"It's going to be lovely." Rose's admiring inspection took in the repeating pattern of green and golden-red leaves. "I would love to learn to sew. I embroider but never learned to sew much."

"It's not hard. But it does require time and patience. I could help you."

"Would you?" Rose responded enthusiastically. This much younger woman constantly amazed her. Born and bred in gentility just as she was, and yet she was coping with near-poverty with such grace and confidence.

"I'm sure to have plenty of time next winter—this might help me with the 'patience' part if I get cabin fever," she added ruefully.

Vera's tinkling laughter cheered Rose. What a good friend she was going to be!

"I should go now," Rose excused herself. "I have some 'settling in' to do before the carpenters come tomorrow."

"Tomorrow? That's very timely. Who did you get?"

"Actually, Brian McKennie got them for me—my near neighbors the Thoresens."

"Oh, Rose, they are the dearest people. Very old country in a lot of ways, but as friendly and industrious as can be. Amalie Thoresen will nurse any sick person she hears of, and Jan Thoresen will do fine work for you for I've heard it said he's the finest carpenter in the county. Doesn't speak much English, but his son Søren is as American as you are."

"On another point, Rose, the Thoresens are a very devoted Christian family. What I mean is that they have a real heart to serve God. I know, because without fail you can find them involved in whatever need there might be. And Rose, God has really used them to help us stay here and build this church."

"Do you mean that they give to the church?"

"Faithfully. We thank God for their family."

Rose digested that while making her good-byes. She recalled Mr. Schmidt's comments on how "the preacher wasn't able to feed his horse well" and they bothered her. The church needed more families like Thoresens. She made a mental resolution for herself and climbed into the buggy.

The drive home went quickly. Rose had a number of things to accomplish and planned them out, the most important being a letter to her family. She had been in RiverBend a week and had made a major decision that would affect her whole life—now she would have to explain it to them.

Rose unharnessed Prince and rubbed him down as Pastor Medford had shown her, then put him in his pasture. It was more like a very large corral, but Rose was glad it was small, because it kept Prince near the house, and she felt less alone. He wandered out a few steps and then astounded Rose by dropping to the ground and rolling in the dirt, legs high in the air. His grunts of satisfaction were hilarious.

Oh, Prince, you're happy to be home too, aren't you, she thought.

Then carefully washing her hands at the pump she started the day's projects. In the large trunk were a number of things to unpack but she chose only her writing desk for the moment. Its rich, well-oiled wood was beautiful to work on and she made herself comfortable on the bed with it. Lifting the hinged lid she selected pen, ink, blotter and stationery. Before beginning, she arranged everything on the desktop and paused to pray again for guidance in writing.

May 2

Dear Mother, Tom, and Abigail,

I am still in the little town of RiverBend. Spring is just breathtaking here. You've never seen the prairie when it's all green and soft, but it's so wide and free. Mother, the grass is the same shade of spring green as my shawl.

About the town: it boasts a train that stops twice a week, a general store that sells just about everything, a boarding house (Mrs. Owens'), a tailor, seamstress, barber, feed store and stable, lumber supply, church, post office, bank, and three schools. Actually, there is one school in town, and two others each about ten miles out. So you can see it is a little town, but quite up-and-coming. At least that is what Mr. Morton of the bank says.

Mr. Morton is the gentleman who took me driving in the country when I first arrived here last week. It was so refreshing to be off the train and in the clean out-of-doors. Mr. Morton is a young, ambitious man (of a good family, of course); nevertheless his company is not my "cup of tea." He did, however, show me a lovely piece of property outside of town right on a little creek, and I thank him for that.

To come to the point, which you may find difficult to understand at first, I have bought the property Mr. Morton showed me. When I came out here I didn't really know what I was looking for. I only know that I believed God was leading me. Now I believe this is where he wants me, at least for now. I hope you can trust him to take care of me and that you can be happy for me also.

The property was a homestead once so it has exactly 160 acres or, as the townsfolk say, one-quarter section. Near the creek is a small house. I'm going to have it fixed up really nice, and I'm now also the proud owner of a handsome old gent of a horse who goes by the name of "Prince." Prince came with a good buggy and lives in my little barn. It is really a small stable, but a prince should live in something grander than a stable, don't you think? My neighbors to the west are a charming family from good Irish stock. A precious collection of china and silver, a dowry for generations, adorns their walls. Mother, I thought I would stare at one of their teacups for an hour, it has such luminous quality. They also have five lovely children, the eldest being a young lady of sixteen by the name of Meg. She is naturally blessed with grace and form and an abundance of rich auburn hair. She is a real beauty. As her dream is to be a teacher, she plans to attend teacher's college and is working to pay for it. In my opinion she is an exemplary young woman and is fast becoming a good friend as is her mother, Fiona.

Tomorrow, the carpenters are coming to begin the refurbishing of my little house. It has only one room right now, about 15 by 25, with a built-on pantry and a very small loft in the pitch of the roof. When they finish, my one room will be two and greatly improved in many ways.

I plan on becoming a member of the church here too. The Pastor and his wife are also from back east, and I know I'm going to enjoy their friendship.

I've included with my letter a list of some of my belongings. Would you please have them crated and shipped to me? I'm looking forward to having some of the comforts of home—like soft sheets! There is also a list for the gardener. One thing I long to do is make my little home bloom. If I receive the plantings before the end of this month, they should have a good start.

I hope my words have helped you envision my new home. Please believe me when I say I'm happy and doing well.

Abby, I am so anticipating being "Aunt Rose." Next year this time I shall have been with you all to introduce myself to my niece or nephew.

Until then, I will write faithfully. Please know you have my prayers and all my

Love,

Rose

Sighing, Rose finished blotting her slanting script and carefully addressed the envelope. When the letter was ready to send, she set it on the table against the lamp and looked forward to more pleasant tasks.

The sounds of a wagon rattling over the rise announced that her coal was here. Pastor Medford drove the wagon up to the pantry door while Rose opened the coal bin. It was a wide, deep box with a lid, on one end of the pantry. When Pastor Medford shoveled it full of coal it only held about half of the load.

"Where would you like the rest of this, Rose?" he inquired. His face was streaked with coal dust and sweat.

"Let me get you a cool glass of water first while I decide."

He nodded and accepted the tin mug gratefully. Tacked on the outside of the pantry was a small lean-to.

"Can you just shovel it in here?" She asked.

"No reason why not. Looks fine to me."

He handed the cup back to her and attacked the remaining coal. Tossing the shovel into the empty wagon bed he grinned.

"Thar, Miz Brownlee, all set fer any o' blizzard that'd dare blow in!"

"Well, I think I'd best get my roof fixed before we have 'any o' blizzards,'" she returned. "And thank you kindly, Pastor Medford."

"Sure thing. Now I've got to hustle. I can finish my sermon today and take Vera on a picnic to the river tomorrow."

"That sounds nice. Have a wonderful time."

She wandered back into the house aimlessly. Finally she got her notebook and began to sketch what she wanted done to the house. After she had it right she began on the outside. Then she started to plan the landscaping.

The gardener would carefully pack a selection of bulbs and seeds and the starts she'd asked for, so she needed to be ready when they came. Much later it occurred to her that the sun was setting again and she had neglected to eat since breakfast.

"What shall I have for dinner?" she asked herself aloud.

With some small pieces of kindling and coal she built up the fire. She scorched a finger and dirtied her skirt in the process. This was going to take some getting used to on her part, she could tell. Next she heated a skillet and sliced a piece of bacon into it, sniffing the delicious odor as it sizzled. When it was just about right, she cracked an egg into its bubbling juices and basted it with the grease until it was perfect. A slice of bread with butter rounded off the meal. Instead of eating at the table, Rose sat on the rickety front step, enjoying the sunset almost as much as the last evening. It seemed to her in her solitude that she had always sat on this step, in this twilight, with this contentment. At last, the shadows indicated it was time to go in.

Tonight she filled the lamps for the first time and lit them both. Taking hot water from the stove, she cleaned up from her simple meal and prepared for bed. Then leaving the lamp on the trunk by her bed lit and blowing out the other, she took her Bible and read until sleepy.

"Tomorrow the carpenters come!" she reminded herself gladly and extinguished the light.

Chapter 14

Rose was up early, washed and dressed in time to watch the sunrise. She treated herself to an extra cup of coffee before planning her day. The crisp air and pale blue sky seemed to indicate another warm one, and she smiled in anticipation.

After setting her work for the morning, she knelt by her bed and prayed. Special consideration was given to each of the two families who had made themselves so indispensable to her; the McKennies and Medfords. Once again she prayed for Mr. Schmidt. It seemed to Rose that he had a good heart, but was far away from finding God and in fact had no real knowledge of what God was actually like, just notions gathered along life's way. *How many "good" folk were in the world,* she wondered, *who were in reality far from God, lost and lonely?* She took time to pray for Mrs. Schmidt too, and included the tailor's hardened old wife and the liveryman.

"Bless them today, Lord, and let them know it's from you so they can turn to you," she whispered. Lastly, she asked for guidance on everything she had planned, giving each thing to his control.

"I thank you for bringing me here, and I really want to obey you in whatever it is you have for me."

Rose heard a splashing from the creek and went to the door. Two large men were sloshing up the slope from the stream. They were both wearing work pants, plaid shirts and sturdy boots. The younger one carried a large wooden box loaded with tools, while the older man had a saw across his shoulder and a tin pail in his other hand. It was the blonde/bronze boy from church and the man with a wagonload of children!

The young man introduced himself as Søren Thoresen and shook her hand politely and with a shy grin. Rose liked him right away. He turned and introduced his father, Jan Thoresen, Rose taking note again that the proper pronunciations were "Yahn" and "Torasen." Mr. Thoresen gazed steadily at her while shaking her hand and rumbled "Gud Morn" but nothing else.

"Brian was right about Søren," Rose evaluated. "He's as much a part of the west as the freight manager at the station!"

Mr. Thoresen impressed her differently. He seemed quiet, reserved, although his size and strong build belied his being the father of a twenty-three year old son. But the most compelling features in his sunburned and weathered face were his eyes. It was disquieting to Rose to be examined with such detachment.

Icy-blue. But not cold. Not exactly, she pondered. The thought of a Norwegian fiord, clear, deep, and still came to her. Søren was a much livelier and comfortable version of his father.

Rose showed them around. Most of the repairs were obvious; Søren and his father held animated conversation in Norwegian, pointing, taking measurements, and "test shaking" was the word Rose coined for it. *Everything* needed to be made sturdy again, Søren informed her, especially the doors and roof. When the blizzards hit, anything not nailed down snugly or firmly built would likely be blown away. They inspected the barn, the lean-to that abutted the barn, the outhouse and, beginning with the roof, the whole house with its attached pantry and lean-to. While they were discussing the front door frame, Rose timidly drew out her notes, and requested their attention.

"Excuse me. I, ah, I know it's important to make everything weatherproof, and I want that of course. But while you're working on the basics, I would like, that is I have some ideas I would like incorporated. Right here . . . on these papers?"

The two men were silent as she spread the sheets out on the table. The rectangle box representing the house was divided into two rooms, parlor and kitchen. The parlor doubled as Rose's bedroom and the kitchen for everything else—working, writing, cooking, and eating. Major improvements were the windows on the east and south walls, the interior wall to make two rooms, cupboards and shelves— lots of them. Last but not least, a porch the entire length of the front and the width of the south side of the house. They studied her sketches, Mr. Thoresen pointing and making comments.

At last Søren spoke. "These windows must be ordered. Mr. Bailey's company doesn't stock them this size, and he only keeps a few on hand anyway. If you are intent on this . . . veranda? My father says it should be built last only after the roof is replaced, the interior work done, doors fixed and windows installed. He means to make you as snug as we can for your money and in the time we have and feels the decorative part should wait. We may not be able to get to it until late summer if we're to do the essential repairs between plantings now. That's about two weeks."

Rose answered. "I see." She couldn't keep the disappointment from her voice, but knew she was being childish.

Mr. Thoresen was looking at her intently, so she mustered a bright smile and responded, "Well then, we will get the essentials done and not worry about the porch until later. But I do want it as soon as is convenient."

Nodding, Søren picked up his tools, and the two men set to business. While they were working, Rose fed Prince and put him in his pasture. He looked questioningly askance at her quick visit so she relented, spending five minutes scratching his forehead and patting his neck. He responded by laying his muzzle on her shoulder. How she loved this horse! Finally, Prince moved away of his own accord to graze, and she fetched her rake, hoe, and hatchet.

Rose didn't know how to go about clearing brush, but she could see what she wanted removed. Brian had cleared the front fairly well, so she widened the area, working around the side in narrow swaths. Each time she hoed down a respectable amount of grass or brush she would rake it into a pile. She made two piles, one on either side of the house. Her hands already stung inside her gloves, and her back protested when she would straighten, but she kept at it. The growing open space was her reward.

At midmorning, every loose board had been nailed down. Søren and Mr. Thoresen were making a list of lumber and materials needed and called for her to come and approve it. Aware of how dirty and disheveled she had made herself, Rose made haste to assure them that whatever they needed was fine.

"All the arrangements are made with Mr. Bailey—you can pick up whatever you need."

Mr. Thoresen spoke rapidly to Søren in Norwegian and he agreed.

"My father suggests one of us take our wagon to town to get the lumber. There are several things to be done here in the meantime, so I'll leave right away."

"That's fine." Rose hurried away to the pump. With her hanky she washed her hands in the cold water. She removed her straw hat and tidied her hair before going back to clearing brush. A new respect for her hoe was in her eye when she began again.

She heard Mr. Thoresen working on Prince's barn, the sound of his hammer blows rhythmic and sure, while Prince stood curiously at the fence watching what he could.

Rose's brush clearing advanced to the back of the house. Again and again she brought the hoe down on the roots of the brush. The largest green roots required using the hatchet to cut through. It was satisfying to see the pile of brush grow and the clearing spread out.

Mr. Thoresen was working on the outhouse now, knocking the old roof off in preparation for a new one. Rose was happy about that, considering the leaky alternative!

For an hour more she labored, going to the pump to bathe her face and hands once. Her back was in pain, but she kept at it, hoeing down the "enemy" (as she now considered all weeds) and raking them into mounds. In her heart she knew she was overdoing it, that it didn't all need to be done today, but she stubbornly kept on. She was struggling to get the last bunch into her pile when turning around she ran right into Mr. Thoresen. She was so surprised, she just stood there. He reached out and took the rake from her exhausted hand.

"Too much," he said mildly. "Sit, please." Without another word he took over her job.

Rose didn't dispute with him. At the pump she washed again and went into the house. In spite of her dusty shoes, she lay down upon her bed and didn't realize she'd drifted off to sleep until the sound of lumber being piled in the yard startled her awake. Her instincts told her it was way past lunchtime. One o'clock! She'd been asleep more than an hour.

"Ohh!" Rose's back protested when she got up. She pushed herself up and, putting on her hat, limped outside. Søren and Mr. Thoresen were just finishing unloading the wagon.

"Have you eaten lunch yet?"

Søren laughed. "No, but I'm hungry enough to. We brought it in that pail, and I'm just getting back as you can see, so we're about ready now."

"Would you like some coffee with it?"

Mr. Thoresen knew what coffee was, apparently, for he responded decidedly, "Ja! Dat's gud."

Rose went to get the water. Most of the back yard was free of brush and grass! In addition, the pile of brush was smoldering, nearly reduced to ashes. She checked the sides. Yes, both piles were burning. Mr. Thoresen had done it while she was sleeping.

Rose stirred up the fire and put the pot on. For her own lunch she sliced bread and cheese, opened a can of peaches, and served out a small dish. When everything was ready, she took a cloth and the coffeepot out to the larger tree and laid them out. Returning to the house she got her plate and three cups. The last item was a pail of icy water from the pump.

Søren and his father, both leaning against the tree, were waiting for her, lunches ready. They looked happy to take a break, and Rose recalled that they had already done the "choring" of their large farm before coming to work for her!

Mr. Thoresen blessed the food softly in Norwegian and Rose and Søren said "amen" at the same time. Then they opened their lunch pail. Rose was astonished at what they pulled out. Great open-faced sandwiches made of thick slices of meat, cheese, and onions followed by pickles, carrot sticks, sliced turnips, cookies, dried apple slices, two quarter-pie sections of squash pie, and a small cheese wrapped in a damp cloth emerged from that bucket. Tucking clean cloths into their shirt collars the two men began to eat. And eat. Rose looked at her bread and cheese. They had both devoured half their sandwiches and several pickles, carrots, and turnip slices when she nibbled her first bite.

Mr. Thoresen said something amusing to Søren who chuckled in agreement.

"What did he say?" Rose asked smiling.

"Oh, he said that the reason you are so thin is that no one has ever fed you properly."

Rose's cheeks and neck flamed in embarrassment.

Mr. Thoresen's eyebrows went up and Søren apologized immediately.

"Mrs. Brownlee, I'm sorry—what he said wasn't meant to be rude. Our women are so hearty that they eat quite a bit. Why, Sigrün eats nearly as much as I do when we are harvesting. I truly apologize if we've offended you."

Rose nodded. After a moment she offered, "I'm not used to working hard—or even seeing men work hard and eat as well, I mean as *much*, as you do. I'm sure my appetite will get better out-of-doors. You see, I was sick a while ago and haven't got my weight back yet. But I will."

Both Søren and Mr. Thoresen nodded in agreement as Søren translated what she said. Mr. Thoresen cut a small wedge from the wrapped cheese and offered it to her.

"Gjetost," (yay-toost) he stated. "Gud, gud for you."

"Goat's cheese," Søren explained. "Our specialty from Norway. It's very nutritious. We have five goats in addition to our cows."

Rose sniffed it dubiously, but was afraid to offend them by not trying it. Cautiously she nibbled the dark brown substance. It was different, quite strong. She thought she could like it so she took another bite. It was all right and she finished the piece. "I like it. Thank you."

"My father wants to know if you have milk here."

"Well, no, but maybe I could buy some from you?"

"Yes, he says we will work something out."

Mr. Thoresen spoke again, and Søren repeated it to her.

"He says if you have been ill you should be careful and not overdo it by working outside too long like you did today, until you build your strength up." Søren chuckled and shook his head. "There's more, too, Mrs. Brownlee, and I apologize for my father's boldness. He's a very kind man, but he basically says what's on his mind without considering if it might be taken wrongly. Please understand that his advice is meant in friendliness. He also says you are too pale (chuckle) and should work outside sometimes without a hat because the sunshine is good for you and will give you color— but, again, not too long at a time (another chuckle), and that you should eat more, of course."

Mr. Thoresen was seriously looking at both of them so Rose thanked him demurely and valiantly ate everything on her plate, including the second piece of gjetost and several pickles and cookies Mr. Thoresen insisted on adding to her lunch.

Rose wondered if her sore muscles would let her get up when lunch was over. Finally the two men stood and stretched. They excused themselves and went back to work so she picked up the dishes, groaning as she did, and shook the cloth.

To her surprise, both men were in the house moving everything to one side of the room.

"We are going to paper and wall the inside," Søren explained. "When your windows arrive in about three weeks, we can put them in. Meanwhile, getting the walls finished is important."

"Yes!" Rose was enthusiastic and helped shift her few things aside. She put a chair by the back door where she could observe them. Beginning in one corner, they papered the front wall between the studs with black tar paper. The paper would make the wall "tight," keeping out wind and dust. They worked quickly, being careful not to drip on the floor. The hot, acrid smell of tar was strong in the room, but Rose didn't mind. She was having the time of her life seeing her plans unfold. After the men finished the papering, they cut long planks and nailed them lengthwise to the studding. Each board was butted up to the next one and made snug by a few soft hammer blows on the side, forcing it as close to the next one as it could go. As fast as they worked, they still only finished the one wall before it was chore time.

"We don't work tomorrow, Mrs. Brownlee," Søren informed her, "because it's Sunday. But we'll be back Monday morning. We'll get a lot done since we have the lumber here now."

"Thank you! It's already looking better! And I'm sure I will see you at church tomorrow. Perhaps I could meet Mrs. Thoresen then."

"I'd be happy to introduce you, Mrs. Brownlee," he replied. They gathered their tools and lunch pail and strode down the slope across the creek and fields to the waiting cows and other chores. Rose watched them and then inspected her one finished wall with satisfaction. Not plastered as she would expect back east, but maybe someday.

Remembering again that the following day was Sunday, she opened her small trunk and unpacked her blue suit and hung it up. Some hand washing took time too, so she was busy. When she should have been thinking of dinner she was still too full from lunch, so she admired her wall again trying to envision all four of them done and the one room made into two, plus the other repairs.

The roof was bad too, they had said, but she had known that from Brian. Rose stared at the little square trap door to the loft and decided to take a look up in it. She'd never been up there. The ladder leaning against the outside of the house was heavy and awkward. By laying it down she was able to drag it in and lift it up until it leaned against the beam next to the door. She tested it gingerly, then climbed up.

Hanging on fearfully to the ladder with one hand she pushed up with the other. The door was quite light and opened all the way over. Rose stepped up another rung but could see nothing in the murky darkness. She descended the ladder and fetched a lamp. Lighting it and trimming the wick, she carefully climbed back up.

This time the dusty outline of the loft could be seen when she put her head through the door. She lifted the lamp higher for a better look. The room was small, because the low pitch of the roof used up much of the space, but large enough for the Anderson's children to have slept in. Rose twisted around to see it all. It was totally empty but dirty. The amount of dirt had to have been from the cracks in the roof. Rose wondered why she couldn't see daylight through those cracks. Brian McKennie had said that the roof had holes or near-holes in its boarding.

An enormous clap of thunder shook the house, making Rose gasp in shock. Before she'd descended the ladder, hard, pelting rain was beating rhythmically on the roof and walls. She hadn't even noticed the sky darken with rain clouds, but that was why sunlight hadn't penetrated the loft. Rose was grateful her stockings were hung inside!

Deciding the rain shouldn't keep her from taking a bath and washing her hair, Rose lifted the galvanized washtub from the nail outside the back door and brought it in, placing it on the floor by the stove. Next she built the fire up good and hot. Then she ran to the pump with both buckets and pumped them full.

The rain was pouring down in cool torrents. Rose liked it. She stood with her face upturned, enjoying the sensation. This was something she had never been allowed to do as a child.

She emptied the buckets into two large pots on the stove and made three more trips. By the time the water was hot she was chilled enough to really enjoy its warmth. Of course there was no way to actually soak in a washtub, but she knelt in it and rubbed herself vigorously with soap and hot water, rinsing with ladles of water from the stovetop.

The heat radiating from the coal fire filled the room with delicious warmth. She toweled off and dressed in her nightclothes before emptying the washtub bucket by bucket. Next she ladled hot (not too hot) water onto her hair as she knelt on a towel before the tub. After washing and rinsing it thoroughly she wrapped it securely in another dry towel and finished dumping the dirty water.

It was late enough to be bedtime when she sat in front of the stove carefully combing and drying her hair with the stove door open.

Chapter 15

When Rose left for church in the morning, gray clouds swirling high overhead in the stiff wind painted the landscape with a dreary, colorless face. She was glad the buggy had its cover up; the rain seemed to hang back ready to pour down at the least provocation. Prince stepped gingerly through the muddy puddles and ruts.

Attendance was actually larger today than last week, and Rose nodded to several families not known to her. Feeling a little bit "the stranger" still, her eyes scanned anxiously for any of the McKennies. Mrs. Schmidt timidly said "hello," while her four children stood solemnly arranged behind her. The smallest broke with tradition by pulling his fingers out of his mouth and waggling them at her from back of his sister's skirts. Rose winked slowly and deliberately in return; he quickly hid his face in his sister's dress, giggling.

Still searching for Meg or Fiona, Rose noticed Søren Thoresen drive into the yard with Mrs. Thoresen and the oldest girl in the buggy. Søren immediately pointed her out to them and Mrs. Thoresen made her way through the crowd to Rose, her face wreathed in smiles, Søren right behind her. Without waiting for introduction, Mrs. Thoresen took Rose's hands in both of hers and spoke in Norwegian for several minutes. The whole time she talked, Rose couldn't help but notice how everything she said was personalized; Mrs. Thoresen looked Rose right in the eyes while speaking and made her feel that they knew each other well—even though Rose didn't comprehend a word! Søren finally got an opportunity to translate.

"Mrs. Brownlee, Amalie is saying she is so happy and blessed to make your acquaintance. Having you for a close neighbor is wonderful news because Mrs. McKennie is too far the other side of you to see often and is so busy with the new baby, too. She hopes that you will feel free to visit our home and to call on us for any help you may have need of while getting used to living out here. Just to start our friendship, would you please be our guest at dinner today following service? You could drive to our home along with us."

Rose continued being held by this strong, outgoing woman during Søren's interpretation. Deciding on impulse that she liked Amalie Thoresen's gregarious greeting, she smiled back to her and replied, "I'm very happy to meet you also, and would be perfectly delighted to come to dinner."

Amalie didn't even wait for Søren's interpreting services.

"Ja?" she asked Rose.

"Er, ja," Rose responded.

"Gud!" She linked her arm in Rose's and turning to the girl at her side made her own form of introductions.

"Miz Brünlee—is Sigrün."

Rose and Sigrün shook hands formally.

The girl was very pretty—pink, beige, and blonde all mixed like pastel ice creams. She shyly bobbed her head but remained silent. Amalie caressed her cheek with her hand reassuringly, and the girl smiled in appreciation. When she did, it seemed to Rose that the sun came out.

Like an angel! Rose thought. *That smile transforms her whole face.*

They made their way into service together, Amalie taking Rose along with them. She still hadn't seen the McKennies but service was starting.

Into the row of bench seating they filed; Søren, Sigrün, Rose, Amalie, three younger boys and the little girl followed by Mr. Thoresen. Mr. Clark stood to lead the singing, and Rose lost herself in the worship, listening and feeding on the verses of each hymn.

> *Whosoever heareth shout, shout the sound*
> *Spread the blessed tidings all the world around*
> *Tell the Joyful news wherever man is found*
> *Whosoever heareth may come*

On the chorus Rose hummed along, learning her way through the words and tune.

> *Whosoever will, Whosoever will*
> *Send the proclamation over vale and hill*
> *'Tis a loving father calls the wand'rer home*
> *Whosoever will may come*

The volume and enthusiasm increased with each chorus and Rose sang out, feeling the hope "whosoever will" spoke to all men and women. Her voice, true and clear, unconsciously rose above the others. She had no way of knowing how her own awakening faith was transmitted into her singing, blessing and bringing a touch of that freshness to many around her.

Song after song, nearly every one unfamiliar to Rose, was taken up and sung with heartfelt expression. Hands would clap out the rhythm and toes tap in time during some; others were sung with such a sweet hush of worship that Rose's eyes would prick with tears. Never had the singing at home been like this! Again and again Rose would open up and express her feelings to the Lord after she felt confident in knowing the chorus. When the song service concluded, Rose was both surprised and disappointed. Forty-five minutes of singing! Unheard of in her other church. And Rose would have gladly sung longer.

As Pastor Medford came forward to deliver his message, Rose glanced to the girl sitting on her right. Sigrün's returned look was full of admiration. Rose smiled, thinking in puzzlement that she hadn't heard Sigrün's voice during the song service but clearly recalled Søren energetically rumbling along and Amalie crooning the choruses by rote.

Pastor Medford called for the ushers to receive the offering. A jubilant emotion ran through Rose as she withdrew her check from her purse, holding it folded and hidden in her hand.

"Oh, God," she prayed. "I am so grateful for all you have done for me just since I've been here. I gladly give this to you for your service and your servants. Please bless Pastor Medford and Vera for their work."

Rose was so excited about putting her offering in the basket that she was actually grinning.

"Silly!" she chided herself. Trying to look suitably dignified again, she glanced to the other side of the church. Ah! The McKennie clan had made it after all. Rose chuckled (to herself this time) over how uncomfortably scrubbed and proper Brian and Fiona's boys appeared.

"My text for today," began Pastor Medford, "is the Gospel of John, chapter 10."

How coincidental! Rose realized. *The very passage Pastor Greenstreet chose the first Sunday I went back to church at home.* A trickle of disappointment threatened to snatch away the joy from the preceding parts of the service as the depressing sermon recalled itself to her.

Pastor Medford began, "It is so essential that every man, woman, boy, and girl hear the message of the Gospel of Jesus. The Gospel simply means *Good News*. Good News!" he repeated. "God sent

Jesus to be the bearer of good news to a troubled world. Yes, everywhere there is trouble in the world. Not one of us, not any life in this room or anywhere in the world is free of trouble. Are you in troubled waters? Thank God, who sent Jesus, that we can be saved in our troubled circumstances."

"Jesus says, *I am the door; by me if any man enter in, he shall be saved, and shall go in and out and find pasture.* Any man means *every* man, and just as the song said, 'Whosoever will' may come. There is no person excluded! No sinner is too sinful. There is no hurt, no problem, no situation that Jesus cannot save you in or from. Only two things can keep Jesus from saving you."

"The first is ignorance. *How shall they believe?* the Bible asks, *In him of whom they have not heard?* Every person can choose to believe on Jesus if they hear about him. The second thing that will keep Jesus' saving power from you is to *not* choose to receive him. In our country today, most people have heard the message of Jesus in someway or another. But many don't realize that to hear is not necessarily to believe. To believe means to choose. Jesus said, *I am the door . . . if any man enter in he shall be saved.*"

"When you enter into the kingdom of God it must be through Jesus. No one else and no other way are effective. If you are desiring to be received by God into his kingdom, the door is wide open today. Jesus is waiting for you."

He paused as if listening.

"There are Christians here today who can testify to the saving ability of Jesus. Do you wish to 'enter in' to his kingdom also?" He looked over his congregation lovingly. "Now is the day of salvation. You don't have to wait!"

Rose's heart quickened in anticipation as she followed, hung on every word.

"If you want to ask Jesus to save you right now and remove your sins, pray with me—from your heart."

Rose closed her eyes and clasped her hands earnestly.

"Pray with me now," he repeated. "Lord Jesus, I ask you to forgive me and receive me as one of your sheep. I turn away from other gods, other desires, other paths. I will follow you. I will listen for your voice and live for you. Thank you for dying for my sins, amen."

Rose didn't hear the dismissal. She was caught away somewhere . . . People left quietly from the service aware that God was at work. Pastor Medford and Vera were praying with a grizzled farmer and his wife, and Rose sat, eyes closed, utter peace resting on her brow.

Peace! Finally. Rose knew she had finally found God. *But how long have you been looking for me?* she wondered.

Her Bible was still open to John 10 and she read it from verse one to the end with new eyes. How could Pastor Greenstreet not see, not understand? It seemed so obvious to Rose at that moment. It wasn't about joining a church. It was about Jesus, the shepherd. He loves his sheep and willingly gave up his life for them. Now she was one of his sheep.

Rose got to her feet, aware that nearly everyone was gone. She floated down the aisle, smiling at Vera on her way out. The Thoresens and McKennies gathered around her outside, hugging and exclaiming in joy.

"You're born-again now, Miss Rose! Praise God for his loving kindness! We're seein' it all over your face. Sure an' it's like glory in your eyes!"

Rose didn't say a word. She hugged Fiona, she hugged Brian and Meg. Amalie squeezed her enthusiastically and Søren shook her hand while Sigrün's beautiful smile beamed on her. Even the smaller boys grinned their appreciation of what had happened.

"I don't know what to say," Rose finally managed. "It's so big! I never knew God was so . . . so . . . "

Mr. Thoresen took Rose's hand, shaking it gently. In his staid, matter-of-fact way he summed it up.

"God is gud, ja?"

"Yes!" Rose declared. "That's it *exactly*! I've always believed that, I've just had . . . some questions." She was unable to go on from there for the time being.

Fiona put in, "We were to be havin' ye for dinner again t'day, boot it's wi' the Thoresens ye've been invited first, I'm hearin'. Well, get 'long wi' ye. An' maybe next Sunday ye'll be coomin' t' owrn home?"

"Thank you, Fiona, that will be a pleasure to look forward to," Rose replied.

Even though the sky began to drizzle just then, nothing could dampen Rose's mood driving the road to Thoresens'. Just beyond the turn off to her house a small bridge spanned the creek and the road continued on to their farm. She was ushered into the large white farmhouse and seated in the enormous kitchen across from the stove.

With a cup of coffee in one hand and the constant flow of activity all around, Rose was happy to nod and smile while Amalie chatted on in Norwegian as though no language barrier existed at all. And indeed, Rose didn't see much problem in differing tongues. By gesture or occasional English word, Amalie indicated the topic and being a very animated speaker, kept Rose interested and entertained.

The children had their jobs to do and went in and out of the house in succession, each time lingering to stare at Rose or listen in on the conversation. The little bright-eyed girl, Uli, made herself useful in the kitchen so as to be allowed to stay and mix with the "company."

Sigrün was there too, hands working the quick bread for the meal, but never saying a word. This puzzled Rose who attempted once or twice to speak to her to no avail. On top of that it seemed that Amalie would intentionally steer the conversation away when Rose spoke to Sigrün. And all along Rose was still blissfully aware of the momentous occurrence in her heart. Nothing dislodged the strong peace that had wrapped itself in and around her.

Amalie's kitchen was as different from hers as Fiona's was—and they were worlds apart too. The ceiling was high and the whole room plastered and painted white. Against the white backdrop, ceramic tiles of blue and white with occasional dabs of yellow were set in the wall behind the stove. Even the stove itself was inset with beautiful tiles on the doors.

One entire wall was given to shelving—also white but trimmed with beautiful and colorful painted designs. An enviable display of dishes and crockery lined the shelves, and the plain wood floor gleamed. Rose was curious as to how Amalie managed that gleam. One door led off the kitchen from which Amalie fetched potatoes, carrots, apples, and the like.

Dinner was wonderful. Not just the food, but the topic of conversation. It seemed that on Sundays the family would discuss the pastor's chosen text and sermon. Mr. Thoresen showed his apt knowledge of the Bible as he point by point led the children as well as the adults into a real discussion. Søren tried, in English for Rose's benefit, to keep abreast of the running and sometimes lively dialogue.

As the conversation ranged back and forth, Rose was amazed how much of the Bible even the children knew. More than a little ashamed of their superior understanding, Rose silently vowed, "I'm going to spend more time reading my Bible!"

After dinner, her offer to help clean up was graciously accepted, and Amalie, Sigrün, and Rose dispatched the dishes quickly, then sat down to enjoy the afternoon off. Before long, Søren found them and invited Rose out, saying, "Father thinks you might enjoy seeing the farm and stock, Mrs. Brownlee."

Amalie objected to her guest being "dragged out to weary herself on some cows," but Rose stood up at once, exclaiming, "Oh, no! I'd love to see *everything*. I've never been on a real farm except McKennies' and that was such fun."

Søren laughed at Rose's idea of "fun" and took her to view the stock. Mr. Thoresen had brought the milk cows out of the rain since it was darkening early and their stomping, shifting, and lowing filled the huge barn. Even the air in the barn was a new experience to Rose. It was warm and moist from all the cows, with its distinct, pungent odor.

A few of the cows had calves with them still although most had already been weaned off. Mr. Thoresen beckoned her to a stall where a newly weaned calf stood, rolling his large eyes at them. When he saw Rose, he startled, jumping backwards a bit. Rose did too, while Søren and Mr. Thoresen laughed at her discomfiture.

Mr. Thoresen took Rose's arm and led her into the stall. Søren handed him a quart-sized bottle filled with milk and complete with rubber tip with which he indicated to Rose she ought to feed the calf.

Hesitantly she offered the bottle to the calf. Rolling his eyes again, the calf edged up and took hold of the bottle. Rose gasped at the calf's pull. She held the bottle with both hands while the calf alternately pulled and pushed against her. When Mr. Thoresen offered to take over Rose gratefully let him.

"He's so strong for just being a baby," she marveled.

Mr. Thoresen nodded, his glacier-blue eyes glinting in the dim barn light. "Haf strong life," he stated.

Rose toured the entire length of the milking barn, impressed with what she saw. Twice a day, Søren, his father and the other three boys, Little Karl, Arnie, and Kjell (Chell), milked thirty cows. Rose wondered why they called the one boy "little" Karl, when even at thirteen or fourteen he was a good-sized lad and far taller than Rose. Arnie and Kjell weren't far behind him either!

"All of these Thoresens are big and hearty. I'm a real 'puny' even compared to the ladies," she remarked to herself ruefully.

Across the barnyard a short distance was another building, a small one. Mr. Thoresen conducted Rose to it. Inside, in one large pen were several goats. Their miniature, dainty bodies were a joy to Rose, who exclaimed in delight over each one.

They obviously knew their master, for they crowded up, bleating and shoving to be caressed and fondled. Mr. Thoresen spoke to each by name and had Rose pat and scratch their tiny, knobby heads.

"Ver gud milk," he stated succinctly. "You try."

Catching up a three-legged stool and tin cup from a peg on the wall, he called a white and brown doe to him. She nimbly leapt upon a milking stanchion, a short, wooden platform with a shallow feed box at one end. Mr. Thoresen placed a handful of feed into the feed box and then placed the cup under her while he milked. Steamy and frothy, the streams of milk filled the cup until he offered it to Rose. She drank readily, but crinkled her nose at its strong taste.

"Make fat." He nodded, satisfied, at Rose's thin waistline.

Rose flushed, a little irritated. Søren was right. His father was outspoken and didn't take feelings, or propriety for that matter, into consideration.

"Thank you for the milk," she answered politely. She hung the cup on its hook and walked away to find Søren. He showed her the pigs. There were three sows with sounders, several just being raised for "feeding out," and an enormous boar kept in a pen off by itself. They were all of them white, except for the newest litter, which were still so young that they were pinkish.

"My father brought that boar's father and mother to America from Norway sixteen years ago. They were from my grandfather's good Norwegian Landrace herd. Actually he brought five weaners on the boat, but only two survived. Praise God they did, too," Søren commented.

Rose listened with interest.

"We will slaughter three of the 'feeders' in the fall for our family and sell the rest. Then of the weaners, we select the best for next year's feeders and sell the rest of them also."

The thought of the tiny piglets growing to the size of the sows in only a year and a half amazed Rose, but Søren assured her that not only did they mature quickly, but the sows also sometimes had three litters a year.

The sky began to look threatening again, and Rose was ready to announce her need to leave when Mr. Thoresen appeared. He spoke authoritatively to Søren and gestured toward Rose.

"Father says I'm to drive you home and put up your horse and buggy so you don't get caught in the rain."

Trying to control her annoyance, Rose responded with a cheerful but firm tone.

"Tell your father thank you, but I was just about to leave, and I can handle getting a little wet. I had better go and say goodbye to Mrs. Thoresen."

Søren shrugged as she walked back to the house and they followed.

Rose was liberal in her praise of Amalie's home and the fine dinner she served. Amalie responded by hugging her tight and asking Rose to come visit often. Then Rose took her leave of Sigrün who nodded shyly and, addressing Mr. Thoresen and Søren asked, "Will I be seeing you both tomorrow?"

Søren answered in the affirmative while Mr. Thoresen, who had been leaning against the wall calmly watching Amalie's affectionate leave-taking, merely nodded and came forward to shake Rose's hand.

The rain was descending in sheets when Rose climbed into her buggy. She hadn't even driven off Thoresens' road before Rose realized how foolishly she had acted in refusing Søren's help. Fortunately, Prince was steady and wanted to go home too. When they slogged at last into her yard, Rose had to fumble with the wet tack several minutes longer than usual.

She led Prince into his stall, left him while she pulled and pushed the buggy into its lean-to cover and went back to feed and dry him. By the time she dried the tack and waded through the yard to her own house, she was thoroughly drenched and cold. Not only that, but a large puddle of water stood on the floor under the trap door.

"Well, so the roof leaks," Rose fumed.

She built up the fire, dropped her dripping clothes on the floor and rubbed herself dry before dressing. Even though it was only near six o'clock, night had come with the rain, so she put on her warm flannel nightgown, wrapper, and slippers. After mopping and wringing, finding a bucket for under the trap door, and hanging her clothes about the bare studding, Rose was exhausted.

She cuddled up in her chair before the stove, supper and Bible on the table beside her. The earlier portion of the day came back to her and eased the irritation of the last few hours.

So many wonderful things to be happy about! she mused as she reread John 10. *I've really found God, just like he promised I would. Soon I'll have the answers to my questions, just as Pastor Medford said.* "In the meantime, Lord," now she addressed him, "Thank you that I didn't die in that river, for I realize I would never have known you!"

Rose found herself drowsing in her chair and forced herself to bank the fire and go to bed. *How strange,* Rose wondered idly, *that Sigrün is so shy at her age. In fact, I can't recall hearing her speak to anyone!* Rose's memories of the afternoon replayed themselves, including Mr. Thoresen's rather rude behavior.

"The Thoresens are good people, even if Mr. Thoresen is a bit outspoken. And I believe Amalie will become a close friend. Amalie and Mr. Thoresen are so opposite each other though. A very contrary union."

She slid into dreamless slumber to the accompaniment of the easing rainfall.

Chapter 16

Mr. Thoresen and Søren returned Monday morning with their tools and lunch pail, and the work went forward quickly. As soon as they saw the damage from the heavy rainfall, they switched their labor from the interior to the roof.

Actually, the roof had been their first concern, but without the materials and needing an entire day to strip off the old roof and replace it, they had opted to work inside the first day. Now with all their needed supplies the old roof would come off and the new one would go on.

Rose's task for the morning was washing clothes. Scanning the sky and finding it once again free of clouds gave her the determination for the job.

While the men pried the rotten boards off and tossed them to the ground below, Rose built a fire in the pit she assumed was used for laundry purposes by the Andersons. Bucket after bucket she pumped and hauled to heat in the washtub until there was enough to respectably soak her clothes.

Since any clothesline was long since gone, Rose strung a piece of rope between the corner of the stable and its lean-to. It was only about nine feet long, but she didn't have many things to dry today.

When the water was warm enough, she soaked and soaped her dress, underthings, and apron. She carried them to the pump, rinsed them in the cold, clean stream of water, wrung them out and strung them on the line.

Her hands were tingling from the cold water when she finished. The roof was mostly off, too, and new pieces of lumber were being nailed on beginning at the top of the pitch or ridgepole. A stack of shingles lay by the house for later.

Rose went inside, grateful to be out of the sun, and began a batch of bread. Its warm, yeasty smell permeated her house, giving it a homey atmosphere, and she set the loaves in their pans to rise, all the while listening with satisfaction to the ring of hammers overhead.

When the day ended, the roof was boarded. Tomorrow, Søren said, the tarpaper and shingles would go on. Rose was pleased by the way the work was going and told him so. He merely grinned and followed his father home across the creek.

During the week while they were repairing her house, Rose drove over to see Fiona with the specific purpose of talking gardening. The end result of her visit brought Brian McKennie with his plow and mule to Rose's next morning.

Brian and Mr. Thoresen greeted each other as good friends. Brian's hearty handshake was returned by Jan Thoresen's rock-solid calm one, but rather than talk they went to work. Mr. Thoresen and Søren were finishing the interior walls today and beginning the cupboards and shelves; Brian was going to tackle the garden spot.

The Andersons had plowed a large piece of sod for their family's general food supply. In only two years however, the grass had entrenched itself again. It wasn't quite as bad as virgin sod, Brian assured her, but plowing wasn't the only work to be done.

"Y'see, lass," Brian began, "When I am cuttin' an' turnin' t' sod up, ye mu' be shakin' t' good dirt from it an' haulin' t' root pack away."

That seemed simple enough to Rose, who had never done a full day's labor of that sort in her life, but she began with a will. Hoe in hand, she chopped and struck at the sod pieces until she had loosened the dirt held in their roots and then shook it out. The leftover clumps of grass she piled to the side. By lunchtime her back pain was reminiscent of the day of clearing brush.

She prepared a meal for Brian, and they sat under the cottonwood with the Thoresens, but Rose only sipped some cold water. She knew Jan Thoresen's steady gaze was measuring her, but she didn't care. She just couldn't eat right then; she would be sick if she did.

After lunch she went back to shaking the sod. Brian finished the plowing and went home, promising Fiona would be over to help plant the garden in the morning. This threw Rose into near panic. Even though Brian had plowed only a third of what Andersons had used for their large family, Rose knew she couldn't get her part of the job done today. She pushed herself as far as she could before lying down on the grass in defeat.

Jan was looking over the garden plot when she opened her eyes a few minutes later. He nodded but didn't say anything to her. Instead, he called loudly to Søren in the house.

Rose sat up and repinned her hair. Jan spoke to Søren and pointed to the garden. Søren smiled at Rose and called, "Well, Mrs. Brownlee, would you like some help bustin' sod'? The three of us can get it done before chore time."

Awkwardly regaining her feet, Rose thanked him. "I really would appreciate it—and I'll pay you, of course."

"No, for the carpentry you can pay, but not for just being neighborly."

"Is this what 'being neighborly' means out here? Back where I come from it means inviting someone to tea or to join your garden club. I think this is wonderful."

The men were expertly removing the grass and leaving the dirt in the garden spot.

"When you have to get your garden in or starve through the winter, you're more willing to help your neighbors when they are in need. When you need a hand, they will help you," Søren explained.

By chore time the edges of the plot were piled with sod. "Take your rake now and level it all out," Søren instructed. They were packing up to leave. "When Mrs. McKennie comes tomorrow, she'll help you get it planted."

"Thank you both so much again," Rose responded in gratitude.

Both men smiled, friendly like, as they left.

Fiona did acquaint Rose with the rudiments of gardening— prairie style—the next day. Rose had far more to learn about vegetables of every kind than she knew about part-time ornamental gardening. Rose struggled to remember Fiona's directives, each with numerous bits of information for this seed or that, sun or less sun, depth, spacing, thinning, and so on.

By noon the seeds were in. Fiona's last charge was to "be waterin' 'em deep, boot nae washin' 'em away."

Rose lost track of hauling buckets of water. Each one would give life to part of her garden, so she kept at it, stopping for lunch with Søren and Mr. Thoresen, continuing afterwards. The men were making good progress in the kitchen and she rested a few minutes to examine their work. Finally, she felt the watering was done, but a feeling of dismay was on her. Would she be hauling water to the garden all summer? Rose knew she wouldn't stand up to it.

"Søren," she questioned. "The garden is about how far from the pump?"

He went to the back door and measured with his eye.

"'Bout 100 foot? Somewhere's close."

"Would there be an easier way to get water to the garden than carry it by bucket?"

He looked from the pump to the garden. His father joined him and they conversed a few minutes. "My father says if he put a hole in your trough, with a 'gate' on it, then dug a channel to the garden, you could control the flow of water and divert it into the rows two at a time. What do you think?"

"You mean, dig little 'creeks' in the garden for the water to run down? Would it work?"

"Sure. Just have to do a lot of digging at first and then keep the furrows cleaned out during growing season."

"Oh, yes! Let's do it!"

"Let's? Do you want us to help?"

"Oh! Well, I would need your father to drill the hole in the trough of course, and make the 'gate', did you call it? Would he do that?"

Søren asked him. Putting down his tools, Mr. Thoresen went to inspect the trough and the garden. He spoke to Søren and Søren translated to Rose.

"This may put us behind on the house a little, but we figure on being done early next week anyway. He will work on the trough, I will dig the channel to the garden, and you are to dig the furrows in the seedbed. I'll show you how."

Rose spent the remainder of the afternoon spading out the ruts between the planted rows. Because she had watered so well, she stood in and hauled away mud as the irrigation system took shape.

"Great!" Rose muttered. Her shoes were soaked and her dress mudstained. Søren's digging was only a third of the way to the garden, but he had to cut through sod to make the canal.

"Why don't you take your shoes off and stand barefoot in the mud, Mrs. Brownlee?" he called. "Your shoes must be getting ruined."

She felt so foolish. Never had she been allowed to go barefoot as a child; she wouldn't have dreamed of it. She pulled her shoes off and wiped the thick mud from them. Walking gingerly to the pump where Mr. Thoresen was fashioning the water gate she washed them thoroughly and sat them in the sun to dry.

"Nei," he spoke up emphatically. "There."

Obviously he thought they should go in the shade rather than the sun. She picked them up and moved them obediently, coming back to examine his work. He had fastened some flat metal strips to the end of the trough, bending the strips lengthwise in half. A fairly thin board

120

was fitted into the space between the strips so that it would slide up and down but still fit snugly against the trough.

Now he was using his auger to drill holes in the trough. The trough was built of solid planks that had baked as hard as iron in the sun, making each hole quite time-consuming. She saw how the pattern of holes was circular, each hole within an eighth of an inch of the next. Since she had plenty of furrows to dig still, she padded barefoot back to the garden.

At four o'clock, Søren put aside his shovel. Rose was glad for an excuse to stop too. They both walked back to the trough. Mr. Thoresen had completed drilling the holes. Now he was holding a very thin chisel and his hammer.

Placing the chisel just between the holes, he struck it with the hammer. It broke the space between the holes. Over and over he re-positioned the chisel and hit it. Finally, one blow more and the entire circle of wood fell out of the trough and a stream of water cascaded into Søren's canal. Quickly, Mr. Thoresen shoved the gate into place and the water ceased.

Rose clapped her hands exuberantly. "Well done, Mr. Thoresen, well done!"

He gave a gallant bow and smiled; Søren clapped him on the back.

"I'll finish the furrow to the garden tomorrow, Mrs. Brownlee," Søren said confidently. "If the rows are done, you'll be watering with ease by tomorrow evening!"

They bid her good night and left.

When Rose climbed out of bed the following morning, her muscles were more sore than she'd ever felt them. Groaning, she stumbled to the back door to get the water bucket.

"Bucket, bucket; let's see, I left it right out on the step—ugh!"

Her shiny new bucket had been the target of a particularly messy magpie. With a grimace she wiped the pail on the sod and limped to the pump.

After her first cup of coffee she was ready to at least consider digging more ditches in the garden. The Thoresens arrived after she'd dressed and breakfasted. Mr. Thoresen continued his work in the house, while Søren and Rose dug. And dug.

Søren grinned wryly at Rose. His channel was getting close to the garden, but it was hard work cutting the thick sod. Her work would be done soon, she hoped. By lunchtime they were very close to finishing. Rose's muscles were warmed again. It wasn't as painful to dig, and she and Søren were carrying on a lively conversation.

He had innumerable questions about her city and what life was like in the east. She was happy to describe it to him. She liked Søren. He was bright, cheerful and had dreams, too, dreams he was willing to work for. When Rose ventured to ask if he had a special girl to go with those plans he shook his head and grinned.

"No, not yet. We Thoresens don't marry young. Most Norwegian men marry between twenty-five and thirty, when they have their affairs well in hand. Father married Mother when he was twenty-eight. They were set pretty well when we came to America and had more to start with than those who came because they had no future in Norway."

"And Norway is part of Sweden right now, you know. Father wanted to come to America where he would have more freedom. Someday, perhaps soon, Norway will be its own nation again."

He paused. "There *is* a girl I admire. But she has plans too, and won't want to marry for quite a while. Besides, she isn't old enough yet, really. So who knows? I trust it to God to give me the wife I want and need."

Rose immediately thought of Meg but didn't say anything. Yes, Meg was still young, only sixteen. Would they make a good couple? Rose smiled approval to herself.

About two o'clock, Rose opened the water gate. Cold water gushed out into the canal and went racing to the garden. It slowed but continued until it reached the furrow across the top of the plot. A board in the furrow stopped the onward flow and forced it down the first two rows. The water soaked slowly into the beds.

Triumphantly, she called, "It works! Look!"

She ran back to the trough and pumped it full, while Søren and Jan watched the water flow. She was jubilant and they were happy for her, chuckling at her excitement.

Jan stood at the head of the garden and moved the board down another two rows. The water shot down to it and then into the dry furrows.

For the next hour, Rose moved boards and pumped but enjoyed it immensely. At four Søren and Jan left and promised to see her at church in the morning.

Another week gone, Rose thought in amazement.

Inside her house, the walls were done, the interior wall constructed, and half her cabinets built. The roof was new and snug (the outhouse roof too!), the stable repaired, and even a real clothesline strung—all in seven days of labor. Only the cupboards remained to be finished, and (Rose's smile widened) her porch! They might have time to get to it.

Rose went through her long routine of bathing and washing her hair for Sunday and sighed deeply when she finally crawled into bed.

Chapter 17

Monday, Tuesday, and Wednesday it rained, tempestuous intermittent showers preceded by hot hours while the cloud cover built up. Søren and Mr. Thoresen finished the last of the cabinets by Wednesday afternoon and Rose was anticipating cleaning up after them and really moving in.

Then, with only the porch left to build, Mr. Thoresen dismissed Søren to work at home again, and carefully laid out the plans himself.

Søren assured Rose, "My father is much better at making pretty things like this stoop you want than anyone else around. I don't have the patience, and never cared to learn beyond basic carpentry. Father is a skilled craftsman from the old country." He laughed, too. "They have a lot of wood in Norway for learning on and you notice we don't here! He will do it right and you'll like it fine."

Mr. Thoresen had only three days of the agreed-upon two weeks to do the job, and Rose was unsure it could be finished in that time. Thursday morning, bright and early, through the fledgling cornfields he strode to work. Rose was both surprised and delighted to see Uli with him, half running to keep up with his long strides. She carried the familiar lunch pail and something Rose couldn't see from that distance, while he toted the tools and saw. Uli's golden curls and healthy frame were a joy for Rose to observe. How much more enjoyable the day's work would be because of Uli's company.

Now that they were crossing the creek, Rose saw that Uli was holding a rope in her hand . . . a little goat!

Whatever? Rose wondered.

Uli proudly marched up to Rose and handed her the line. Bleating and pulling fearfully, her small brown and white charge danced at the end of the leash.

"Mr. Thoresen, what is this?" Rose inquired, itching to comfort the distraught little creature.

"Goat," he replied matter-of-factly. He set down his tools and untied a small stanchion Rose hadn't noticed was strapped across his back.

"I mean, why is she here? I don't understand."

Uli tugged her sleeve. "She's a present, Mrs. Brownlee!" she lisped. "For you! Isn't she just beautiful?"

Rose was so overcome that she didn't say anything. The doe's delicate face studied Rose nervously while trembling at the end of her tether. All four of her dainty feet were pure white just above the tiny hooves while her body was varying degrees of brown and tan highlighted by a flash of white on her face.

"I'm to show you how to milk her," Uli continued, "so you can have milk every day like we do. You can even make gjetost."

Rose lifted her hand slowly to pat the little animal. Still quavering, the goat tolerated it and then pushed her head into Rose's hand and settled.

"Oh, my," Rose whispered.

Uli beamed. "I knew you would like her. I helped pick her out for you. Her name is Snøfot—Snowfoot. Isn't she beautiful?" This last was an anxious repetition.

"Oh, yes! Beautiful indeed!" Rose hugged Uli. "I am thrilled with her, sweetheart. Thank you so much."

"Oh, the goats are Onkel's. They are his favorites because he grew up taking the goats into the mountains above their fiord every summer in Norway. He tells us about it sometimes, where our Grandpa still lives. They would stay all summer in the mountains—even sleeping there. Do you suppose there are any mountains in America?"

Laughing, Rose answered, "Uli, there are more and bigger mountains in America than anywhere in Norway, but unfortunately we live a long ways from them. Perhaps someday you will ride on a train like I did and see them."

Leading the goat with them, Rose approached Mr. Thoresen. Her porch diagram was tacked on the outside of the door and scribbled notes and figures covered the margins. He was measuring the distance from the wall to what would be the outer edge of the porch.

"Mr. Thoresen," Rose interrupted, "I want to thank you."

He didn't lift his eyes from his tape measure, but asked mildly, "You like?" and drove a stake into the dirt with a blunt hammer.

"Yes. Yes, I do. I don't have any idea how to take care of her, but she is the loveliest creature I've ever owned."

"Uli teach." He gestured at the yard, still concentrating on his figures. "Snøfot eat grass, all here. Make gud milk."

He turned to her now and said deliberately, "You get fat, ja?"

This time Rose wouldn't allow herself to be offended. *The Thoresens have proven themselves to be genuinely concerned about my well being, and I have been both foolish in not taking advice given in the spirit of friendship and very nearly rude in return*, she repented silently.

Out loud she responded, "I will try. Thank you, really." She offered her hand.

He nodded and shook it, then turned back to his chore.

Uli was anxious to show her everything about caring for Snowfoot.

"First, Onkel says her home is to be in the stable by your horse. He says your horse is very gentle and won't mind. Also, Onkel fixed it up just for Snowfoot last week before you knew she was coming."

"He did? Well! You two have thought of everything!" Rose took Uli by the hand and they showed Snowfoot to her new domicile together. The recent repairs weren't news to Rose, but now she understood why the feed box had been lowered. Uli tied Snowfoot's rope to a new tethering ring in the wall.

"We need a bucket now, Mrs. Brownlee," she announced. "It has to be a good, clean one."

"All right, Uli. I'll get one." Rose fetched a pail from a hook inside her house and scrubbed it thoroughly, rinsing it with hot water from the teakettle.

Uli knelt down and placed the bucket where Snowfoot could examine it. The goat was already acclimating to her new home, helping herself to strands of hay projecting from under Prince's stall wall.

Leading the goat up onto the stanchion and giving her a little feed, Uli demonstrated her milking technique for Rose.

"It looks simple enough," Rose considered. "But that's what I believed about 'busting sod,' too!"

"Now you try it," Uli urged.

Rose knelt down where Uli had been and gently grasped and squeezed Snowfoot's teat. Nothing happened. Two golden eyes with horizontal slits paused to examine Rose and the tiny mouth ceased chewing.

"What am I doing wrong, Uli?" Rose lamented.

"Grasp higher, ma'am, and squeeze downward."

Rose tried again. This time the teat twisted under her pull and a hot stream of milk splattered the wall.

"Point it down, Mrs. Brownlee," Uli encouraged.

"How humiliating," Rose inwardly ridiculed. "Poor little Snowfoot! I hope she survives my learning."

It took five minutes for a reasonable amount to collect in the bucket and Rose's hands were cramping. Uli finished, stripping the remaining milk with her capable little hands in under a minute.

"You will get good in no time," she insisted.

They took the milk to the house where Rose also got a lesson in straining and keeping milk.

"Shake it up before drinking it and drink all you can every day," she was instructed.

"Is that what your father told you to say?" Rose inquired, wondering if anyone had ever drowned in goat milk.

Uli looked puzzled for a moment. "That's what Onkel said, yes," she answered. "He doesn't think you will make it through the winter if you don't get strong like us Thoresen women." She stated "us Thoresen women" proudly.

"I'll try, dear. I promise."

"What were you sick from, Mrs. Brownlee?" Uli questioned without preamble.

"Oh! I was . . . it happened . . . and well, Uli, I was in an accident and it took a while for me to get well."

"Is that when Mr. Brownlee died?" It came out before Uli could stop it, but Rose still responded sharper than she meant to.

"I don't like to discuss my private affairs, Uli."

Large tears formed immediately in her blue eyes, eyes just like her father's, Rose realized.

"I'm sorry, Mrs. Brownlee; Mamma says I don't think before I talk. I'm sorry—truly I am."

Rose wanted to shake herself. "Uli. I'm sorry too. Don't worry about it, all right? It just hurts still to talk about it." Rose stroked her sunny head while Uli wiped the dampness from her face.

"I had a little girl who might have looked a lot like you. She was six."

"Oh!" Uli was quiet and then timidly asked, "Did she die too?"

"Yes she did."

"Oh." Meditative silence reigned for a moment. "So now she's with Jesus, isn't she? Just like my cousin Kristen."

Rose hadn't examined it from that angle before.

"I suppose she is, Uli." The realization gave her a small smile. "Yes, she must be, mustn't she?"

Uli nodded her head "yes," smiling, too.

"O.K., then. We have a little secret, Uli. No one else knows about it so we'll just keep it that way, hmm?"

Uli nodded again. Impulsively she hugged Rose around her waist. "I won't let you get lonely, Mrs. Brownlee! I will be your friend."

They went back to the barn arm in arm and fetched out Snowfoot.

"You must use a stake and put Snowfoot out to eat in the grass every day," Uli informed Rose. "She will keep your whole yard clean and eat all the weeds too. Only don't let her eat any milkweed or bad grass that will sour her milk. And never let her near your flowers. She will eat them right up! Mamma had beautiful sweet peas one year, and the goats got loose and ate them all. Ohh, she was *very* angry! We have to be very careful to keep them tied up or in the pen. But you'll like how she keeps the grass down in your yard. Snakes don't like to live where the grass is short either."

Rose was quick to see the benefits to that and selected a patch of grass by the well for Snowfoot to dispatch for her. Uli got a mallet from her father, and they pounded Snowfoot's stake firmly down. Tiny green shoots were finally making their way out of the hard-bought earth in Rose's garden. She was determined not to allow Snowfoot to lunch in style on their tender beginnings.

Uli showed her ability to handle a hoe when they worked in the garden that day, too. The recent rain was giving both the vegetables and the weeds a real boost. Rose and Uli took turns chopping at the resilient prairie grass while the other gathered them up and carried them to the burning pile.

Lunch was companionable. Uli chattered happily and Rose and Mr. Thoresen ate in leisurely silence, content to take a quiet rest from the hot sun.

After clearing the lunch things away, Rose and Uli worked on sanding the cabin floor. First it had to be sanded smooth, then oiled deeply and rubbed. Rose was determined to have a "shiny" floor when her things arrived.

"Another two weeks at the most, I hope," she told herself patiently. Counting on her fingers, she estimated that her mother, Tom, and Abigail received her letter no later than today. Barring a flat refusal on Mother's part to send her belongings, a few days to pack them up and nine to ten days for travel made two weeks. She pressed harder on the stone she was rubbing the floor with. Only about half of the floor was done at the end of three hours, but she refused to be discouraged.

"Out here I'm learning that everything worth doing takes twice as long as it should, and anything else only half of that. Well, at least I am developing perseverance!" Rose sat back on her feet. "Uli, how about tea and cookies?"

Uli's face brightened. They washed the dust off their hands and faces out at the pump and brewed the tea hot and sweet. While it was steeping, they examined the progress of Rose's porch.

"Oh, it's going to be big!" Uli exulted.

Mr. Thoresen had dug the holes and planted half the poles that would support the porch frame. Sweat dripped from his burnt brown face. They watched him heft the next twelve-foot pole into its hole and pack dirt around it. When the pole was steady, Mr. Thoresen used a mallet and a short post to pack the dirt down, hitting the post with the mallet all around the foundation pole. Finally the pole stood rock solid.

"Tea, Mr. Thoresen?" Rose invited.

"Ja!" He spoke a few words to Uli before disappearing around the side of the house.

"Onkel is going to wash up too, Mrs. Brownlee."

Rose spread the tea things (such as they were), and they sat down to wait for Mr. Thoresen.

"Uli, I just remembered something," Rose puzzled. "Who is Kristen?"

"Kristen was my cousin, but she died."

"Cousin!" Rose was surprised, but Mr. Thoresen entered right then, thirsty for his tea. He drank deeply of the strong brew and sighed appreciatively.

"Cookie, Mr. Thoresen?" Rose offered the plate of plain sugar biscuits. He helped himself to two. She poured him another cup of tea and asked again. "Another cookie, Mr. Thoresen?"

"Nei." A few more sips drained his cup, and he waited while Uli finished her cookie before stating kindly, "Uli, home now."

She reluctantly but obediently rose and cleared off her dishes. Mr. Thoresen stood too and bowed to Rose. "Takk, Mrs. Brownlee."

"You're very welcome, sir." She saw them to the door where he gathered up his tools.

After they left, Rose untied Snowfoot and scratched her pretty head affectionately. Snowfoot was feeling frisky and gamboled about Rose in circles, but came tamely when presented with a bucket of cool water.

"How sweet you are, little one," Rose crooned. Prince hung his head over the pasture fence, curious about the newcomer, so she introduced them. Snowfoot hung back, but Prince looked her over thoroughly before losing interest.

Since it was only four-thirty, Rose moved Snowfoot's stake to fresh grass and tied her up again. Down the creek she wandered, girl-like, slipping barefoot over the rocks and grassy banks. She had discovered that she *liked* to walk barefoot occasionally. She also enjoyed letting the breeze blow freely through her unconfined hair. Yes, she was working "without her hat" some of the time, too. The result was a brightening of her complexion and bright streaks in her ash hair. Rose knew the hard work coupled by good food and fresh air was improving her health, even if she was still thin.

"Not," she added, "as thin as I was a month ago."

Uli came with Mr. Thoresen Friday and Saturday also and kept Rose company while he worked nearly nonstop on the porch. Rose grew so fond of the little girl that she knew she would sorely miss having her every day.

Friday, Mr. Thoresen completed the frame and laid the planks. Saturday the roof went on and in the afternoon, the steps took shape, one set from the front door, another off the southwest corner of the house in the back. At the end of the day, Mr. Thoresen, hot and obviously tired, told Rose he was finished.

Rose admired the porch, walking its distance across the front and down the one side, exuberant over the shaded view.

"It's a beautiful piece of work, Mr. Thoresen," Rose told him. Uli translated. "I'm sorry you had to work so hard to get it done on time—I very much appreciate it."

"You like?" he queried. Even in his weariness his blue eyes were unreadable, scrutinizing.

"Yes. It's everything I wanted and more."

He smiled briefly and bent his head once. "Dat's gud den. Come Uli, go home." Without another word he gathered his tools and trekked across the wide field just beyond the creek. Uli's small figure in the distance turned once and waved.

Chapter 18

Saturday night or rather Sunday morning in the dark, still hours before dawn, Rose awakened from deep sleep. She lay entirely alert, listening. Something had penetrated her slumbering consciousness and triggered an alarm. She heard nothing, however. Even the crickets were silent. But they shouldn't be, should they? Unless somebody or some*thing* . . .

Rose threw back the covers and stealthily found her slippers. Opening the back door just a crack she peered out. Minutes went by, but she still didn't see anything amiss. Then Prince snorted angrily and kicked at his stall. Whatever it was, was by the stable.

"What do I do?" Rose was frantic for her animals. She glanced in agitation around the cabin. The largest skillet hanging behind the stove caught her eye. Softly she removed it and a long metal ladle from their hooks. Fear for Snowfoot and Prince made her bold as she crept out the door.

Desperate bleating broke out from Snowfoot and Prince was thrashing inside his stall. Rose threw caution aside and sprinted for the stable. There she saw three shadowy figures leaping at the stable doors and trying to pry them open. Shouting, she rushed at them banging the ladle and spoon together angrily. The dark forms melted away into the tall grass and she charged after them, pounding her "weapons" and yelling crazily.

Finally Rose came to her senses and rushed back to the stable calling reassurances to Prince and Snowfoot. Inside, the two animals both expressed their relief at seeing their mistress. Rose patted and stroked Prince, speaking gently to him while he calmed down. Snowfoot trembled and bleated plaintively until Rose opened the stall door.

The little goat came to Rose's arms like a frightened child so she sat in the straw and cuddled her. Afraid of another attack that night, Rose decided to stay in the stable. She went back to the house and pulled a blanket from her bed. Back out in Snowfoot's stall with the stable door tightly closed, she made herself as comfortable as possible wrapped in her blanket and sitting against the wall. Prince was quiet and Snowfoot lay beside her, her knobby little head resting on her thigh.

She finally drifted off fitfully until just before dawn when a chorus of yapping and howling in the distance stirred her again. Coyotes? She was sure they were her visitors—would they be back?

When she departed for church, bleary-eyed and fearful, Rose left Snowfoot in her stall and securely tied the doors of the stable closed. Only human hands could undo those knots! But the tracks of several four-footed animals were all over the yard. They had been through the garden, on the porch, and even at her pantry door! They seemed to have no fear at all, and Rose was outraged by the intrusion.

After service Rose couldn't wait to pour out her indignation to Brian and Fiona.

"Sure an' them coyotes be terrible thick this year," Brian commiserated. "Folks wi' large flocks o' sheep be takin' the worst o' it for th' divils go after th' wee lambs an' even t' growed sheep if they be bold enow. Yer goat is being their look-out, an' a tidy morsel she'd be makin' for five or six o' 'em."

"But what do I do about them? They came into my yard while I was asleep! Should I get a gun?" The idea seemed ludicrous even to Rose, who had never handled a firearm in her life.

Brian's mouth twitched. "Well, an' that's bein' the 'hit an' miss' idee to be sure. Jist be doin' what ever'one does. Get a dog."

Rose's face fell. "I don't like dogs, Brian. They scare me almost as much as the coyotes do."

Yet Fiona nodded agreement when Brian responded, "Ye'll have to be gettin' o'er yer fear, Miss Rose. A farm is needin' a good dog whether for one woman or a whole family. I'm thinkin' a woman alone is needin' one that much more."

"Aye, Miss Rose. My Brian is tellin' ye true. Had we a right proper watch dog th' day we 'cleaned' yer stove, he would have been lettin' us know directly 'bout t' snakes afore we found 'em our ownsel's."

Rose nodded and turned away disheartened. Her little world was going to be invaded further—by a stupid dog!

Brian was passing the information of Rose's night visitors to Jan Thoresen, who nodded gravely. They both glanced her way, and she turned her back on them so as not to let them see her mutinous expression. Then Sigrün tapped her on the shoulder.

"Oh. Hello, Sigrün. How are you today?" Rose attempted to be cheerful.

Sigrün smiled and nodded, but didn't say anything, as usual. Rose noticed Mr. Thoresen talking now with a young farmer by the name of Harold Kalbørg. They both exhibited the same staid characteristics—hands in pockets or arms crossed, quiet, steady voices, and rigid, work-toughened carriage.

"That is a fine young man your father is speaking with, Sigrün," Rose commented. To her surprise, the girl blushed and looked down in confusion.

Oh! Rose thought, putting it together. Right then Vera approached, inviting her to dinner, but Rose declined, explaining her worry for Snowfoot.

"I'm going to need to let her out today for a while and watch her closely. I'm sorry not to be able to come. Would you and Pastor Medford be my guests next week?"

As she got ready to go home, she found herself watching Sigrün and this man Harold to see if they spoke together. But all the Thoresens got in their vehicles to leave and so did Harold. She directed Prince out of town, and expected Harold to turn north toward his own farm. Instead, they all followed each other down the road toward Rose's and beyond that was Thoresens'.

"Aha!" she chuckled. "The young man is invited to dinner!"

Sure enough, the Thoresens' wagon and buggy led the way for young Kalbørg's rig and Rose turned off on her own road.

"Wouldn't it be wonderful if Sigrün and Harold fell in love and married," Rose daydreamed. She recalled her own excitement the first time James had dined with her family. Tom had teased her unmercifully. "Sigrün is a capable girl and old enough to marry. Would she ever talk to Harold though? Does she ever talk to anyone?"

Rose unhitched Prince and put him in his pasture. In the bright sunlight, last night's events seemed distant, even foolish. Imagine! Chasing coyotes through the grass in her nightgown with a frying pan! She led Snowfoot out and allowed her to run free for a few minutes before staking her out. As a precaution, Rose put the stake inside the pasture. Prince would help guard little Snowfoot.

That evening, Rose securely tied the stable doors again. The idea of setting traps came to mind. She would speak to Brian about it in the morning.

She didn't get the opportunity though. About eight in the morning, after she had milked the goat and put her and Prince out,

Jan Thoresen rode over the rise from the direction of McKennies'. He was riding one of his bays and across the saddle in front of him was sprawled a very miserable dog. Behind him rode Uli, holding tightly, for she bounced regularly to the horse's gait.

"God-dag, Mrs. Brünlee," he began. He swung Uli down and then dismounted himself. Uli ran up and chattered to Rose enthusiastically about another "present." Mr. Thoresen tied a rope to the dog's collar and set him on the ground.

It was, as Rose feared, one of the McKennies' half-grown pups.

Ugly didn't satisfy her need for a word to describe him. In the weeks since she'd first seen the mongrel he'd gotten a lot bigger, too, even though it was easy to see from his gangly legs that he hadn't finished growing.

"See, Mrs. Brownlee? We brought you a dog to chase away the coyotes. We had to carry him all the way here 'cause he didn't want to come."

"Good boy!" Rose encouraged silently.

Mr. Thoresen led the dog to Rose. The pup pulled at the rope and growled at Jan. Suspiciously, he eyed Rose. Rose eyed him back with distaste.

"Put your hand out to let him smell you," Uli suggested.

"Will he bite me?" Rose asked.

Uli looked surprised. "Why would he? He's only mad at Onkel for making him lie quietly on the horse." She held out her hand to the dog. "See?"

The dog licked it.

"Ugh! I don't want him to lick me."

"Why, Mrs. Brownlee, don't you like your dog?"

"I don't care for dogs, Uli, especially big ones." And extremely homely ones, she added to herself.

"But you don't want the coyotes to get Snowfoot, do you?" Uli persisted.

Mr. Thoresen had listened and watched quietly. Now he spoke to Uli who nodded.

"Onkel says if you are afraid of him he will know it. You must be bold because you are his mistress, and he must learn to mind you."

Thoresen's blue eyes challenged her. Squaring her shoulders, Rose held out her hand to the dog. He sniffed it and then her skirts. He looked up expectantly so she patted him.

That wasn't too bad, Rose admitted.

Jan handed the rope to her and spoke to Uli again.

"Onkel is going to drive a stake for you to tie him to; otherwise he may try to go home. You are to leave him tied up for two days and feed him. Then he will think this is his home and stay all by himself. Also, stake Snowfoot near him—not too near at first, though. Soon he will know Snowfoot lives here too and will protect her."

Mr. Thoresen went about cutting and driving a stake while Rose held the dog's rope uncertainly. He gazed hopefully at her—one of his droopy eyes was blue, the other golden, she realized.

"Don't ever look in a mirror," she muttered. The pup wagged his tail when she spoke. He never took his eyes off her.

The stake was in, the dog tied, and the goat placed nearby. Immediately the dog began to pull at the rope and whine.

"He isn't used to being tied up, but he will be all right."

"What do I feed him, Uli?"

"Oh, most anything. He will catch his own food later—you know, rabbits and ground squirrels. That's nice too, because they eat a lot from your garden. Well, we have to go now. G'bye."

Mr. Thoresen pulled Uli up in front of him on the horse. Rose decided it would be polite to at least thank him.

"Hm. Thank you very much, Mr. Thoresen."

He glanced at the dog and back to her. She was certain for once that he was laughing behind that impassive expression.

"Ja, sure," he replied.

Rose was busy with her usual chores all day. The dog alternately pulled on his rope or wound himself up in it and yelped piteously, so she was constantly untangling him. His reaction when she came near him became friendlier as the day wore on. Moreover, he came near to knocking her down in his exuberance. This was repugnant to Rose and she became more put out with the inconvenience each time, but the fact that Snowfoot seemed relaxed made her tolerate it.

That night after Snowfoot and Prince were inside the stable, Rose brought the pup a large plate of Prince's oats, cooked and cooled. He ate them gratefully and drank deeply from the pan of water next to them. Then he lay down quietly so Rose went to her own dinner relieved.

The sound of the pup's angry baying that night awakened Rose. She rushed from the house and slipped the rope off his stake, freeing him. Fiercely he charged across the yard and around the stable, disappearing into the darkness beyond. His bark (a sort of cross between a deep cough and a howl) echoed back, farther away. Rose checked the stable; the door was secure, and Prince and Snowfoot, awake and alert, seemed fine.

Rose waited by the back door more than an hour for him to return.

"He probably saw a shadow, and now I've let him run home," Rose fumed. "Brian will bring him back tomorrow and tell me how foolish I am. Well, I'm going back to bed!"

When Rose opened the door to fetch water in the morning, there across the threshold on the top step lay the dog. The rope was gone—no, six inches of it hung from the collar and his coat was a mess from his jaunt. But he seemed happy to see her. His tail thumped as if to say, "See? I'm a good dog!"

"Well!" Rose went to the trough and began to pump. The dog stayed close beside her, not exactly underfoot, but nearly. After starting the fire and putting coffee on, she went to the stable.

On the ground, mingled with her own footprints, were new coyote tracks. They led off in the direction the dog had gone last night.

Rose examined him closely. He wasn't just dirty—his left ear was slightly torn and bloody, and some of the other marks on him were dried blood too. Getting on her knees, Rose patted him and spoke in genuine praise. "You are a *good* boy. Good boy!"

She scratched his head, and he closed his eyes. Rose was so impressed that she gave him half of Snowfoot's milk as a reward. Afterward, he crawled under the house and slept several hours.

Later in the day she saw him marking the perimeter of the yard. He swaggered around, sniffing everything and letting everyone know he was there. Even Snowfoot endured his close examination and then astounded Rose by playfully butting him in the side. Maybe it would work out to have a dog, she admitted. When it was evening again and time to milk the goat, the dog and goat were both fast asleep, the dog's head resting protectively on her rump.

"All right, dog," Rose relented. "It looks like you'll be staying. But you don't own the place. I'm the boss—even if you do act like the 'Baron of Brownlee Estate'!"

He merely thumped his tail and stretched nonchalantly. He had no doubts about staying.

Chapter 19

The calendar showed it was almost the first of June. Rose had been in RiverBend for five weeks, and her life had taken on the feel of regularity, each day flowing peacefully into the next. The repairs to her house were finished, including three windows large enough to let in light and allow Rose to enjoy the view. Moreover the hard work of living by herself out in the country with three animals and a new garden to care for demanded all her attention and strength. Yes, it was hard, but she thrived on it and ate and slept better because of it.

There was no way she could compare her life with many of the other women living in the district, though. She had her money to buy whatever she needed or just wanted and the option of leaving for the comforts of an easy life anytime she chose. Her heart ached over the stark poverty of some of her new acquaintances, a few really on the point of destitution. They had begun with little and by sheer sweat and determination managed to feed their growing families. But the children had to have clothes, shoes, and schooling, the roof needed repairs, the mule went lame, or father or mother couldn't work. Their existence hung by such a fragile thread—how real a God must be for people in desperate circumstances!

One woman in particular Rose had only seen once yet her look of emptiness went to Rose's soul like a knife. "I must have looked like that when I lost James and the children," she realized. "God reached out to me; could I reach out to her for him?"

The woman glided through town with her family, silent and wraithlike, stopping at Schmidt's for only the most meager of purchases. She stared bleakly at the bright bolts of fabric and colorful pots, pans, and dishes but never touched them. Her children were as silent and drab as she, gazing at the glass candy case without a flicker of emotion. Rose wasn't fooled. Inside those malnourished, veiled expressions lived little boys and girls who longed to run and laugh, lick peppermint sticks, and have all they wanted to eat for dinner every night. The father, Rose noted, could afford his plug of tobacco and spoke roughly to his wife for "gawkin' at them fancy doodads."

Rose observed the woman's involuntary cringe. *Does he beat her?* she wondered, and indignation welled in her breast at his arrogance. A desire to help somehow was born in that instant.

Evenings when she spent real time praying, she asked the Lord to show her what she could do. How could she help these women? Would her money be of use? "It belongs to you, Lord; I will always have enough. Whatever you tell me to do with it is what I will do."

So the unnamed woman and her family were on Rose's lips daily.

Then, since the time for her things to arrive was close, Rose went to town both on Wednesday and Friday that week. The perishable freight sent by her mother's gardener could not be allowed to sit in the sweltering sun without disastrous effects, so she must check with Mr. Bailey after each twice-weekly train. On Wednesday after the Tuesday evening train there was nothing for her. On Friday, a letter had arrived.

> *Dear Rose,*
>
> *We have had our struggles accepting what you've decided, but have reconciled ourselves for the most part. Mother, of course, has cried, complained, and run the gamut of emotion. I believe if your letters continue to express the satisfaction and happiness of your situation it will help.*
>
> *We are all in good health. Abby is growing with "expectation" and Mother is spending her attentions on helping to prepare for baby. Of us all, Abby was most supportive of your venture. She has even suggested that we visit you next year! What a woman. It seems your descriptions of spring on the prairie really sparked her inner eye.*
>
> *Oh, yes, we are shipping your requested items directly following this letter. Mother adamantly refused to send anything at first until I pointed out that as a woman past the age of twenty-one you have all the rights and privileges of managing your own affairs as Mother has of hers. It may have come as a shock to her to recall that you are not a child anymore, but it did the trick and getting your freight together began soon after.*

*I turned the list of landscaping items over to Abby
who remains enthusiastic about beautifying your
prairie cabin. Maybe that is why she wants to come
next year and has added several pieces of her own
inspiration as a gift. I have not yet developed a
craving to spend more than a week on a train one
way anywhere with a family to care for, but who
knows? I may miss my dearest sister enough by then
to suffer the discomfort with joy.*

*Mother is enclosing her letter with the freight, but we
all send our love and best hopes for the success of
your schemes. Remember—you can always come
home if by any chance things don't work out.*

I am always your loving brother,

Tom

"What a precious message," Rose murmured. "And my things
will be here next week!" Because the following train would arrive
Tuesday, she could be fairly certain of that. She sipped her coffee
slowly and reread every line. What if they did come next spring? Her
imagination went wild with delight. Somehow she knew both Tom
and Abigail would love it.

Rose usually saw Meg and went visiting when she was in town,
but that was regularly on Wednesdays. Today, Friday, Vera was out
in the country herself with Pastor nursing a sick family. Rose
decided to invite Mrs. Schmidt to have lunch at the boarding house.

The bell jingled merrily when she breezed through the door.
"Hello, Mr. Schmidt!" she called out.

He didn't answer and a strange tension permeated the store. By
the cash register stood a dark-haired young man of about twenty-
eight or so. His hair was long and unkempt, his clothes slovenly. In
his hand he held a lovely glass platter, one of the few pretty items
Mrs. Schmidt had in stock.

"I guess I didn't hear ya right, Schmidt. I thought I heered ya say
I don't get no more credit?"

Mr. Schmidt's face was red with suppressed anger. He reached to
take the plate from the man, but it was jerked out of Mr. Schmidt's
reach.

"Hey, old man! I'm a-lookin' at this!"

"Mr. Grader," Mr. Schmidt spoke tightly, "unless I get some money on your account, I cannot gif you anymore credit! It's been four months now."

"Really? Well, don't worry 'bout it. I'll pay ya next month. Right now I need me some beans, cornmeal, and tabaccy. Jest put it on my tab."

"No. I cannot anymore."

"Well now, I didn't know you were gonna be unreasonable and not take my business! That could lose you money."

The plate slipped intentionally from his fingers and smashed on the floor.

"Oh, gee—what'd I tell ya?" He picked up a glass sugar bowl and pretended to examine it.

Mrs. Schmidt heard the breaking glass and came bustling out, concern written on her face. She took in the situation at once and looked helplessly at Rose still standing just inside the door. Grader's eyes followed her nervous glance to Rose.

"Hey—you must be thet widder lady from back east they telled me about." The man seemed to have just noticed Rose. He looked her over rudely and called back to Mr. Schmidt.

"Why don'tcha introduce us, Schmidt?"

Mr. Schmidt hesitated. The sugar bowl fell to the floor, shattering. Stifling a hurt cry, Mrs. Schmidt looked to Rose again. Rose walked forward and stopped in front of the man.

"My name is Mrs. Brownlee. Do you intend to pay for the damage you have done?" She tried to sound as authoritative as possible, but knew she was only bluffing.

He bowed sarcastically in return. "My name is Mr. Grader," he mimicked. "But you kin call me Mark." He looked her over again.

"By God, I believe you *do* have money. Bet she don't owe you none, huh, Schmidt?" He picked up a vase now and stared with meaning at Mr. Schmidt.

"Why don'tcha add some coffee and sugar to my order, old man? And hurry it up."

Beaten, Mr. Schmidt gathered the items and stacked them on the counter. He didn't bother to write up a charge. Tossing the vase to Mrs. Schmidt and laughing raucously, Mark Grader picked up the groceries and strode out. Just at the door he turned and lifted his hat in mockery.

"Good day, Mrs. Brownlee!" His laughter followed him out onto the street.

"That man just robbed you! Don't we have a policeman, constable, or sheriff or something?"

Mrs. Schmidt answered, "Ve haf only a mayor and a council. Ve will complain to them and they will do something, ve hope. That man Mark Grader is bad, but his brother is worse. They put him in prison last year for hurting a man who made him angry, and now Mark is half crazy—like he is looking to fight mit someone."

Mr. Schmidt was ashamed. "I apologize, Frau Brünlee. That you should be spoken to in that way in my store . . ." He shook his head sorrowfully.

"No, please don't feel that way. You are not responsible for that man's actions. We're friends here. I came to ask Mrs. Schmidt to have lunch with me at Mrs. Owens' parlor. Are you free to be my guest, Mrs. Schmidt?"

The good woman looked the question at her husband with pleading eyes. He nodded immediately.

"I get mine hat, Frau Brünlee!" she said eagerly.

Her face was shining as they strolled over to the boarding house. A bought lunch! Rose became infected with her excitement and they both ordered gleefully. Hot tomato soup, chicken sandwiches, and cool peaches shimmering in golden syrup were followed by rich chocolate cake with thick icing and coffee. Mrs. Schmidt was having such a wonderful time that she became like a girl for a few minutes, shedding the weariness of hard frontier life. Rose thoroughly enjoyed her company and her tales of life in native Bavaria before coming to America.

"Ach! It's beautiful in Deutschland, aber the land is all owned by the rich, and ve pay very much to use it. Many years of hunger and getting no better made us think to come to America. Ve vork hard, very hard and now ve own land and store and haf good life for children." She paused. "I find Lord Jesus here, too, dank the good Gott! If Heinrik find him, too, den ve have best life together."

Rose agreed. "I want you to know, Berta, that I'm praying for you, but mostly for Mr. Schmidt to know Jesus. If friends pray together, they can expect good things to happen."

"Ja? Are you really? How dat gifs me hope! Can we pray now, together, bitte?"

Rose and Mrs. Schmidt put their heads close together and prayed. When they were done, Berta squeezed Rose's hand.

"Dank you so much! And for saying you are my friend."

How many new friends did she now have, Rose wondered on her way home. In five short weeks—almost a month and a half—her life had taken on new meaning and purpose.

Sunday the Medfords spent the afternoon with her. It was the first real hospitality she had given, but soon, she told them, her things would arrive, and she would have dishes and chairs. They laughed uproariously because dinner was served on cheap tin and Jacob Medford sat on a box at the table. Rose didn't even own enough plates so she was using a bowl for her food.

"I'll have you back properly, I promise!" she assured them.

"If we enjoy ourselves less than this, Rose, it won't be worth it!" Vera chuckled.

"Well, anyway, I believe the shipment will be here on the Tuesday night train. Would you be able to drive it out here Wednesday morning, Pastor?"

"I could on Thursday, Miss Rose. I'm sorry, but I have several appointments that day."

"Of course. That's all right, but some of it really shouldn't wait until Thursday. There are some perishable items that can't sit in the sun. Could you suggest anyone else?"

"Why don't you have little Karl Thoresen drive it? He's young, but Jan raised him to be very conscientious and dependable."

"Thank you for the idea! I'll ask him tomorrow."

The morning was soft and misty when she drove to Thoresens'. She felt familiar on her second visit and greeted Amalie as warmly as she was welcomed.

It was impossible to actually tell Amalie what she came for though, even if Rose did enjoy her coffee, pastry, and chatter, so Rose employed Uli to interpret. The child took her job seriously and endeared herself further to Rose by her solemn manner.

"Uli," Rose began, "Would you tell your mother, first of all, how much I enjoy her hospitality?"

Amalie responded to that with what pleasure it gave to have a lady visit her—that Rose's company was a treat.

They smiled at each other with perfect understanding. "This is going to work out well," Rose rejoiced.

"Uli, next let your mother know that my household things are arriving on the train tomorrow night. I need a driver to bring them home, and Pastor suggested Karl. Would he be willing and available to do the job?"

Uli translated dutifully and brought Rose Amalie's reply.

"Mor says we would be happy to help. She says maybe little Karl and Onkel both should come because she thinks it would take two men to do a good job and not drop your pretty things."

Rose made a note to herself that Norwegian for mother and father must be Mor and Onkel. She had heard Uli use "Mamma" several times also. "Mor must be a little more formal," Rose decided.

"I hate to take Mr. Thoresen from his work here at home when this is such a busy season," she objected.

"Oh, Jan works much too hard. I will insist he take a few hours to go to town. It will be good for him," was Amalie's response through Uli who, waving her hand at Rose's concern in such exquisite imitation of Amalie, nearly made Rose giggle.

"What an interesting relationship this couple has!" Rose marveled, wondering if Mr. Thoresen would do as Amalie expected.

Early Wednesday morning as Amalie promised, "little" Karl, accompanied by Mr. Thoresen, drove their two bays and wagon into Rose's yard and found her ready, indeed eager, to leave for town.

Karl was at that stage of youth where growth of limb and leg had seriously outstripped social maturity. Rose found him so shy and unwilling to speak that she gave up on him after only a few futile attempts. Mr. Thoresen was not quite as reticent, but there were no subjects they could converse about for more than a line or two before they came to the end of his English vocabulary. So Rose sat back and enjoyed the drive, observing from her seat on the second wagon bench how Mr. Thoresen related to the young boy.

He made a few comments on Karl's driving that made the boy grin and change his grip on the reins slightly. Since they were speaking Norwegian, Karl seemed to lose some of his shyness and began to talk about something that interested him, because his eyes sparkled while telling Jan. Mr. Thoresen, in return, nodded and added his thoughts here and there.

The boy respects and loves him, that's obvious, Rose thought in approval. *All of their children are well-behaved and brought up.*

Rose looked anxiously at the freight dock when they drew near—what if her things weren't there yet? She had been so sure they would be; this was the first time that it occurred to her that maybe they had been delayed for some reason. Mr. Thoresen helped her down, and she searched around for Mr. Bailey.

"Howdy, Miz Brownlee! Glad t' see ya got yer self some hardy men." He punched Karl's arm good-naturedly and the boy blushed and grinned. "I b'lieve all the boxes came fer ya will fit in that one wagon—cept'n that 'un." He pointed to the crate stenciled liberally with the words "Fragile" and "Do Not Drop" under the eaves of the station. "Reckon you'll hafta take my wagon, too. My boy kin drive it back when it's empty. He's a mite small yet, but he kin handle the horses okay. Over here, Mr. Thoresen. All these boxes here."

In the shade around the side of the freight office were Rose's things. She was taken aback at how much there was.

"Just what did Mother and Abby add to all this?" she asked herself. "Mr. Bailey, which are the perishable goods?" Rose inquired.

"Well, they're inside here." Pointing to his little house next to the office he added, "Mrs. Bailey saw the things needed waterin' and brought 'em in overnight. Seems ta have perked 'em up some, but there's a few I'm feared didn't make it."

Rose knocked on the door and introduced herself to Mrs. Bailey. She seemed to be an exact female counterpart of her husband, rough, easy-going, and cheerful.

"Landsakes, Mrs. Brownlee, do come in! It's a pure pleasure to meetcha finally. Hope ya don't mind me bringin' yer bushes and such inside, but they looked pretty poorly. Last time they's watered was three days ago. The boxcar ain't even been opened since then. Sorry ta say, it looks as though these four didn't make it, but t' others may."

"I'm most grateful to you for caring enough to water them— thank you so much! And I would be pleased if you would accept a few bulbs from me for your own garden when I get them unpacked."

"Why, sure, I'd be likin' that fine, Mrs. Brownlee."

"Good! Then I'll be seeing you with them soon. I'm surprised I haven't met you before, Mrs. Bailey. I'm in town for church on Sundays and have met most everyone who lives here."

Mrs. Bailey's open face didn't flick an eye. "I reckon we ain't church-goin' folk, Mrs. Brownlee. We came once a few years back but t' preacher said we weren't proper Christians and couldn't belong." This was stated matter-of-factly but still, Rose's mouth dropped open.

"What! Whatever did he, I mean what was his objection?"

She shrugged. "Mr. Bailey and me's both raised in the Roman church. Hadn't been fer years though, an' ain't one 'round here anyway. Preacher said we'd just have to do without."

Rose burned with shame. "Mrs. Bailey, our present pastor doesn't believe that at all. My good friends, the McKennies, are Catholic too, but they worship with us. They do because they love Jesus just like we do, like I do. That's what counts!" She struggled to explain, to apologize.

Mrs. Bailey shrugged again. "Guess it don't make no never-mind, 'ceptin' if you don't 'ssociate with non-Christian folk. Don't you worry none about it now. We get 'long all right. Well, the fellers should come git yer bushes an' stuff."

Rose hurt so badly that the joy of having her things arrive went out like a candle. She wandered outside and told Jan and Karl where to find the other crates. Mr. Bailey was with them.

"Mr. Bailey," she said boldly, "on behalf of Pastor Medford and our church, I want to cordially invite you to come to service anytime—this Sunday in fact. You will be most welcome!" This last line was said almost defiantly.

Mr. Bailey's eye's narrowed slightly but he acknowledged her invitation. Jan and Karl stared at Rose in surprise, then finished the work of loading the rest of the crates and got ready to leave. Karl and eleven-year-old Jeremy Bailey sat in one wagon while Mr. Thoresen helped her into the other one. She saw Mr. Thoresen go back and say a few words to Mr. Bailey who looked down at his feet. Jan put out his hand and they shook.

Out of town and down the road, Rose spoke. "Mr. Thoresen, what did you say to Mr. Bailey just then?"

He didn't answer right away, but finally replied, "Say, 'Mr. Bailey, come church. God luffs you. God vants you.'"

"Oh, Mr. Thoresen, how wonderful! I feel so shamed that the Baileys have thought they weren't welcome in our church. Why, I think they've believed that God didn't love them! And I—"

He clucked his tongue. "Mrs. Brünlee, talk so slow, please."

Rose laughed. "Sorry, Mr. Thoresen. It was kind of you to tell him."

"Ja," he answered. "God is kind, gud. Ver . . . " He couldn't find the word and shrugged. "What in boxes?" he asked later.

"My dishes and some household goods from back east."

"Ah! So, you like stay?"

"Yes. This year anyway. Then . . . we'll see. It's very pretty right now."

He looked around at the fields and the vast prairie. "Need rain." He pointed at McKennies' wheat field that edged the road. "Too dry."

"It rained last week," Rose offered.

Something in the way his mouth twitched told her she'd spoken ignorantly.

"I guess we need more than that, though?" she amended.

He removed his straw hat and wiped the perspiration off his neck and forehead with his sleeve. The years and rigors of dry-land farming showed in the leathery brown of his neck, but his full head of white-blond hair made her think how much like Søren and Karl he must have looked twenty-five years ago.

"Ja," was all he said.

Rose recovered her excitement when they began to unload and pry open the cases. At first, Baron raised a fuss about the strangers, especially Mr. Thoresen, so Rose had to tie him up. Then she didn't think there would ever be enough room for everything as it piled up on the table, bed, and even floor. Rose had them open the large crate whose boards were stenciled "Fragile" and "Do Not Drop" repeatedly outside. Inside, the packing was wadded solidly around its contents. She stood on a stool in the yard pulling it out.

"Now," she indicated to Mr. Thoresen, "you can pull the other boards off—but carefully, please."

He got his crowbar and glanced inside before attacking the casing.

"Hah!" he grunted with interest.

The crate came apart under his efforts revealing a cherry-wood spinet piano.

"Oh, isn't it sweet?" she crooned, caressing the glassy veneer. "Let's put it inside right away—out of the sun."

Jan, Karl, and Jeremy (who stayed to see all the interesting things unpacked) picked the piano up and gently placed it against the wall built halfway across the cabin. Rose followed with the winding stool and set it in front of the instrument.

Mr. Thoresen examined it closely, stroking the grain, scrutinizing the workmanship.

"Play, please," he requested.

"Oh! Well, maybe just to try it . . ." She ran her hands lightly over the keys and played a few bars of an old air she'd known most of her life. Several notes were sadly out of tune. Still it was soothing to hear.

Jeremy Bailey was thrilled. "Gosh, Mrs. Brownlee, that 'uz beautiful! Never heered nothin' like it afore."

"I will have your whole family over sometime, and we will have a regular concert. I play guitar, too. My guitar should also be in one of these boxes."

That reminded them of the crates still left to open. While unboxing her goods, the two boys splintered the crating into a large stack of kindling by the back door and Mr. Thoresen toted the other contents inside. By the time they were ready to leave, Rose was surrounded by piles of linens, unpacked dishes, and miscellaneous goods.

"May I pay you all now?" Rose asked, getting her purse.

Jeremy was enthusiastic and Karl was, too, although he tried to disguise it as she paid them. Mr. Thoresen just clucked his tongue and shook his head.

"Nei," he stated mildly. "*Venner*."

"Pardon, Mr. Thoresen?"

"*Venner*," he repeated. "Friends."

Rose was touched. "Thank you! You've been so kind to me. I do thank you so much."

Jan Thoresen's glacier-blue eyes glinted and he nodded. "Come, Karl."

Rose was left alone amid her "plunder." She sank down and decided to eat her very late lunch before putting things away. The Baron scratched at the door to be let in, but Rose had no intention of letting him in while everything was on the cabin floor! She ate on the porch, keeping him company, excited about getting organized, and turning her house into a real home.

Lifting the lid of a large trunk, Rose began to systematically remove its contents. She pulled out a winter coat, woolen stockings and warm underthings, umbrella, several pairs of gloves, scarves and shoes; boots, hats and an afghan. Under them lay books; one layer of good reading: Bronte, Austin, Dickens, Browning—all her favorite authors. These she stacked on the shelves the Thoresens had built for her.

Below the layers of clothing were also pictures and mementos. Not many, but each tenderly wrapped and packed. A photograph of her and James on their wedding day. Rose gazed deeply into his eyes, remembering their hazel color and how his look had warmed her. Quickly she put it aside. She removed pictures of their children and set them resolutely aside also. Others were watercolors and pastels, just pretty scenes to hang upon a wall.

Far into the evening she worked. First she cautiously unpacked her good dishes, expensive china that had been her wedding service, silverware, her everyday dishes, glasses, cooking utensils, and kitchen linens. The dishes went in the cupboards Mr. Thoresen had fashioned, and she distributed her kitchen things between the drawers, the walls, and the shelves built below the work surface.

Next, a quantity of linens, towels, blankets, and an unexpected supply of fabrics and yarns from Abby were carefully laid on shelves. A set of irons and sewing baskets followed.

Rose made her makeshift bed with fresh linens, humming contentedly. When she snuggled contentedly in her bed, happy to have her things at last, the Baileys came to mind, and she prayed for them.

"Oh, Lord! You love them and sent Jesus for them. Let them have the courage to look for you again. I will do my best to show them what you are like!"

She thought about the Schmidts, how Berta, so different in background, was not any different as a woman than she was or the wretched unnamed wife and mother Rose felt for. She even prayed for the angry young man, Mark Grader, whose brother was in prison. She thanked God for the Thoresens whose help had gone past simple "neighborliness." The McKennies, Thoresens, and Medfords: Vera, Amalie, Sigrün, Meg, and Fiona's friendships were a dear part of living here. All these people made up the fabric of this new life, this new home.

Rose stroked the coverlet on her bed thoughtfully.

"I believe if I didn't have these things I would love living here anyway. The people who are my new friends are not impressed by 'things,' and they, not the relative comforts of this house, are the pieces of my new home."

Chapter 20

The next few days Rose took her time really making her little house what she had envisioned. As she put her linens in order she found her mother's letter in the stack of towels:

Dearest Rose,

I cannot begin to express my concern over this unexpected and inadvisable lifestyle you have undertaken. As you requested, we have sent your things—but Rose, dearest, you are so far from your family and acquaintances, even the very manner of living in which you have been raised and are accustomed. It has been difficult to explain to my friends just what it is you are doing and your purpose in doing it.

Let me encourage you to consider returning home after you have rested and had your little "experience," but certainly before winter. We understand how you must be struggling to begin life again; just please remember that your real home is here with us, your family.

We will be waiting to hear from you soon, darling.

With love,

Mother

Rose folded the letter carefully and put it in her lap desk. It was the kind of response she had expected and it didn't hurt her.

"Mother will not understand, at least for a while, why I won't be coming home, but she will be consoled by her friends, and Tom is there for her," Rose concluded.

She laid her personal things neatly in drawers. Most of her dresses and suits, too fine and therefore out of place, she covered and hung on hooks to preserve them. Doilies and scarves, cut-glass lamps and vases, knick-knacks, books, music, and an exceptional old clock all had their places now, and the windows were hung with frothy white-lace curtains. Even the floor boasted two beautiful, thick carpets, one in her parlor/bedroom, the other in her dining room/kitchen. A plain throw rug was laid in the kitchen to stand upon while working and foot mats were at each door.

All of this did not take precedence over her yard, though. Rose knew that any starts to survive the trip and the lateness of the season must be planted in the cool of the day. Because of this, she dug their holes during the day and as soon as the sun went down in the evening she began to plant. The roses and the trumpet vine went in first, followed by the several varieties of flowering shrubs and climbing vines. Mr. Thoresen had put two trellises on the porch as she requested; one was on the northeast end just to the left of the front door. She planted a sturdy trumpet vine trunk there. The other trellis was on the south side of the porch right in front of the parlor window, and she set a climbing rose there. In addition, she planted lilac, forsythia, wisteria, and Virginia creeper starts. Abby had sent more than she'd asked for, and Rose earmarked several for Amalie and Fiona. One risky extravagance on her part had been fruit trees. Only four out of eight looked to have survived—a cherry, two apples, and a plum. Without other cherry and plum trees in the neighborhood they wouldn't bear, but Rose planted them anyway, promising to acquire "mates" for them next year.

She looked fondly at the four tiny saplings on the far side of her garden.

"Maybe someday there will be a real grove of fruit trees here, even if it does take five or six years," she predicted.

By nightfall all the shrubs, trees, and starts were in and watered. Sad and sickly looking though they were, Rose believed enough of them would endure to make the effort worthwhile, and admired them for their expected effect on her homestead.

Early, before the sun rose, she watered again. The thirsty ground drank the moisture greedily so after chores Rose watered once more. To her gratification, a few bushes with straggly leaves appeared a little "perked up." She stared skyward anxiously—if it was tremendously hot today her new arrivals might all die anyway, still in shock from the trip and transplanting. Since she would gain nothing by worrying she went about her other yard work, sowing flower seeds and planting bulbs in the bare beds beside the house.

Along about two-thirty she was delighted to see a thundershower begin to form up. There had been several of those in the last weeks—Rose was getting good at recognizing the signs: hot, humid, still air and thick, dark clouds that piled up overhead like railway cars plowing into each other. Around four the weather broke and large drops of water pelted the ground for an hour. Afterwards, a twilight sunset took place and the sweet, steamy smell of warm earth filled the evening. Rose felt sure her plantings had benefited from the cooling shower and would now start well.

On Sunday next Rose invited several of her friends to have a special lunch at her house: Berta and Vera from town, Amalie, Sigrün, and Fiona from the neighborhood. Meg was working as usual and couldn't attend.

"Uli must come too," Rose insisted, delighting that little person. Rose had more than one reason in mind for including Uli. She wanted to be able to talk with Amalie and enjoy her conversation and her companionship, and Uli was indispensable in that capacity.

The menu was to be special too, but not too elegant. Rose planned cold chicken salad; assorted muffins, biscuits, and crackers; and cool tea. And as a distinctive treat, a plate of exquisitely fine chocolates, a gift sent by Tom to his sister, found packed with care amid the other household goods.

Rose laid a delicate beige lace cloth and added her fine patterned china and silver candlesticks, transforming her plain wooden table. Rose had brewed tea, light and lightly sweetened that morning. It was chilling in a pitcher set in a bucket surrounded by cracked ice. The ice had been a block in Brian's icehouse that Rose had tried to pay for. Truthfully, ice became scarce as summer went on, and Rose deserved to pay for it, but Brian set his jaw in mock resentment and insisted on giving it for the festive occasion.

"That's the way it is out here," Rose mused. "There is a tremendous gift of giving at work in many people—and instead of having less, they seem to always have more. It's like God blesses them for blessing others."

Her guests were scheduled to arrive at one o'clock, late enough to have set their men's dinners before leaving for the afternoon out. Rose dressed with care, rechecked every detail, and was in a dither of excitement before they arrived. Fiona was first, heralded by the Baron's deep barking. She was carrying baby Sean, and Rose hugged her warmly when she stepped through the door.

"Oohing" and "ahhing," Fiona examined the house. She was still exclaiming over Rose's finely crafted kitchen cupboards when Berta and Vera drove into the yard at the same time Amalie and Uli crossed the creek. The Baron ran circles around the house, baying the whole time. Rose and Fiona hugged and welcomed the other ladies while Amalie and Uli dried their feet and put on their shoes and stockings. Laughing and gay, they entered the cabin. The women spent twenty minutes admiring Rose's home and its changes and ornaments, but nothing took their attention like the piano. Vera was spellbound.

"Oh, Rose! How did you ever? May I play it, please?"

The other ladies were quick to add their hopes so Vera sat down, sheer joy on her brow. The minute her fingers touched the keys, Rose realized that Vera was no dilettante on the instrument. From her hands flew Mozart, Bach, Chopin. Enchanted, the women listened on. Even Uli was transfixed.

When Vera finished, tears stood in her eyes. "I'm sorry," she apologized. "I truly thought it would be years before I played again."

"You have a gift, Vera," Rose stated. "And you gave it up to come out here."

"It's worth it," Vera replied.

Rose took her hand and kissed the young woman's cheek.

"I salute you," Rose whispered. Out loud she announced lunch and seated her guests. Every possible contrivance for sitting that Rose owned was at the table, including an upended crate for herself. That's when she at last realized they were one seat long.

"Amalie! Why, where is Sigrün?"

Uli answered for her mother.

"Sigrün was too busy to come today, but Mor says really it's because it's too hard for her to be with all the ladies. She's sorry for the trouble."

"No, it's no trouble; I'll merely clear this setting off and now you can have the chair, and I'll take the stool, and we'll put this box in the corner, all right?"

Rose poured iced tea into the glasses, garnishing each serving with ice chips and mint sprigs. Then she seated herself at the head and served the salad and passed the breads. With everyone enjoying themselves, it was tremendous fun for her, too.

"Amalie," she remarked when an opening came in the conversation, "Mr. Thoresen worked so hard and did the most excellent work on my cupboards and porch. What a blessing it must be to have a husband so skilled. He did a wonderful job of your kitchen, too."

While Uli translated, it became very quiet, and Rose glanced around curiously. The other women were staring at her with puzzled expressions—even Uli.

"Well, I'm bein' jiggered," Fiona chuckled.

In fact they were all beginning to laugh.

"What is it?" Rose demanded, beginning to redden.

"What ye said," Fiona choked out. "Oh, 'tis rich, 'tis!"

A gale of laughter rocked the table at that. Gradually the women recovered their decorum. Rose insisted they explain. Amalie took charge, swamping poor Uli with explanations.

"Mor says," Uli began seriously, "That surely you knew that Onkel is not her husband."

"*What?*" Rose was astounded, and the ladies roared in hilarity. It was several minutes before Uli could go on.

"Mor says, didn't you know that Onkel is my papa's brother? Didn't you know that, Mrs. Brownlee?" she added of her own.

Rose shook her head dumbly.

"But Mrs. Brownlee, how can Onkel be my papa if he is my onkel?" Uli persisted.

Onkel. Uncle. Rose finally connected it.

"Mor says to tell you that before I was born, my papa died. So did Onkel's wife, Aunt Elli, and my cousin Kristen. I told you about Kristen, remember?" she added.

The women were sober now and listened respectfully as Amalie explained and Uli translated.

"Onkel and my papa came to America together with their families and filed those two farms." She pointed across the creek. "There was Onkel Jan, Aunt Elli, Søren, and Kristen, Papa, Mamma, Sigrün, and Little Karl, Arnie, and Kjell. I wasn't born yet when the plague came. Then a lot of people got very sick and Papa, Aunt Elli, and Kristen died."

Rose was watching Amalie's face as she spoke. The reality of her tale came home to Rose when she saw the sad light in Amalie's eyes.

"Sigrün was a little girl then, just older than me," Uli continued. "She had the fever, too, but not really bad. Only, after Papa died she never talked anymore."

Amalie sighed and went on. Uli nodded in agreement. "Mor says, she thinks there's nothing wrong with Sigrün why she can't talk; but she just wouldn't afterwards and hasn't since. She's very shy too."

The story was over and the ladies were quietly finishing their lunches.

"I . . . apologize, Amalie," Rose managed at last. "I had no idea . . . Mr. Thoresen is so good with the children and everything . . ." She still couldn't grasp it all.

Fiona chuckled again. "Aye, he's bein' a wonderful father for Karl and Amalie's children, and Amalie has been grand for Søren. Ah, Rose. If'n ye could've been seein' your face when she told ye."

"I guess we all just assumed you knew, Rose," Vera put in kindly and added, "this chicken salad was delicious!"

Gently recalled to her duties as hostess, Rose set all this new information aside and got up to brew coffee. Vera cleared the table while Rose laid the coffee service and called Uli to her.

"Look, Uli," whispered Rose. She lifted the corner of a linen napkin covering a footed crystal plate. The elegant assorted chocolates were arrayed temptingly underneath.

Uli's eyes grew large and her tiny mouth said "Ooooh!" so softly.

"Would you like to pass these as I serve coffee?" Rose's expression was shining at Uli's obvious pleasure.

"Oh, yes'm!" she whispered back.

Uli administered her charge scrupulously, enjoying the guests' exclamations and praise over the unaccustomed treat.

"Frau Brünlee," Berta uttered, savoring the melting delight, "ist wunderschön!"

The other accolades were sweet to Rose's ear too. "They are a gift from my brother Tom. He was very extravagant, don't you think? But I shall tell him how much they were enjoyed, and it will please him greatly."

They lingered over their coffee another half hour, sharing and chatting; not many such days of leisure could be afforded by busy farms and businesses. Rose knew her luncheon was a success.

Chapter 21

Summer had arrived in its fullness. The heat began early each day before the sun was fully up, driving Rose into the house by mid-morning. When that was too unbearable, she sheltered under the cottonwood trees where a hot breeze and a cold washcloth gave her an hour or two of relief.

Now she chored as early every morning as she could get up. By watering and hoeing in the early light she did half a day's work by eight or nine. After milking and putting Snowfoot and Prince out she had her usual washing and cleaning. At noon she fixed her large meal of the day with a little left over she could eat in the evening. The less she used the stove, the better.

The garden grew up before her eyes, taking quantum leaps overnight, it seemed. New peas were on and baby radishes, onions and carrots supplemented her diet. The squash and pumpkin blossomed and spread out. Beans and cucumbers had to be staked up, and she watered, weeded, thinned, watered, weeded, thinned. In those late afternoon hours she rested, dozing or reading. When the sun declined, choring began again and life seemed to revive in the evening as it cooled to tolerable levels. Even then, Rose slept fitfully in the stuffy, muggy house to wake early and begin the long, hot process again.

The Baron became more and more Rose's companion these days. He exuberantly displayed his loyalty and affection whenever they were apart for even a few minutes and then reunited. He was fast maturing physically, too, and it was difficult for Rose to control his zeal. He was so strong and heavy! He literally knocked her over when she wasn't expecting his onslaught of "tender" affection. This was a big problem, but there was another, too. The Baron was a great watchdog. He kept the coyotes out of the yard and discouraged the 'nibblers,' but he liked to dig. Not just anywhere, mind you. Only in the garden or in her shrubs. Now that the starts and flowers were doing so well along with the green garden, she cried tears of vexation when she came upon his destruction. And she couldn't seem to stop him.

Every week Kjell or Uli would bring fresh eggs, butter, and cheese to Rose, and she would pay for them. After a particularly weary morning of replanting a bush that obviously wasn't going to 'make it,' she snapped at Kjell in desperation, "Please tell Mr. Thoresen that the dog he gave me is tearing up my yard and garden. Ask him what I should do, for heaven's sake!"

Kjell must have delivered the message effectively, for an hour later Mr. Thoresen was knocking on Rose's front door. The Baron growled menacingly at him.

"Kjell say dog bad. Here." He handed Rose a thin, resilient stick.

"What do I do with this?" Rose inquired indignantly.

"Come see." Jan walked down the porch steps and around the house. There, the same poor bush victim had been dragged out of its hole and was gasping its last.

"Baron!" Jan's voice was stern and commanding. Even Rose's eyes grew big, and Baron skulked behind her skirts.

"Baron, come!" he demanded again.

When the pup refused to move, Jan reached behind Rose and took him by the collar, gently, but firmly.

Immediately Baron snapped at him, and Jan switched him soundly on the muzzle.

"Nei. No."

He dragged the struggling dog to the bush and rubbed his nose in the shrub and its roots, punctuating his actions with "No!" and a firm smack with the stick on his hindquarters every few seconds. Having thoroughly acquainted Baron with the adverse results of his hobby, Jan turned to Rose.

"Now, Mrs. Brünlee—must do if dog bad. *All* times." He was very solid on this and his inflexibility scared Rose a bit. He must have seen her shrinking back for he added gently, "See?"

Baron was slinking repentantly toward them, baring his belly in submission and his teeth in a comical parody of a grin.

"Must teach dog be gud." Jan glanced around. It had been weeks since he had been to Rose's.

"Look nice. I see?" He didn't wait for an answer but inspected the little shrubs and bushes, her garden and the flowers from seed just now beginning to shoot up. He even examined with interest the four fruit saplings.

Grunting in approval he commented, "Four, five year, get fruit."

"Yes, I know. I . . . just wanted to start them, to see them grow."

He nodded. "Garden grow gud."

"Isn't it doing well? I should have beans soon, and I even have a little salad every day from the greens. It's more than I can eat by myself, really, and with the new potatoes and peas I—"

Holding up his hand he smiled, fleetingly. "Talk so slow, please, Mrs. Brünlee." He seemed weary for an instant and it made Rose feel badly.

"Mr. Thoresen," she began again, "I'm sorry. Thank you—takk takk—for helping me with the Baron."

He bent his head once and turned to leave.

"Mr. Thoresen," Rose hesitated. "May I fix you some cool tea?"

Shrugging, he turned back around.

"Ja. Denk you."

She poured two tall glasses of sweet, cold tea, and they sat on the porch in the shade of the house looking at his cornfields, house, and barns, the brown, gold, and green fields and the prairie away beyond. She refilled his glass almost immediately.

He seemed to be relaxed, so she ventured, "The day I had Sunday dinner with your family?"

He nodded for her to go on.

"At dinner we talked about the Bible." She spoke slowly.

"Ja?" He was interested.

"I enjoyed that so much. Since then I've been studying—reading and trying to learn more."

"Ah, dat's gud. I try, too."

"You do? I thought . . ."

"Hmm?"

She searched for the right, simple words.

"I thought you knew already."

He snorted and his eyes gleamed with humor. "Not all; not . . ." he sought for the word.

"Not possible?" Rose suggested.

"Ja, not possible. Have Bible?"

"Do I have a Bible? Yes, of course. Do you want me to get it?"

He nodded and she went to bring it. Turning to Colossians 3, he pointed out verses 16 and 17.

"Read, please."

Rose read slowly, with articulation:

Let the word of Christ dwell in you richly in all wisdom;
teaching and admonishing one another
in psalms, and hymns and spiritual songs,

> *singing and making melody in your hearts to the Lord.*
> *And whatsoever ye do in word or deed,*
> *do all in the name of the Lord Jesus,*
> *giving thanks to God and the Father by him.*

"See?" he gestured in approval. "God's word 'dwell'—stay, live *here*." He pointed to his chest. "Keep try to learn. Here. Not here." He indicated his head.

"I see! Yes. Thank you." She marked the passage so she could come back to it.

Draining the last of his tea and setting the glass down he stood. "Go now, Mrs. Brünlee. You make dog gud."

Reminded of what he expected her to do with Baron, she grimaced but agreed.

"Proverbs 13:24," he quoted succinctly and swung off the porch. Rose leafed through her Bible until she found it.

> *He that spareth his rod hateth his son;*
> *but he that loveth him chasteneth him betimes.*

"For my dog?" Rose burst out laughing. Quiet, solid, reserved patriarch of his clan, Mr. Thoresen, had a sense of humor!

She had an opportunity to try his method out on Baron soon. The following morning while she was watering, he was excavating the marigolds from around the trumpet vine. Now, nothing could have been better designed to raise her ire than an attack on her favorite vine, so with a determination fueled by her anger she called Baron to her.

Maybe the dim light of understanding flickered somewhere in his small brain for as he came bounding toward her, tongue lolling, ready to fawn and lick her hand, he took note of the flowers scattered by her feet and the switch in her hand. Suddenly, he wasn't nearly as enthusiastic about seeing her so she strode to him and using all her might and main pulled him to the scene of the crime. It was ludicrous, really. Rose couldn't force his nose down to the ground, so she held him and thrust the flowers up into his face while shouting "No! Bad dog!" then dropped them and picked the switch up to use on his rear.

In a contest of strength, Baron would win "hands down," but due to his loyalty to her, and the fact that she had never struck him before, he was submissive and abject for several minutes.

Then after lunch she caught him in the very act of demolishing a lilac. Stick in hand, and vengeance in her eye, she descended on him. It was easier for her to do a thorough job this time, and Baron's yelps of surprise and pain didn't deter her.

Several sessions more followed in the week and then "miraculously"—it seemed to work. Baron took his excavation projects elsewhere, and Rose's garden and yard endured a season of peace.

As summer drifted by, Rose bought a used saddle and copied Fiona by riding Prince on short trips although she feared she would never be a graceful horsewoman. Just mounting Prince required the use of her front porch and patience on both parts. Of an evening she might ride across her unused fields behind the house the three miles to the McKennie farm. Their family made room for her like a favored relative and often Rose would bring a treat or game for the children and a book for Brian while she and Fiona talked and worked or occasionally visited another neighbor.

Through Fiona Rose met several other families in the area. A few miles opposite McKennies' was the Gardiner farm. They had come from Tennessee five years before and had just "proved up" their claim that spring, one that had previously been filed on and abandoned when the former owners failed. They had a grown daughter, Sally, who was engaged to be married in the fall, and two sons still in school who farmed with their father. Beyond them lived the Bruntrüllsens, a Swedish family whose only son, Ivan, was Søren's best friend.

Sundays and spending Sunday dinner and the afternoon with friends, either as guest or hostess, was the high point of every week for Rose. The whole McKennie family, including Meg, or Jacob and Vera Medford, all the Thoresens, the Schmidts, and the Gardiners had been her guests. When delivering the promised bulbs to Mrs. Bailey she had asked them to come, but Mrs. Bailey amiably declined, and Rose continued to pray for them and to try to express God's love in some tangible way. They had not come to church as yet.

She remembered the soddy one Sunday when McKennies were visiting and asked Brian about it. He agreed to open it up and take a look. Rose had a small collection of tools bought one or two at a time when she needed them. They were stored in the stable and Rose showed them to Brian, who selected a crowbar and a mallet before they made their way through the dry, overgrown prairie grass disguising the soddy against the hillock.

Brian felt for the edges of the door and used the end of the crowbar to scrape through the dirt and grass grown around it. He pulled and fussed a few minutes before it came open.

The inside was small—about eight feet, but cool and empty. A musty, earth smell permeated the air. Rose was impressed that a family of four had lived several winters in its small confines.

"When they built the house it must have seemed like a mansion after this," Rose commented.

"Aye," Brian replied. "Our soddy was 'most twice as big, but we were havin' more young 'uns at t' time than Andersons did."

"Is your soddy still around, Brian?"

"Nae. We was usin' it for cool storage many o' year 'fore we were diggin' t' root cellar closer by. Then we tore it doon. An' we should be diggin' a cellar for ye, too, Miss Rose. This is bein' too far from t' house, especially in winter—and ye must be havin' a place for t' store yer garden produce."

"I hadn't thought about it, but I suppose you are right."

As June melted into July and July passed by drowsily, Prince grew fat and sassy along with Snowfoot. Sometimes, on a hot day, just for pleasure, Rose would take Prince and Snowfoot with Baron tagging along and walk up the creek. She turned them loose to wander and play, nibble or graze on the green growth by the water. Prairie dogs, birds, garter snakes, rabbits, all were observed in their tramps.

Across the creek, beyond the Thoresens' fields, unplowed prairie or other farms stretched out. Very few farmers actually used all 160 acres of their homesteads yet. But every year they could, they would break more ground, sow more crops. Thus, the wild spaces were being pushed back, a little at a time.

Rose was happy to dip her bare feet in the creek and feel the sandy gravel between her toes. Days they would ramble aimlessly in the sunshine became her fondest memory of that summer, her first year out west.

Chapter 22

Corn stood higher than a man in every field, golden-tasseled and heavy-eared. More times than Rose could count she heard the words "bumper crop," and hopes were running high. The winter wheat crop was in; now the second sowing approached maturity.

Rose's garden, too, was yielding enough to keep her canning, pickling, and drying hours every day. Between watering, regular chores and tending the produce, Rose felt there was only enough daylight left to meet herself getting up in the morning. She dined on the best of everything each day: fresh carrots, beans, potatoes, turnips, cucumbers, and tomatoes to her heart's delight. She anticipated her own sweet corn any day now, too.

The result of Snowfoot's abundant milk supply, the fresh, plentiful produce coupled with Rose's increased appetite was apparent when she dressed that dawn.

"Dear Lord! My skirt is snug around me again!" Rose studied herself critically in the mirror. What a change! Instead of the thin, inadequate, and pale creature she had been months ago her mirror showed a wiry, healthy—and heavens!—*brown*, yes, brown woman.

"You look like a pioneer, Rose. Whatever would they say back home? Well, *I* say you look alive and *feel* alive!"

The Baron thumped his tail in agreement. He was waiting for the day to begin; chasing gophers, rabbits, and other "nefarious creatures" was his first order of business.

For Rose, milking Snowfoot, putting Prince in the pasture, staking out Snowfoot, straining the milk, making breakfast and a long list of other "firsts" were on her mind. Bible reading and prayer followed breakfast and, as today was Wednesday, a trip to town for mail and visits. It was still early, only eight thirty when she left for town.

After checking the Post Office, she had coffee at Mrs. Owens'. She wanted to enjoy her letter from Tom and Abby. Had the baby come? She forced herself to wait so as to derive the most possible pleasure from the letter. Meg served her coffee and stood by to swap news for a minute. Rose would have loved to share her letter with Meg, but she was working and could not stop long or sit down.

Rose creamed and stirred her coffee before meticulously slitting the envelope.

Dear Aunt Rose, (Aunt Rose!)

We are all happy to tell you about your new nephew, born August 3. He is as handsome as his father and as sweet as his mother. I'm sure if you saw him you would agree!

Abby is fine, too. I'm not able to judge what it costs a woman to bring a child into the world, but I value my dear wife for the struggle she went through, for it was not easy. However, we are both glad of the results.

Mother is overjoyed to be a grandmother again. She sends her love, as we both (all three of us!) do.

By the way, your nephew's name is James Jeffrey Brownlee Blake. We think it's beautiful. He will wear it with pride.

Our love and affection,

Tom, Abigail, and Jamie

Rose took her hanky from her pocket and dabbed at the tears. Precious baby! Tom and Abby couldn't have honored her more.

She flagged Meg with her fluttering kerchief.

"Oh, Meg! I've had the most wonderful news! My brother Tom and his wife Abigail just had a baby boy, their first! And such a blessing! They named the baby—"

Rose caught herself.

"What were they namin' the bairn, Miss Rose?" Meg's eyes were sparkling with happiness for her.

"They . . . named him James Jeffrey Brownlee Blake," Rose said lamely.

"'Tis a foine name, Miss Rose. Is it having a special meanin'?"

Crookedly, Rose smiled at Meg. "Yes. It has a very special meaning to me. It is . . . was . . . my husband's name and also my son's."

"Yes'm. That would be makin' it most special," Meg was gentle and compassionate.

"Well, anyway, I'm an aunt now, Meg. That's good news."

"As ye were sayin'—'tis a blessing!"

Finishing her coffee, Rose paid a few calls. Vera was pleased to hear her news, and as they quietly talked, Rose found herself opening up, sharing her joy for Tom and Abby. Somehow she found herself sharing the details of her own losses, felt afresh in the shadow of their gain.

Her young friend listened, nodding and patting her hand occasionally while Rose unburdened herself.

"In one respect I thank God for this change in my life," Rose pondered. "I mean if I hadn't needed him so badly when it happened, I might have gone on as before, without him and not seeing that I was lost myself. But one thing still bothers me, Vera. The Bible says that God is good, that he loves us as a father. Can you tell me, did God do this? Did God kill my family?"

Vera shook her head. "I don't believe so. Do you remember the Sunday you were saved? Jacob preached from John chapter 10. In that chapter Jesus says he is the good shepherd who cares for his sheep. A caring shepherd lays down his life to save his sheep. In verse 10, he says it is the thief who comes to steal, kill and destroy— that Jesus came not only to give life, but to give it abundantly."

"So who is this 'thief,' Vera?"

"He is God's enemy and our adversary, the devil."

"The devil! Is there really such a thing?"

"Not a thing or a person, but a being. The devil was formerly an angel who lifted himself up in pride and rebellion against God. God had him thrown out of heaven, and because we are created in God's image and likeness and because God loves us, the devil hates us fervently. He tempted Adam and Eve and tricked them into sin. Ever since, sin has been in the world producing sorrow, sickness, and death. But God didn't leave us without hope, Rose! He sent Jesus to buy us back from sin's grasp. Legally, sin has no more control over us when we believe on him, but because we still live in this fallen world in fallible bodies, we struggle and fight against circumstances and yes, against real personal attacks by the devil. The Bible says 'your adversary, the devil, goes about like a roaring lion seeking whom he may devour.'"

"But how do we protect ourselves from him? What can we do?"

"Jesus said that he gave us authority over the devil. When we use God's word against him and trust God to be our deliverer, we can win in our situation. Sometimes we don't win at first, for one reason or another, but God will always make a way for us through any circumstance. And his peace is our greatest joy in every situation."

Rose pondered this. "It's hard for me to understand what you are saying, but if I hear you correctly, then God didn't cause or direct the accident that took my family?"

"That's right. This world is caught in sin and death, but God sent his own Son to die so that you would have help in your time of need. Has he helped you, Rose?"

"Oh, yes, but I've been blaming him, you know, for being ultimately responsible."

Vera understood. "I can't answer all your questions, Rose. I do know that God wasn't responsible for sin, and we are all sinners in one way or another. Yet he still sent his precious Son as the answer. He didn't have to, you know."

Rose felt like she was as close to having a real solution to her enigma as she had ever been. For nearly an hour more they talked on. Vera had such a great knowledge of the Bible that Rose was envious. She not only shared bits of good things with Rose, but where to find them herself so Rose could have them later to study. Once again Rose was utilizing her now dog-eared notebook.

Reluctantly they parted.

"I've enjoyed this time so much, Rose," Vera said with sincerity.

"But not as much as I have! And what's more, I will continue to enjoy it all week." Rose felt inspired just then. "Vera! What would be the response from ladies in the neighborhood to having a sort of ladies' tea or lunch every week for the express purpose of learning the Bible?"

"Why, I know several who would most definitely be interested. Why don't we try it?"

"If no one else ever comes I would be there. Yes! Could you ask Pastor? Maybe he would make an announcement on Sunday!"

"That I will. Where shall we have it? Our apartment isn't large enough, and it should be in town, don't you think?"

"Vera, I have a daring plan. How about Mrs. Bailey's? I believe if someone showed her God's word that she would become a Christian almost immediately."

Vera looked doubtful.

"You don't know her like I do. She's so hungry for God's love. Our meeting would be perfect there; the ladies all know her, and the unsaved ones would come to her house."

Becoming thoughtful, Vera answered slowly. "It may be right. Yes, I think so. Listen, I will discuss this with Jacob. Oh, he will be so thrilled! On Sunday I'll let you know what we can do."

Rose drove down the road in such excitement that Prince must have felt it. His ears pitched forward, and he trotted quickly, taking little, short jumps now and then that jerked the carriage.

"Oh, Lord! Oh, I know you are going to do something wonderful through this—starting with Mrs. Bailey. This could be the way to the ladies I've been concerned about!" She found herself praying so earnestly that tears ran down her face in her desire to see God show his love and mercy in a personal way to Mrs. Bailey and especially the lonely, unknown woman Rose had seen only the one time.

The sun was hot overhead as she neared McKennies'. She saw a wagon turning in and another right ahead of it down the lane. Rose scanned farther back—more wagons! What was happening? On the track behind her she heard another rig rattling along. It was coming at breakneck speed. Rose moved her buggy over and saw Harold and his team fly by. What was in the wagon bed? She looked again, anxiously, toward the McKennies' house. No flames, thank God! No perceptible difference. Her eyes scanned the fields behind the barn. Nothing. No, wait; was it her imagination? She made the turn into McKennies' herself. Down the long lane she kept her attention fastened on the far fields. They were planted in corn, she knew. What was bothering her about the way they looked?

She pulled Prince up behind Harold's team. Everyone was on the far side of the house toward the fields; Brian, Fiona, Mr. Gardiner and his two sons, Harold, Jan, Søren, Søren's friend Ivan, about five other men and several of their wives.

"What Jan says will be workin', boot 'tis meanin' we've got t' break our backs in t' next hour or two, three at t' moost, or our chance will be goon. Your fields may be next!" It was Brian, voice harsh with strain and fear.

Søren spoke up. "My father says if Brian McKennie is willing to sacrifice his corn, we should be grateful to take advantage of such an offer." There was a buzz of talk and Brian spoke again.

"Well, laddies, let's to it! Th' Lord be blessin' ye all. Even ye women what feel ye can help, we'll be needin' ye."

The group of men dispersed into action, but Rose still didn't know what was happening.

"Fiona! Fiona, tell me what it is!"

Fiona's usually ruddy face was ashen gray. "Look, Rose, 'tis a cursed thing."

Rose did look. In the far part of the cornfield it seemed that the tops of the corn lifted slightly, in a wave, or a blanket. The blanket lifted several feet and settled down again, a great, gray-brown blot on the field. Her mind took several seconds to understand what it saw.

Locusts.

The men were hitching up their plows, following Brian's directions even as he hitched his own. Meg's brothers with shovel, hoe, and scythe, were already running into the fields, circling far to the right of the hideous enemy.

"What can I do, Fiona?" Rose fought down her panic.

"I'm takin' me shovel out to t' field. Do ye be thinkin' ye can handle a hoe?"

"You know I can. What's to be done?"

"The idee is t' be makin' a swath around th' field—a fire break they calls it. We will set t' corn all afire around th' field at t' same time. If it works, them divil's own will be caught in t' flames or t' smoke."

"Let's go then." Rose sprinted to the right side of the field and spaced herself about 50 feet from one of the boys. The area to clear had to be at least three feet wide, judging from what she saw them doing. Rose attacked the corn, Brian's beautiful corn, hoeing it down and throwing it back into the field to fuel the fire. All around, the sounds of hacking and shoveling grew. More farmers were arriving. Where the corn was cleared, the plow turned up the damp, dark soil.

If the locusts lifted, Fiona repeated, they had instructions to torch the field immediately, but without the firebreak, the possibility of a wildfire across the dry prairie was nearly as terrifying as the locusts.

Gunny sacks of burlap to beat the fire if it went out of bounds were being distributed along with torches made by tying rags securely around stout sticks and dousing them in kerosene. Still the firebreak was unfinished, not wide enough in many places and disconnected yet for several lengths. The men were heaving from the sheer fury of the work, driving their horses or mules at a merciless pace. The women and children went before, chopping and cutting, ripping up with bare hands even, to clear the corn before the plow. Others followed behind, spreading the dirt out, tossing any remaining cornstalks into the field, hacking deeper into the field to widen the swath.

A great warning shout lifted, and Rose caught her breath as the cloud swarmed upwards. Torches were readied for the signal shot—but the hovering mass descended again, just a trifle farther from where it had been feasting.

One hour, two hours; no rest, no water. Rose could see that few would be able to continue much longer at that frantic rate. She was dizzy and nauseous, and Mr. Gardiner, plowing behind her, was drenched in perspiration, and his face was pinched and gray.

Up ahead, a swath was growing toward them. Jan Thoresen drove a mule harnessed to a disker, followed by several boys and Søren with shovels and rakes, spreading the dirt. Mr. Gardiner swung his plow to the left, and they drove by each other, connecting the swaths. Shouting orders, the men unhitched the animals and had them led away to safety. Torches were given to each person able to hold one and they lined the perimeter of the field, waiting for the signal. Several men were liberally sprinkling kerosene on the edges of the cornfield. One of Brian's sons lit Rose and Fiona's torches, continuing down the line. The acrid smoke burned their already dry and hurting throats.

A gunshot. Every torchbearer plunged his or her torch into the cornfield, touching off flames in row after row. It seemed to Rose that the corn was too green to burn, that the fire couldn't possibly take.

"Lord, I rebuke the devourer in Jesus' name, according to your word," she prayed aloud.

A breeze freshened. Its coolness soothed her face. From the cornfield thick, dense smoke billowed upwards, growing, spreading. The fire caught and began to burn freely and the slight wind helped it. Through the smoke Rose strained to see the locusts. What would they do? The men and women on the other side of the field were working hard to keep the fire on the right side of the break, while the breeze drove the fire on Rose's side into the field, toward the infestation.

Then she heard a strange whirring, clicking noise, the sound of thousands upon thousands of insect wings. The smoke and the locust cloud seemed to merge; the insects fell away in the other direction, escaping. That's when it happened. The wind veered. It shifted. On the other side of the field, the fire roared up before the flight of the locusts. The sounds of their frenzied buzzing coupled with the crackling flames. She heard shouts and the beating of burlap bags. The circle of men and women tightened around the field as the flames moved inward, where its fuel was.

Out of the air fell dead or stunned insects. The beaters descended on them with their bags. Rose felt a fury toward the winged creatures that drove her beyond her own strength. Beating and slapping the burned areas and the fallen bugs was her only goal. It seemed that it was all she had ever done, all she would ever do. The other people became shadowy and vague. Only killing the enemy was real. On and on, deeper into the field, over the hot ashes and smoldering stubble.

Rose didn't remember quitting but eventually it came to her that she was sitting against McKennies' barn. Fiona was slumped at her side. All around the yard, men lay prostrate on the ground, and women and children were scattered by the buildings. Every piece of shade was occupied.

She wiped her face and eyes wearily. Had they won? She couldn't see the cornfield, only a haze of smoke.

Some ladies were hauling buckets of water to the workers. With ladles they ministered the reviving liquid. Many of the men poured it over their heads, swallowing only a few sips.

"Fiona? Fiona, did we get them? Did we stop them?"

"Aye, I'm b'lievin' so." She struggled to her feet. "Onyways, we'll be knowin' soon. I best be lookin' to me family an' seein' if Brian be all right." She stumbled off, her clothing and features blackened by smoke and ash.

Rose got up too. Her skirt was ripped badly around the hem. The other damage was more apparent to an observer but as she wandered through the recovering army there were worse than she. One of the Gardiner boys was sitting bent over, coughing and retching from the smoke. Rose went to look for Fiona and found her by the pump, fussing over Brian, tears running down her face. Brian's hands were badly blistered and swelling, and Fiona had them soaking in icy water while she tore up clean cloths to wrap them in.

"Oh, Brian!" Rose commiserated.

"Aye. Not s' pretty—nor handy."

"But the locusts?" Rose asked hesitantly.

"I'm thinkin' we've done wi' 'em. Tomorra' will tell." He bowed his head on his chest. "Th' corn is gone, too, of course, boot we can be gettin' by somehow. Th' Lord will be supplyin' what we're lackin'.'"

Mutely she nodded. She helped Fiona wrap Brian's hands before moving off. Trying to find anything needing done she meandered around the yard. Prince was still hitched and waiting dejectedly in the front. She rubbed his neck and patted him fondly.

"Poor boy! It's so hot and miserable for you." The morning with Vera, her good news from Tom, all seemed a very long time ago.

Folks were leaving now, by ones and twos making their way in exhaustion to their wagons for the long drive home under the declining sun. By the front fence Jan Thoresen was waylaying them as they left the yard, seriously conversing with each one until the man gestured acquiescence. Søren stood by his father, helping him with the right words.

When the young man saw Rose he nodded. They both grinned at the same time—Rose didn't know what she looked like, disheveled and dirty, but *his* face was nearly black with soot while his blonde hair, sticking straight out, looked a hilarious sight. Hearing Søren's chuckle, his father looked and smiled broadly when he saw Rose.

"So! Mrs. Brünlee like play dirt?"

"And it doesn't appear that I am alone, does it?" she joked back. The tension was ebbing away, and Rose sighed. "What a shame! Brian's corn is all gone, but we did get the locusts, didn't we?"

"Ja. And help Brian now."

"How? How can we help? Can I help?"

"You help . . ." He asked Søren for a word. "You help already, Mrs. Brünlee. We . . ." He consulted Søren again.

"We share corn, all farmers . . ." He waved his hand to include those living in the area. "*All* safe now. We share for Brian."

Chapter 23

The corn harvest came in big the following three weeks, just as many had predicted. The remaining locusts were too few to swarm, and the damage from them could be lived with, so the harvest went forward, and when it was finished, the oats and wheat were ready. Rose had never experienced the fever of a real harvest time. She watched from her porch as every male in the Thoresen family, as well as Sigrün, worked from dawn to dusk to gather it in. Her own garden was yielding more tomatoes than she would be able to use by herself, along with sweet corn, dry beans, and plenteous table vegetables.

Cheese making followed on the heels of the grain harvest, and Amalie insisted that Rose participate. She loved learning how to curdle and press the milkfat and form the cheeses. Along with the mellow and cheddar cheeses, Rose was instructed in the making of the pungent gjetost—so that she could eventually make her own at home, Amalie reasoned.

There was a chill in the air when Rose got up in the mornings now and nights were becoming shorter. She took Fiona's lead and dug her potatoes, carrots, and turnips, storing them in her new root cellar to keep them cool and dry all winter. Up in the loft, she stacked pumpkins and squash next to bags of beans, baskets of onions, and strings of herbs and spices. Rose began to feel truly prosperous as she surveyed the jars and jars of produce in the pantry and under the work table in the kitchen, the cheeses carefully wrapped and laid individually on their shelves, and her small crocks of butter purchased from Amalie. It was more than she ever dreamed of using for herself, and she took comfort in the thought of having more than enough for any who had little. Only the meat for winter remained to be "laid up."

When the ground began to really freeze at night, slaughtering commenced. All of Rose's neighbors killed their hogs or calves, and Rose was inducted into the art of making the sausages, head cheese, soap, and candles, all at Amalie's side. In helping, Rose earned her small share of each and made arrangements to buy two hams and a side of bacon when they were smoked and cured.

Patrick McKennie was hired to plow Rose's green garden under so that the remaining vegetation would mulch it for next year. That day, Rose realized harvest was over, and she was ready for winter.

Now Sally Gardiner was to be married and the whole countryside turned out for the event. Rose felt a little like a stranger still amidst the gala gathering in the Gardiner barn, but the excitement and release after the grueling harvest was contagious. The bride and groom, blushing and happy, said their vows before Pastor Medford and the guests, then everyone sat down to a huge feast prepared by all the women present. When the dinner was over, hot coffee, punch, and desserts of all kinds—including the wedding cake of dark spice and fruit—were set out on tables lining the wall on one side of the barn, and everything in the center of the floor cleared away.

Two men with violins (or fiddles she was told) stood on a box platform at the end of the room along with a woman holding a "Jew's harp" and a boy with spoons. Rose had never heard anyone play spoons before. When the fiddlers tuned up and began playing, the boy produced a lively tattoo, slapping and clicking the spoons against each other and off his thigh and opposite hand. Together, the four in the ensemble made music that caused her hands and feet to go crazy with wanting to dance. And dance the folks did! Reels and jigs, polkas and waltzes, one after another the fiddlers called and the people danced.

Rose sighed. "I certainly wish I'd brought my guitar."

She could easily have played along with the other musicians. As it was, she helped with the serving, washing dishes and keeping the coffee and punch replenished.

Fiona sidled up and muttered out of the side of her mouth, "Be lookin' at that, will ye?"

Søren had Meg and was leading her through the paces of a reel. Meg's hair was curled today, tied with a bottle-green ribbon and hanging long and loose in a golden-red fire. Søren's eyes never left her glowing face as they promenaded and turned.

Rose grinned at Fiona. "They are beautiful together, aren't they?"

"Aye, that they are!" she agreed. "An' I'm wonderin' what temper an Irish-Norwegian offspring would be havin?"

Rose burst out laughing at Fiona's bold tongue-in-cheek.

Then the music slowed to a waltz and the floor cleared for the groom and his new bride to dance their wedding waltz. The scene was so precious, so full of hope and young love. Many older folks watching wiped a tear from their cheek; the sweetness of first love was never forgotten through the years of life. Others joined the dance and Rose observed with tender reminiscences of her own.

"Fiona!" Rose whispered suddenly. "Look there!"

Harold Kalbørg was asking Sigrün to dance. Her pretty face was a brilliant red and she shook her head "no" while he talked. Harold just grinned and insisted.

Then he took her hand and gently pulled her to her feet. She cast around for "help" and saw Rose. Her eyes pleaded with Rose to be rescued, but Rose mouthed the words "Go dance with him!" and smiled encouragingly. Reluctantly she went out on the barn floor, and Harold reverently took her in his arms.

"Ah, that 'uns fair goon, if I be a-readin' him aright," was Fiona's comment.

"Yes, that is a young man in love, I'm sure. But Sigrün is so shy. How will he ever win her?"

"Ye canna be thinkin' love can be stopped. If there is bein' a way, likely he'll be foindin' it."

It didn't seem to bother Harold that Sigrün kept her eyes down while they danced. He talked softly and wooed her gently, patiently. When the music ended, he appropriated her hand and drew her to the punch bowl where he served her and then seated her while continuing to press his advantage.

Rose fetched more coffee from the kitchen. When she came back, they were dancing together again. Sigrün still kept her eyes down, but Rose thought she smiled while Harold spoke. Rose found herself silently cheering for his success. At the end of the evening, Harold was conversing with Jan Thoresen, and Rose had a feeling the Thoresen farm would be seeing much of young Mr. Kalbørg soon. She was glad for Sigrün.

School had been in session for the last month with only the small children attending. Now that the older students were through with harvest, the school year began in earnest. Out past Thoresens' about two miles stood one of the school houses and every day children for a five-mile radius walked or rode horseback to learn their lessons. Rose had understood that the schoolmaster usually boarded with the closest family to the school, so she was surprised when Fiona told her he was staying at Thoresens'.

"Seems Jan asked special for t' teacher to board with them this winter. Even was agreein' to the loanin' of a horse t' ride."

Rose figured there was a reason if Jan had especially asked, but didn't let it concern her. With harvest over, the ladies' Bible study could begin, and she was going to Mrs. Bailey's after church to talk to her about it. They had developed a casual friendship that Rose felt would allow her to approach the subject.

"Hello, Mrs. Bailey," she greeted as the door opened.

"Well! Come in, come in! Yer jist in time fer supper, no doubt about it!" Mrs. Bailey's rough face creased with smiles.

"I'm sorry, I didn't mean to intrude at mealtime; it's just that I was already in town and wanted to visit."

"Ain't no never-mind! Jer'my, git Mrs. Brownlee a plate—set right down here now."

"Hello, Mr. Bailey." Rose was acknowledged by a nod and gesture toward a chair.

"Jist sit right there. Plenty o' stew and my woman's good hot biscuits to go 'round," he smiled.

"Thank you, it's very kind of you."

"Ma," Jeremy piped up, "Ya shoulda heered Mrs. Brownlee play thet piani—it was plum fan—tastic!"

Rose thanked him for the compliment. "I did tell you we would have a concert sometime, too, didn't I? Well, I've found out that Mrs. Medford not only plays also, but was trained as a concert pianist in a fine music school back east. That is a performance I would love to hear."

"Makes a body wonder why she'd be a comin' 'way out here where there ain't no concert halls or recitals if she's that good," Mrs. Bailey asked slowly.

Rose nodded. "I asked her the same thing, more or less. You know what she told me? That it was worth it to be doing what they are doing."

"Pass the biscuits, please," Mr. Bailey put in.

"Mrs. Medford and I have an idea for the ladies in town and who live within driving distance. We thought it would be fun and . . .educational to give a small luncheon or tea once a week in a lady's home to visit together and, well, mostly study the Bible."

"Study the Bible?"

"Yes. I've been reading it for about six months now and really like it, but it would be even better to read together and then talk about what it says; you know, figure out what it means."

"Dunno. S'pose some'd care fer it. Don't know as I would."

Rose swallowed. "Well, that is one of the things I came to talk with you about today, Mrs. Bailey. We, that is, Mrs. Medford and I, thought you would make a good hostess for our lunches."

"Me?" Mrs. Bailey was disbelieving.

"Yes, you! Why, everyone knows you, and you make people feel so friendly and at home—we think it would be perfect!"

Mrs. Bailey glanced at her husband but he was studying his stew. "Dunno. Hev t' think on it."

"Certainly." Rose's hopes sank.

Mrs. Bailey cut and served a pumpkin pie. Each slice was covered with thick cream and smelled deliciously spicy. As she poured the coffee she remarked, "This Bible study idee'd be fer any woman t' come to? Even if'n she didn't belong t' no church?"

"That's exactly it. We want any lady to come and be comfortable. All Christian churches believe in the Bible so no one would be left out." Her hopes rose up again.

"Cream and sugar, Mrs. Brownlee?"

"Cream, please. Thank you."

"'Spect I could be havin' that there lunch thing in my settin' room. Hev t' bring in the kitchen chairs if more'n six be here. That be all right?"

"That would be perfect. And every week you could make coffee and tea but two other ladies would bring the lunch or tea cakes so everyone gets a turn."

"I do have a mighty fine chocklit cake receipt I wouldn't mind fixin' up sometime." Now she was getting interested!

"Is Wednesday a good day—say, at 10 o'clock?"

"I'm supposin' so."

"That's wonderful! Oh, we are going to have a lovely time together—thank you, Mrs. Bailey."

After dinner, Rose went straight to Vera's with the news. They agreed to begin a week from the coming Wednesday and to deliver invitations to all the women they could think of.

"But if they all come, Rose, will Mrs. Bailey's be large enough?"

"At least fifteen can be accommodated without too much discomfort. If we grow bigger, the only place I can think of is Mrs.

Owens' parlor and by then Mrs. Bailey and her friends will feel a part of it and come anyway."

"Yes! Oh, Rose, this is a great opportunity to lead women to Jesus and see their lives really changed for the better."

They agreed to meet the coming Wednesday and complete the details then.

It was the end of October when the Bible studies began. Seventeen women, three with nursing infants, crowded into an astonished Mrs. Bailey's sitting room.

Instead of being overwhelmed, she cheerfully accommodated them as best she could and amazed both Rose and Vera by displaying an innate gentility that they had never observed before.

Mr. Bailey, however, fled at the sight of so many women in his home.

Simply, Vera led the group through the passage in John chapter three. Women who didn't bring a Bible or own one shared with those who did. Even, Rose discerned, the few women who couldn't read made like they could. Vera encouraged questions, but being new as a group, not much discussion evolved.

"They will get over their inhibitions soon," Rose was sure. She had asked Vera to explain a verse and the women had listened with interest, some of them nodding as it came clear to them.

For lunch, Mrs. Schmidt and her friend Gertrude served cabbage rolls, sausage, and apple kuchen. Happy chatter filled the house and no one was more enthusiastic than Mrs. Bailey.

"Mrs. Brownlee! Mrs. Medford!" she urged, "tell the ladies next week we go to Gertrude's. She says twenty ladies can fit in her house 'cuz the kitchen and settin' room hook together. And Mrs. Kalbørg and Mrs. Svensen want to fix the lunch—what should I tell them?"

"Tell them 'yes,' Mrs. Bailey, and I will announce the change to Mrs. Grünbaum's home." Vera and Rose clasped hands joyfully.

Over the next several weeks the study grew. Even when the first snow came, attendance continued steady. But the greatest reward was when one of the Christians could pray with a lady to receive Jesus as their savior. Many times in the back room of Gertrude Grünbaum's house a teary voice lifted itself to God and received forgiveness and entrance into a holy, unseen Kingdom.

Attendance at church increased—for many a wife and mother brought husband and children where their ears, too, could hear the words of life.

Not everyone responded. A few hurting and a few bitter souls rejected the message and did not return to Gertrude's, but the Sunday Robert and Mary Bailey came to church was Rose's happiest day. Few knew they were there since they came late and sat in the back, but Pastor Medford made a special point of welcoming them after service before they could leave so Rose saw them at last. She hugged Mrs. Bailey with fervor that touched her heart.

Because of the work with the ladies and the days she spent with Vera visiting and teaching the new Christians, fall slipped away almost unnoticed. It was Thanksgiving. Rose was invited to eat with the McKennies, Thoresens, Baileys, and Medfords. She hardly knew what to do.

"Somehow, I would like to spend this Thanksgiving with all my friends, but I know it's not possible," she confessed to Vera. "I wish they could all come to my house."

That was how the plan of the Thanksgiving concert began. Rose declined all her invitations graciously and insisted on Jacob and Vera coming to her home for dinner. Then she told McKennies, Thoresens, and Baileys that dessert and coffee would served be at her house at five o'clock. Thanksgiving evening followed by a piano recital by Vera Medford and a sing-along.

Counting on her fingers the number of guests, Vera shook her head. "I hope your house can hold everyone. Have you counted? There are going to be twenty-one counting us, and most of those are energetic youngsters!"

"We-ell . . . " Rose hedged. "The little ones can play in the loft. I suppose that is just Uli and Martha though." She thought a minute more. "Everyone will sit somewhere, I will serve dessert, you will play, we'll all sing—and no one will be allowed to move until it's time to go home!"

They broke out in peals of laughter, but Vera insisted while trying to catch her breath that it was the only plan that would work. They couldn't stop laughing then for several more minutes.

Rose spent all Thanksgiving morning cooking and baking. Jacob and Vera were bringing several pies as well as part of the dinner. Figuring that the boys and men would have two servings of dessert, she baked a spice cake, two pumpkin pies, two apple pies, and a large plate of cookies.

"That ought to hold them!" she concluded, satisfied.

The Medfords arrived at noon, and dinner was served at one. In blessing the food, Jacob took particular notice of the families back east that they were away from that day.

Rose remembered fondly how her mother loved to be the hostess on Thanksgiving. Tom, Abigail, and baby James would be her guests about this time. Tom would joke and tease, keeping everyone laughing and cheerful . . .

Dinner was cozy and family-like with Jacob and Vera. They ate all they could and hardly made a dent in any of it.

"No cooking for a week!" Rose and Vera gloated.

Guests began to arrive just before the set time. Merry, laughing greetings were exchanged, and the children ran around outside playing tag or catch (to the Baron's dismay) while the adults visited and sipped coffee or hot, cinnamon-spiced cider.

The day grew dark early, the children trooped in, and even with all the small children sitting on the floor, Jacob and Vera were still sandwiched in between Meg and Sigrün on Rose's bed. But no one seemed to mind; just being together, sharing the evening was enough for them.

"That's another thing I love here," Rose reflected, smiling to herself. "People love people, not things and social status."

Her daydreaming had caught the attention of Jan Thoresen who raised his coffee cup when she came out of her reverie and realized he was watching her with his intent blue eyes. She saluted him back warmly in friendship.

Vera and Rose served around pie, cake, milk, and coffee. A few minutes later they served it around again.

"All right, Vera," Rose motioned. "Knock 'em dead."

The chattering and fidgeting ceased when the young woman seated herself at the small instrument. After a moment's pause, soft, delicate, notes seemed to float in the room as she began. The tiny rivulet grew into a mountain stream, a rushing, sobbing torrent that took their breath away.

Many of the youngsters sat still, riveted in place. Vera ended the prelude and launched into a spirited sonata that defied the ability of untrained ears to follow—let alone fingers play.

The glissando that ended it would have more appropriately been played on a ten-foot Steinway in a cavernous concert hall, but was no less appreciated. Deafening, spontaneous applause filled the little house.

Vera, flushed and pleased, stood and bowed while the applause continued. Reseating herself, she started a well-loved Gospel song that was taken up in a flash. Feet patting, hands beating the rhythm, they burst out in harmony. It was too much to be resisted. Through one after another, Vera led them, at last bringing the evening to a close with

Amazing Grace! How sweet the sound,
That saved a wretch like me!
I once was lost, but now am found,
Was blind, but now I see.

Jacob stood where all could see him and prayed. Yes, they were all thankful and, the Lord knew, they had much to be thankful for.

Chapter 24

When Thanksgiving had passed, Rose realized with a start that she had only two weeks to finish the Christmas projects to be sent home to her mother, Tom, Abby, and the baby. The shipping would take around two weeks if there were any delays.

At the same time, the temperature started to drop. That night, when she banked the fire, the room had already chilled and by morning a thick coating of frost covered the lower half of her windows and her teeth chattered as she fed the fire and added coal. A glance out the window showed a whole world covered in frost.

The box she was sending sat on a dining chair near the table and through the next week she snugly packed in it two dainty jars of raspberry jam, a sausage, a good-sized wheel of cheese and a small one of gjetost—fruits of her own labor under the watchful eye of Amalie.

For baby Jamie she had plied her needles and created a knit sweater and bonnet of soft blue edged in fuzzy white. The last item was a watercolor portraying her house and yard from the vantage of the road just above them. She had labored hard to capture the view of the creek, the protected, serene effect of the house and stable with Prince and Snowfoot grazing contentedly in the pasture. It wasn't finished yet.

Rose sat with her eyes closed to recall the green of the cottonwood trees in spring, the way the grass waved on the hill in the breeze. She gave herself two more days to complete it—no more—and went on to write a Christmas letter. It grew in length rapidly as she described in detail the last busy weeks of harvest including her new experiences and skills up to the Thanksgiving gathering and concert.

Under her pen, the people she knew became real and visible to her family. Concluding with her love to each of them, she signed her name and stood up to stretch. Snow was falling in the yard, thick, heavy and silent.

"Beautiful," Rose admired.

Throughout the day it came down until just after dark, when the moon lit the sky and revealed the clean blanket covering everything.

Baron scratched at the door to go out and paused confused on the porch.

"Go on, Baron," she laughed. "It won't hurt you!"

He stepped tentatively into the snow, lifting each foot high and shaking it. Suddenly, he leapt into it, nosing great sprays of snow into the air, snapping at them, and running crazily in circles. He stood still and barked at Rose as if to say, "Come on!" but she shook her head and declined.

"No, you go have your fun, boy."

He took off, scattering the fluffy whiteness as he went.

The month went quickly. The schools hosted recitals that Rose attended, clapping enthusiastically for each of the children she knew. Arnie Thoresen stole the show with his unconventional rendition of "The Charge of the Light Brigade," complete with cannon and rifle fire, bugle calls, and shouted orders much to the discomfiture of the schoolmaster, Mr. Letoire, and the delight of every boy and girl. Refreshments were served afterwards; coffee, punch and cookies provided by the parents. Rose sought out the teacher to compliment him on his fine work.

"Thank you, Mrs. Brownlee. I do enjoy instructing a fine mind. We have quite a few outstanding pupils including the Thoresen boy who gave us that memorable performance this evening. All the children of that family will make their mother and uncle proud, I am sure."

"You must enjoy living with the Thoresens then, Mr. Letoire."

"Indeed! Mrs. Thoresen makes every meal a delight to sit down to, which is certainly a desired improvement from cooking for oneself. And Mr. Thoresen is making rapid progress too, for a sound mind in any language is a blessing to work with."

"I beg your pardon, Mr. Letoire? In what way is Mr. Thoresen your pupil?"

"In the study of the English language, of course. This was his prime consideration in requesting I board with his family this term. We have an hour most evenings using the English Bible as our text. His knowledge of scripture in his native Riksmaal makes for some very enjoyable discussion for improvement of English vocabulary and grammar."

"And you find Mr. Thoresen an educated individual?"

"Oh, certainly. You know, he and his younger brother did not come to America in desperate circumstances as many émigrés did.

No, I am given to understand that his father is a landowner in the mid-coastal region of Norway, someways north of Bergen. Not rich by any means, but secure and prosperous. I believe they came for what Mr. Thoresen would term 'spiritual opportunity' in addition to financial."

"I see. Well, once again, it was a lovely and well-prepared evening. Congratulations to you, Mr. Letoire."

They sang all the beautiful Christmas carols at service the next day. Rose sang with her whole heart, allowing her voice full rein for a change. The message Pastor Medford preached was about the birth of a baby who brought deliverance to each heart that allowed that baby entrance, just as Joseph went from inn to inn looking for a welcoming door for his wife and expected baby. It set Rose free inside and it came as a revelation just then how each thing God did had to be received, believed on if you will, individually. Her faith was no good for someone else, and theirs no good for her, because God was looking for love in return from each man and woman.

"I love you, Lord," she whispered, "for what you have done for me."

That night was Christmas Eve and she was going to spend Christmas day with the McKennies. Meg and Fiona both begged her to come early "for t' be see'n th' wee ones wi' their socks and presents" and Rose accepted.

Thoresens, too, asked, but she had already made her plans, so it was with both surprise and pleasure that she heard the music of sleigh bells that evening across the rise descend into the yard. There was a whispered conversation out in front and giggles before voices commenced a familiar carol in an unfamiliar tongue.

They trooped up the steps and sang lustily to Rose who opened the door to them. Bundled and red-cheeked with excitement all the Thoresen children stood singing, even Søren. But Uli stood in front, a wreath encircling her head like a crown, lit with candles.

"Oh, how lovely!" Rose exclaimed.

The children pushed forward, eager to deliver their packages, and Rose waved them all inside. Amalie, Sigrün, and Jan came behind them, smiling and wishing her a Merry Christmas.

"But what is this?" Rose demanded of the children. "Explain it to me."

"It's Saint Lucia," Karl began. "She lost her eyesight but—"

"And God gave her new eyes," Arnie finished when Karl took a breath.

"I'm Saint Lucia!" Uli bragged. "See my candles? We're looking for my new eyes but we found you instead!"

The boys hooted with laughter at Uli's explanation while Søren added,

"It's traditional to visit one's neighbors between Saint Lucia's day, the 13th of December and Christmas to bring candies and sweets. You are our only close neighbor so here we are—even if we are nearly late!"

Amalie helped Rose undo the packages of cookies and cakes, which were promptly handed around. One bundle was definitely *not* candy by its smell, and Rose handled it suspiciously.

"Lutefisk. Ver special," Jan explained. He took the brown paper package and cut its cord with his pocketknife. As he unwrapped the unmistakably strong fish, the family sniffed appreciatively.

"Ver special for Christmas. Codfish hard get here, so ver much treat, ja?" The children echoed their relish.

"Try, please?" The fluffy fish meat was steaming with warmth still, but the odor was having an unpleasant effect on Rose. Reminding herself that it was just codfish, she forced herself to try the offered bite. It was light and buttery and melted away in her mouth. The children giggled at her surprised expression—but the smell! Her stomach pitched uneasily.

"It has a very pleasant taste and texture . . ." Rose commented weakly.

Reading between the lines, Jan chuckled and re-wrapped the fish. "Lutefisk not for ever'one. We take home and eat more, eh?"

"Thank you, anyway."

Then the children bestowed a present on her wrapped with shiny red paper, sprinkled over with silver stars.

"I'm sure I didn't expect a gift," she protested.

"Open it! Open it!" they urged.

She did and found a colorful wooden trivet painted in traditional Scandinavian rosemaaling.

"Wonderful work! It's truly beautiful—thank you all, very much!"

"Sigrün did the rosemaaling," Uli volunteered. "And Onkel carved the wood."

"I might have known so, he has such a grand skill. And Sigrün—I didn't know you did painting. Would you show me sometime? I dabble in watercolors a little."

Ducking her head in shy pleasure, Sigrün nodded.

"Now I have a gift for all of you."

The children expressed their approval. From under her bed Rose pulled a small box. She set it on the table and invited them to look. Kjell lifted the lid and "ohhed" softly. The other boys and Uli crowded up to see. The box was lined with shells, starfish, coral, and sea horses.

"What are they?" Uli breathed.

"Let's take them out and see," Rose suggested. Carefully they removed each one and laid them where everyone could inspect them and Rose could comment. They listened attentively as she described each piece, where it came from and what it was like in the ocean before it died or washed up on a beach.

"However did you collect them all, Mrs. Brownlee?" Karl asked. He was holding a large, red star-fish and poring over its intricate construction.

"My son collected them over the last four years," she stated. "It was a hobby of his, but I knew you had never seen anything like them so my mother sent them to me for you. Do you like them?"

"Yes'm." They looked curiously at the shells in the light of their absent owner but refrained from asking further questions. The uncomfortable moment passed and the children, even Søren, Sigrün, and Amalie continued to admire the box's contents while Rose plied them with their own sweets.

When they left, Rose gave each of the youngsters a candy cane and a hug. She hugged Sigrün and Amalie, shook Søren's hand and Mr. Thoresen's.

"Merry Christmas, Mr. Thoresen."

"Ja, and a ver Merry Christmas for you. And I denk you."

She looked questioning.

"Denk you for special gift to children," he repeated. "Ver special." He pressed her hand and bowed.

It seemed to Rose that when the Christmas season ended, the blizzard season began. Rose was pumping water when she noticed the northern vista had assumed a hazy aspect. A few minutes later she was sure there was something odd about it. She took the water in and came back out to pump another bucketful for Snowfoot. Glancing over her shoulder she was amazed to see that nearly all of the prospect just north of Thoresens' was gone—obliterated.

Even while she watched, their pastures disappeared from view and the cloud advanced. It dawned on Rose that her first blizzard was nearly upon her. In a panic, she yanked Snowfoot's stake up and dragged her to the barn. Moments later Prince was deposited in his stall unceremoniously, and Rose hurried to pull down double portions of feed into their mangers. She'd been told how often a blizzard could keep a family from tending their stock, occasionally causing them to starve. She called loudly for Baron and found him already by the stable door, anxiously whining for her.

"Good boy! You wanted to take care of me, didn't you?"

She ran for the house, Baron at her heels, and pulled the shutters closed, fastening them securely, top and bottom. Thoresen land was gone from sight, the blizzard upon the cornfields, when she slammed and bolted the front door. It was quiet, unnaturally so, moments before the storm hit. Rose was trying to remember if she'd left anything undone or forgotten when a shriek surrounded the house and the wind-driven snow blasted every wall.

Rose sat still in the rocker, her heart racing wildly. She felt as if a fantasy monster was attempting to pull her home apart in order to pluck her out. When the roar continued unabated but the doors, walls and roof held, Rose began to relax. She built up the fire, thankful for the load of coal inside her pantry's bin, and made dinner, adding a little extra for Baron. He wouldn't be going out to catch his meal.

The blizzard went on and on. Rose worked quietly, first tidying up, then on a quilt she was attempting for Jamie. It was going to be robin-egg blue on the back and a pattern of stars and crescent moons on the front in yellow, orange, and white. A blue border would tie it all together.

Vera had helped her to start, and Rose was conscientiously following her instructions, even pulling out uneven stitches which, Vera insisted, were signs of an impatient nature. Rose was sure of that, and struggled to keep her temper under control, even as she struggled to get stitch standards high enough to win Vera's approval.

"Knitting is easier," she fussed.

The continual roar and scream of the wind was deafening. If anyone had been there to talk to, no conversation could have been held anyway. She went to bed early and lay awake both feeling and hearing the barrage against the house. Fitfully, she dropped off to sleep, exhausted by the commotion.

In the month of January there were three blizzards with heavy snowfall in between. Rose enjoyed the snow, but it did make traveling difficult. She didn't have a sleigh like many families did by taking the boxes off their wagons and mounting them on runners, so she rode Prince to service and to Bible study on Wednesdays.

It was slow going at times and often cold; also lurking in the back of Rose's mind was the scary idea of being caught in a blizzard away from home alone with Prince. She never left the house without first putting Snowfoot in her stall with adequate food and water.

The ladies' meetings continued to produce good results. Jacob and Vera's work grew and prospered too as the church grew. They were able to rent a small place of their own in town with a kitchen, tiny sitting room, and bedroom. Vera confided to Rose what a blessing the privacy was and, even more, the room.

"We're going to have a baby, Rose, probably in late July." Vera's face glowed with happiness.

February blew in much the same as January and the sheer boredom of being inside so much started to tell on Rose's spirits. She finished the quilt for Jamie, began another for her mother, knit mittens for several neighborhood children, read most of her books, and played her piano sporadically.

Visits were infrequent because the weather was so severe most of the time and just plain cold. The temperature stood often just above zero. More and more she understood what she'd heard called "cabin fever" although to Rose's way of thinking, one good friend . . . or husband . . . would have made all the difference in the world.

It was the loneliness that did it. The days held few interests or visits. Her nights became infiltrated by dreams of James, memories of James, and a great, dull, heavy longing settled on her as if a stone were tied to her heart.

Without realizing it as it happened, she slid into a slough of depression that was draining her spiritually, day by day. She continued reading her Bible faithfully and was deep in the book of Psalms, but when she encountered David's songs of anguish, she failed to hear David's answer from God because of her own dark thoughts and, instead, became more depressed.

Her trips to town twice a week were the only things she looked forward to. Then, the last Saturday in February a blizzard set in and stayed until Tuesday preventing the ride in for church. She reassured herself that nothing could hinder her trip in the morning to attend Bible study until she awoke early before daylight to the incessant roar of yet another storm. Through that day and the next she trudged, lethargic and downcast.

Friday afternoon the weather cleared and Rose stared dully out her window, not really perceiving the brilliant sunshine on the drifted fields. She sat in her chair, letting the tears run down her face unheeded, uncaring.

The ring of sleigh bells entered the yard and little feet padded up the steps, followed by heavy, firm ones. Rose answered the door, without thought of how she would appear.

Bounding in, Uli announced joyfully, "Mrs. Brownlee! Onkel is taking me for a ride; do you want to come?"

Smiling wanly, Rose nodded. They stepped inside while she went for her cloak, bonnet, and gloves. Moving slowly and mechanically, it took her several minutes to find her things and begin to put them on. Uli frowned and looked up at her Uncle Jan.

His face was impassive, almost stern, but he stepped forward and assisted Rose as she fumbled to put her cloak on. Unconsciously she sniffed and rubbed her cheek with a gloved hand.

Jan suddenly became loudly cheerful and sent Uli into gales of laughter by snatching her up and "whiskering" her cheek. It seemed to wake Rose up a bit, and he added for her benefit,

"Sun is ver shining today, Mrs. Brünlee; ver gud day drive, Ja?"

He hustled them out into the sleigh, wheeled the team around and back up the hill. Flying across the snow-crusted upper fields of Rose's property they sped, the wind whipping their hair and faces, Uli whooping in delight at their speed. Her squeals of excitement were not curbed by Mr. Thoresen; rather there was something in his manner that seemed to encourage her exuberance and glee. With the gleam of reflected sunlight on her face and Uli's happy chatter in her ear, Rose came to herself gradually.

They rode for miles that day and Rose thought the air had never been fresher, the sun brighter. She smiled, she laughed, she sang "Jingle Bells" with Uli as many times as she wished and she talked companionably with Jan when Uli grew sleepy and snuggled against her between them.

"Vinter most gone, now," he mentioned. "March haf many nice days; some storm too, but most getting nicer."

Rose sighed. "I guess I don't care much for winter out here, but I can't say I wasn't warned."

He shrugged. "Vinter ver hard, all. Must busy. Must outside some and also vit' people."

"I know. I just haven't been able to see anyone recently. I guess I let it get me down."

"Not eat gud, also?"

"Hm? Oh. Food hasn't tasted good to me lately."

"Mrs. Brünlee, body belong God; must take care for him, ja? Take care mind, too."

"Your English is improving, Mr. Thoresen," Rose commented, changing the subject. "Have you been working on it?"

Glancing sideways at her he responded slowly, "Ja, am learn some."

The sun was dipping low when they let Rose off. From around the side of the house Baron streaked, yipping his pleasure at seeing her, displaying his displeasure at the "intruder," which made it difficult for Rose to say "thank you" to Mr. Thoresen. She managed, while pushing Baron down and over his growling and whining, to say how much she had enjoyed the drive.

"I take Uli Monday," he responded quietly, staring out over the snow-laden fields. "You like come too?"

"Yes, I would. I would greatly enjoy it."

Rose was able to pull herself out of the deep despair after that. She went to church on Sunday and spent the day with Jacob and Vera; Monday Jan and Uli came as promised. The days were lengthening slowly too, and she found Jan was right; there were some nice days as March approached. On Saturday evening Meg and Fiona drove their sleigh over and spent a few hours sipping tea and sharing the latest news from town.

Eyes sparkling, Meg predicted, "An' I'm havin' it from a very reliable source that there's t' be a weddin' fair into May what's bein' announced next Sunday!"

"Meg, I wonder who this 'reliable source' might be?"

Keeping a straight face, Rose stared innocently at Meg, who blushed and hedged. "And could the happy couple perhaps be Harold Kalbørg and Sigrün Thoresen? But probably not; after all, he's never at their house."

They laughed gaily. It was well known that young Kalbørg was present for nearly every Sunday dinner at Thoresens' as well as Saturday afternoon rides and Saturday evening company.

"Aye, an' ye know 'tis," Meg giggled. "Mrs. Thoresen has ordered for the weddin' dress already t' be makin' and Harold is t' be addin' t' his house soon as t' snow is clearin'."

"He's not the only one waiting for spring," Rose sighed. "I've planned my garden three times thus far."

"Well an' 'tis bein' a while afore ye kin be plantin', Miss Rose," Fiona wagged her head knowledgeably. "Spring is bein' a ways off, and terrible fickle she is too when coom. Many as sowed in April has froze in May for not waitin' long enow."

Late winter storms pounded the area again the first days of March as if to emphasize Fiona's words and left a six-inch layer of fresh snow. It seemed that just as Rose wanted to go crazy from the inactivity, Uli would skip up her front steps to include her in a ride out in the brisk air with "Onkel."

How much Rose enjoyed and needed those hours skiing atop the brightness, leaving her gloom at home, she couldn't say. Mr. Thoresen was always the same: kindly, aloof; reserved, yet friendly. Still Rose felt that her thanks was received with a subtle satisfaction and he always left mentioning the next time he would be taking Uli driving so that Rose began to expect the jingle of the sleigh bells and Uli's trip up her porch steps.

The second Sunday in March as she left church after service, Mary Bailey met her. Rose hugged her warmly and received a fond greeting in return. There was a restraint of some kind in Mrs. Bailey's manner, though, that prompted Rose to inquire with concern,

"Mary, is something the matter?"

"A mite, yes. I've brought you a wire from your brother, come this mornin' early." Her face was expressionless and a chill went through Rose as she took the folded paper. Mary patted her on the arm and moved off a few steps for Rose's privacy.

Mother passed away in sleep Saturday a.m. Funeral Tuesday. Come anyway. Tom

Great, silent sobs welled up inside her, and Rose bowed her head on her hands.

Chapter 25

Rose spent two weeks with Tom and Abigail. When they met her train she requested to be taken directly to the cemetery as if it would somehow make her mother's absence more real or tangible.

It did in a way. She stared intently at the new stone side by side with the discolored twin bearing her father's epitaph and part of her grief subsided. Tom and Abby described the funeral, the friends and loving tributes paid to Mrs. Blake, and it helped Rose to hear all the details.

When Rose was ready to leave, Tom hesitated.

"I had thought we would be coming here tomorrow and would have an opportunity to tell you that, well . . . we want you to come with us over there, too." He pointed to a stand of trees near the center of the yard. Rose knew it was the Brownlee family plot.

"James," Rose whispered.

"Yes."

She walked steadily toward the black iron fence enclosing the plot and opened the gate. Tom and Abby followed at a discreet distance. In a tidy little row the markers stood; James, Jeffrey to the left, a space to the right, Glory and Clara.

"The space is for me," Rose realized.

Tom's hand touched hers. "We had a memorial service in July. You never asked, and I felt there was no need to mention it before you came back to visit. I just didn't know Mother would be here too when . . ." His voice broke.

Rose consoled Tom as best she could. It struck her that she was somehow now cast in the role of the comforter, that a change in their relationship had made her the "strong" one—or was it just a change in her?

They stood there, arm in arm, Abby, Tom, and Rose, gazing at the row of graves, and the torrent of grief that Rose expected did not materialize. Instead, in the bottom of her soul where she had thought the desolation and despair of the last year would take her, a deep peace rested, but pulsing and alive.

It was as if she'd opened a door that she'd really believed contained the ultimate in pain and fear and found instead Another, the One who contradicted death by being Life himself.

Oh, Lord, it's you! I can feel you! Tears splashed on her coat, and she smiled tremulously through them. *Death cannot hurt me ever again because of you living inside of me! I know that now. And I don't belong here where they have made a place for me. I'm not dead! I have a life to live and I have a mission, a work to do for you. Maybe someday someone will put my poor body in this piece of ground, I don't know. But it won't be 'me' because the* real *me will never die! Oh, I'm so glad, Lord, Thank you.*

Rose took her hanky, dried her face, and suggested, "Isn't there a little nephew waiting at home for me to meet?"

Tom and Abby looked surprised, but Abby embraced Rose. "Yes, and he's been wanting to meet his Aunt Rose, too!"

Purposely, Rose made an effort to draw their attention from the sad events of late by describing her winter in RiverBend, the Christmas celebrations, sleigh rides, and most of all, her precious ladies' meetings. Everything intrigued Abby who questioned Rose vociferously, and Tom showed a keen interest too, especially in her descriptions of milking Snowfoot, the amount of work she did caring for her animals, and her little farm.

"Rose, you were so fragile and timid before you left home. You never did a lick of hard work in your life! I see now you've grown hearty—not overly plump yet, more than that, you have an air of . . . I can't put my finger on it exactly . . ."

"Self-assurance," Abby nodded in admiration. "I like it very much, Rose."

Tom lifted his brows at his wife. "And would you like me to advertise my business for sale this week so as to engage in such a venture, my dear?"

"No, Tom, but we should visit there this summer without fail," she responded positively. "And it isn't as though there were any reason not to now . . ."

"Now that Mother is gone? Yes, Rose is my only kin, and we can afford to. We'll see."

"Thank you, darling."

They ushered Rose into the Blakes' house where they had taken up residence only the last week, and Abigail called for the nurse to bring Jamie. Before Rose even got her coat off she was face-to-face with a chubby little fellow, wearing honey brown curls and brown eyes in a rosy face that displayed no fear, only curiosity. While Abby held him, Tom intoned formally with a grin:

"Mrs. Rose Brownlee, I have the pleasure of introducing Master James Blake; Master Blake, your Auntie Rose."

While crooning a "hello," Rose slipped her coat off and a servant took it away. She casually fingered her brooch, making it glint in the light and, as she hoped, Jamie noticed it and after a moment, reached out a pudgy fist to "see" it. Soon he was cuddled in Rose's arms and examining all her buttons and bonnet ribbons gleefully, perfectly content to sit with his Aunt Rose all that evening.

"I have a beautiful pull toy for him, Tom," Rose mentioned after dinner, "carved by my nearest neighbor Mr. Thoresen. The man is a genius with his hands and so thoughtful. When their family heard I was to leave in just two days after your wire, they came and took my animals to their farm to care for them, and Mr. Thoresen drove me to the train with his little niece Uli."

"Mr. Thoresen is a widower and his sister-in-law, Uli's mother, is a widow. They share a home all together. Uli is the darling of their family and a very staunch friend of mine. She told her "Onkel" that I should have a present for Jamie, and he made the most darling thing in just a few hours."

"Speaking of your stock and farm, Rose," Tom began carefully, "You know, we are both inheriting Father and Mother's house and properties; there's more than enough room here, more than enough money for—"

"Tom," Rose interrupted gently, "if it had ever been a matter of money, you know that I never needed to leave here. Believe me, I have found a happy home where I am and cannot imagine leaving it to live here again."

Tom frowned. "Is there any man out there paying you attention, like that Morton fellow?"

"Mr. Morton?" Rose was astonished and chuckled. "He is so pompous that I embarrass him just by living on a homestead. And attending church for that matter."

"What about that Thoresen guy?" he shot back.

"Tom, Rose is not here to be interrogated. Be polite," Abby remonstrated. "Now, what about this Mr. Thoresen, Rose?"

"Well, you both wouldn't even ask if you knew him. He must be twenty years older than I am. We are good friends, though."

"Oh." Abby appeared disappointed, but Tom put in a last remark.

"Hmph! Just because there's snow on the roof, doesn't mean there's no fire in the stove."

Rose dismissed the suggestion and moved the subject to more comfortable things. The week went quickly, and even though they begged her to stay longer, she refused gently. Her old acquaintances and connections seemed superficial and her friends' lives were entirely concerned with improving their social positions and their children's accomplishments. Not one meaningful relationship from her hometown induced her to lengthen her stay except for the time spent with Tom, Abigail, and baby Jamie. She would miss him the most, she knew.

"Tom, everyone at home is getting ready to plow. The prairie is turning green and coming to life, something I have pined for all winter. Even my own garden needs planting and my animals will be missing me, too. Won't you promise to come this summer? Come during harvest! It gets into your blood and you'll never forget it," she begged.

"If I have any influence at all, we'll be there, Rose," Abigail replied with confidence.

Tom merely repeated, "We'll see."

The morning Rose left she insisted Jamie ride to the station with them, and she held him during the drive. What she would have given to take him with her! All the tears she shed when the cars rolled away from the platform were for missing his sweet baby face already, and she had again pleaded with Tom to come out the end of summer.

"If business holds steady, it's possible, Rose," was all Tom would promise before he hugged her boyishly and kissed her loudly on the cheek.

"Tom, behave yourself!" Abby chided.

"He is," Rose just laughed. "Like he always does and has. That's my baby brother!"

"All right! Time for you to get on the train," he responded, chastened. "At least I feel better about this than last time. Take care, Sis. We love you."

As the train steamed west, Rose looked anxiously for the signs of spring. It was only two weeks earlier in the year than when she had come out last year, but it had been a harder winter, folks were saying, and longer, too. Miles of farmland, as yet still bare and gray, lined the way home. Rose curbed her disappointment, but still she impatiently longed to get home and plant her own little crops.

"This time last year Fiona had planted hers," she reminded herself stubbornly and counted off the hours before she would see the longed-for prairie.

Every part of her being beat with gladness and with relief when Rose descended the train steps back in RiverBend. The scents of the prairie filled her nostrils; the breath of spring had touched it while she was away.

Quickly, she located her bag, smiling at the folks she knew, looking for someone dear, Vera and Jacob, the Thoresens, or McKennies. Her wire to Vera had requested her to arrange transportation out to her home, and Rose's thoughts kept turning to Prince and Snowfoot—had they been all right at Thoresens' while she was gone? Oh, to be back at her little house watching the sunset with Baron contentedly sprawled by her side!

Golden hair and short skirts flying, a small, sturdy form raced toward her.

"Mrs. Brownlee! Mrs. Brownlee!"

Rose scooped Uli up and smothered her round cheeks with kisses while Uli squeezed Rose's neck and matched her kiss for kiss. At a more dignified pace, Amalie and Jan Thoresen followed, and soon Rose was engulfed in Amalie's loving arms and enthusiastic chatter while Mr. Thoresen stood calmly waiting his opportunity to shake her hand and say, "Velcome home!"

They had brought their wagon to take her out to her homestead, and while Amalie ran on, with Uli trying to translate, Rose found out that the boys had been sent ahead to put Prince and Snowfoot in their stalls and open the house for her.

"And Baron? How is Baron?" Rose questioned.

Jan snorted and through Uli responded.

"Onkel says your dog is fine even if we did give up trying to keep him at our house. He chewed through two ropes and went back home, so we just let him stay there. He's waiting for you right now."

Rose smiled broadly, and Jan clucked his tongue in mock disapproval.

"Dog ver gud now, eh?" he commented wryly.

When they let Rose off, she babbled her thanks and good-byes and ran to the porch. A long, drawn-out howl from back by the stable was her first greeting from Baron, and by the time she reached the steps, she heard his fast-approaching barks. Around the corner he flew and unleashed his excitement and joy. Rose was nearly as overcome and allowed him to jump up and muddy her dress while she patted, scratched, and hugged him. Søren and Karl joined them in the yard right then and over Baron's yips and barks "hello-ed" and grinned.

"Say, Mrs. Brownlee, Prince and Snowfoot are really glad to be home," Søren said reassuringly.

"Thank you, thank you for taking care of them!"

And she ran off to look them over, leaving the boys behind.

Everything and everyone, (meaning Prince, Snowfoot, and Baron) was fine, she concluded happily. The Thoresens had gone by the time she wandered back to the house. Sighing in deep contentment, she seated herself on the porch and watched the shadows fall on the prairie and fields. The fields were a soft, hesitant green, not really fully awakened yet, but the evening was warm and promising.

She readily readjusted to the daily flow of chores and weekly events that she looked forward to. At services on Sunday she was greeted cordially, even warmly, by most but Vera was overjoyed to have her back.

"Rose, how I've missed you! The ladies' study group is growing so well but it just isn't the same without you."

"The ladies' meeting isn't the only thing growing!" Rose teased. Her friend's figure had expanded considerably in her absence.

Vera blushed and laughed prettily. "Yes, baby is coming along fine. Just about three months to go. We can hardly wait."

"And are you getting ready?"

"Oh, Rose, God is so good! Our parents are so excited that they have sent quite a few things including a baby bed. I've been sewing merrily the last few weeks too!"

Fiona joined them, and Rose squeezed her fondly. Meg and Fiona hadn't waited for Sunday to pay a visit to Rose, and she had already been welcomed heartily. A half-dozen steaming Irish scones in a basket had been in their hands when they knocked at her door.

"Aye, ye've been sewin', girl," Fiona chuckled. "Few babes coom t' the worl' wi' sech a foine layette as this 'un has already. Why, what she does wi' needlework an' embroidery on plain cotton tis fit fer t' crown prince o' England, I'm thinkin'!"

"And a crown prince or princess is what they are getting, too, Fiona. As if you don't remember how we all fuss over our first one so." Recalling her new nephew, Rose added, "and I can't tell you what a darling little man my brother's boy is—why Jamie Blake is every bit as big already as Sean, Fiona, and besides that—"

She would have bragged on but they laughed her into giggles so she couldn't continue.

"Well, he *is* a cutie!" she finished triumphantly.

"Oh, an' have ye heard Sigrün's weddin' is fixed last Saturday o' May?" Fiona filled in the details of the big event being planned "far grander than Sally Gardiner's for 'tis Amalie's first child t' marry and Jan has set his mind on it bein' everything Sigrün an' Amalie would be wishin'."

Rose was happy for both Sigrün and Amalie, and Jan Thoresen rose in her estimation as a man who showed he understood what was important to female thinking. "The weather will be lovely then," she thought aloud.

A little frown puckered Fiona's brow, and she answered slowly, "Ye-es. Should be at that, boot a fair cold spring we've been havin' s'far, an' t' almanac has bid farmers t' be sowin' late—not 'til mid May even. We've seen it snow afore in June. Nae a freezin' snow, boot there 'as been killin' frosts in May, too."

Vera listened placidly to all this, but Rose grew alarmed. "I'm going to put my garden in this week, Fiona. Do you believe it's too soon? Yours was in this time last year."

"Aye, an early spring we were havin', too. Best be waitin' loike ever'one else and plant mid-May. Mind ye an' that's nae guarantee neither."

Another three weeks! At home Rose examined her shrubs and bushes. They were budding out nicely—slowly, she admitted—but coming along still. Her beds were full of the tender tips of tulips and iris; the daffodils, hyacinth, and lily-of-the-valley were poised on the brink of bloom.

Still there was something to what Fiona had said, for the day's warmth was often just a bit too tentative, the evenings a little more brisk than one cared for. Rose asked Little Karl Thoresen to plow the garden, *so I'll be ready*, she told herself, and he arrived mid-week with the wagon and plow horse. The plow was in the wagon's bed. Within a quarter hour he was hollering "gee-up!" and crisscrossing the plot back and forth, turning over the soil that had been asleep all winter.

Rose and the Baron lounged near the garden. Rose, girl-like with feet bare, was watching the dark, damp earth as it came up, enjoying the gentle breeze. She heard Baron's growl of disgust before the step behind her and a greeting.

"Gud day, Mrs. Brünlee. Is Karl do good job?"

"Goodness! Hello, Mr. Thoresen, how are you?" She discreetly hid her feet under her skirt, but he merely looked away with a soft grin and squatted down a few feet off.

"I fine, denk you," he answered her question and repeated his. "Is Karl do good job?"

"Oh! Oh, yes, certainly. I'm just anxious to plant soon, you know and—" she remembered to slow down. "And I'm very ready for spring and summer again."

He wrinkled his leathery face as he squinted up at the sky and around the yard. "Ver cool time still, eh? Maybe yes can plant now and all right." He shrugged his shoulders. "Maybe come hard freeze, kill everyt'ing." He smiled wryly. "Get plant again!"

They both laughed at his joke, then Rose questioned seriously, "So you think it may be late enough now?"

His slow, steady smile took in her anxious query.

"If soft snow come," he struggled for the words he wanted and Rose sensed his frustration. "If snow not freeze, if melt away quick, okay then. If snow or frost hard on plants, then some die. We see, ja?"

Rose understood and nodded. It was up to her to take the chance, the risk.

Jan helped Karl load the plow into the wagon and lifted his hat to Rose when they left later. She wandered around the plot several times in contemplation before she decided.

"I'm going to do it. Tomorrow morning."

Actually, the day was gloriously warm and everything she wanted when she put the garden in. By herself this time, not as Fiona's protégée, she marked off the plot, staked her rows, and planted the seeds. The dirt was warm to her bare feet as she padded along. When she stood still and dug her toes into the coolness it was nice, not uncomfortable.

By afternoon when she finished, the day was verging on being hot. She took a short break for lunch and returned to work, this time with a hat on, to dig the furrows while the ground was soft and easy to move. Stretching her sore muscles around three she surveyed her day's labor and was content.

"I can easily trench the rest tomorrow. The important thing is, the garden is in!" Her spirits continued to climb as throughout the week the weather moderated and continued warm.

The leaves on her bushes and shrubs and her tiny fruit saplings unfurled and turned up to the sky. White lilies of the valley dotted the flower beds along the porch along with yellow and purple crocus, bonny yellow daffodils, pink and lavender hyacinth, and the shoots of other, later blooming bulbs and tubers stretching up in the warmth.

She even breathed a sigh of relief when Fiona told her a week later that she had put her garden in, too. All over, spring was "happening," and the farmers were busy in their fields, working from dawn to dusk to make up for the few weeks they'd been delayed.

The height of Rose's joy was when the buds began to form on her roses. She checked the calendar carefully. If all went well, the first of her blooms would grace the most sacred of all occasions.

Then two weeks into May the wind shifted in an afternoon and the temperature dropped ten, twenty, thirty degrees as night descended.

Chapter 26

The chill wind had blown until dark clouds scudded across the night sky and in the morning when Rose awakened, the Baron was scratching and whining imperiously at the door. When she opened it, he bounded through, shaking fresh snow in all directions while Rose stood in the doorway staring. At least several inches of soft, wet, spring snow lay everywhere, and the sky glowered threateningly. Rose would have judged it to be before sunrise if she hadn't known better.

Remaining calm, she sought her memory. What was it Mr. Thoresen had told her? If the snow were soft and melted off quickly, the damage would be minimal? Rose grabbed up her shawl and walked out to check the garden. Traversing the porch to the south side of the house she first examined the roses then strode into the snow to the garden, then the "orchard."

Everything was thoroughly coated, but the snow was so heavy with moisture that she was sure it would melt off as soon as the sun came out. The sun, however, was not to be seen and Rose shivered as a bone-chilling gust of wind struck her. She was hardly dressed for the present turn in the weather.

Back in the house she changed into warmer clothing and went through the chores. Ever-present was the worry about the snow and drastic change in the temperature. Not only her small garden but the whole community's crops for the next year were at stake. The coffeepot sent forth its usual appealing aroma, and Rose took no notice. Breakfast held no allure. She viewed the long day ahead trapped inside with disappointment and an irritable temper.

Finally Rose sat herself in the rocker before the stove, ottoman beneath her feet and a cup of coffee beside her, and took up her Bible. If winter would persist a little longer, then so must she.

Turning to where Vera had been teaching, Rose reread her careful notes. They were studying the book of Ruth. Oh, how she ached as Vera described the young Ruth's circumstances: a widow and a foreigner in Israel, not even welcome in her husband's country and forced to work each day among unfriendly strangers just to glean enough grain to keep herself and her mother-in-law from starving through the winter.

Then, out of the blue, a relative of her husband begins to assist her efforts. Acting on her mother-in-law's advice, Ruth calls upon this relative to "redeem" her and her husband's property by marrying her! In the end, he does so, giving Ruth and her mother-in-law a home and security, and her husband's name and property to their firstborn son.

Vera pointed out how the relative had not been a young, handsome man. It had been a marriage of necessity and convenience, yet out of commitment to the God of Israel and great mutual respect for each other they formed a lasting union resulting in the eventual birth of King David—and also the Lord Jesus.

It was such a tragic and romantic tale the way Vera presented it. Rose considered Boaz' words to Ruth:

Blessed be thou of the Lord, my daughter:
for thou hast shewed more kindness in the latter end
than at the beginning,
inasmuch as thou followest not young men,
whether poor or rich.
And now, my daughter, fear not;
I will do to thee all that thou requirest:
for all the city of my people doth know
that thou art a virtuous woman.

Seemingly, Ruth understood a man's character to be more important than youthful romance and chose it as a superior match, even though she was still young and attractive.

Engrossed in her thoughts, Rose put her Bible away and straightened the kitchen. All activities must be done inside today, so she made herself look over her clothes and begin a mending project, occasionally opening the door or going to a window to check the weather as the day wore on.

Around three, Rose was considering hitching Prince to the buggy for a drive. The threatened storm had not materialized and the clouds showed promise of breaking up and letting in a bright day's end. The knock at the door startled her and then Baron's unfriendly attitude as he tore up the side porch and around to the front let her know who it was before she opened the door.

"Mr. Thoresen, hello!" Rose was so glad to see another face.

Ja, god-dag," he greeted her. "You please to take ride?" He indicated his buggy in the yard pulled by his team of bays.

"Yes, yes!" Rose, in her haste to enjoy the unexpected treat left Jan on the porch with the Baron while she scrambled into her long coat, bonnet, and mittens. Glowing and anxious to get out into the fresh air, she bustled through the doorway and distractedly shooed Baron as he pushed against her. Jan's eyes glinted with humor, but she didn't notice.

They drove away, slowly, sloshing through the wet and melting snow, the breeze catching at their clothes and whipping their cheeks. The urge to sniff the air and see all about was like a thirst to Rose, and she closed her eyes in bliss.

"Day to ride—not to house, ja?" Mr. Thoresen observed.

Rose agreed heartily. "I was feeling so 'cooped up' because of the snow. I'm glad you came."

Across the snow-clad plain on little-used roads and tracks the bays charged with a will. In her own enjoyment Rose never wondered at Jan's coming today. They drove on and after a while Jan spoke, loudly enough to hear over the swish of the wheels and the wind whistling by,

"Ve go, look river. Ver big now. Ver *grand*."

Rose hid a smile. "Grand" was not a word she'd ever heard Jan Thoresen use. He'd added that one recently!

He pulled the team up as they approached the brow of the overlook and laid the buggy alongside the edge. Below and running from the north was the very creek that divided their properties. It was wider and deeper here where it emptied into the much larger river. Fresh snow covered the banks of the creek and hung over the sides of the small torrent in outlandish, drooping pillows.

The junction of the two streams was swollen and swift, wickedly so in Rose's imagination. It was both "grand" and disquieting to her. The still, white plains in the distance seemed surreal in their picture-like quality as the sun's late rays broke through and touched them. All was silent save for the shifting of the team.

Watching the river, she was reminded of that night when heavy, heaving chunks of ice floated in another river . . . the horses screaming, Clara crying—she shivered and shook off the oppressive memory. Jan was speaking, very slowly and carefully forming his thoughts.

" . . . name vas Elli. Vas gud, best, and kind woman."

Rose saw that he was holding in his hand a small tintype set in a morocco case. Instinctively she reached out to examine it. He set it gently in her palm, and Rose beheld a woman's face, unsmiling as the custom was, but nevertheless with some quality that made Rose smile back into the sweet likeness. A familiar something, too . . .

"Who . . .?" She looked up inquiring and Jan was studying her steadily. Could he sense her preoccupation of the last few minutes? Her lack of attentiveness couldn't have gone unnoticed.

"Mine vife, Elli." He spoke patiently; Rose knew he was repeating what she had not heard the first time.

He continued. "Fever, ver bad come. Our *dottre* Kristen, mine brot'er Karl, and mine Elli die. Go to God. For eight year."

Re-examining the image of the woman, Rose now saw the resemblance Søren bore her in the cheeks and the nose. His mother in this picture was young still.

Why, she was closer to my age when this was taken, Rose thought. *Yet she is dead, gone from her family like James.* Tears of sympathy sprang to her eyes.

"I haf much luf for Elli. Ver hard life vit no Elli," Jan said slowly. There was a pause before he went on, each word chosen, practiced. Rose had never heard him speak so much in English. "You luf, too. Your man." And very softly, "He die, too, ja?"

His understanding undid her. Voice shaking, Rose tried to answer back. "Yes, he died. And my children, my sweet little ones, too." She gestured at the water. "Our carriage slid into a frozen river like this one. They all died. They drowned. *Except for me.*" Rose wept and felt shame. She'd been so strong, so *healed* at their graves yet now, here where the memory was more real, she struggled with but couldn't seem to stop the grief.

The buggy pulled away from the high bank. Making a wide circle, they turned back in the direction of her home. Now, before them and off every snow-clad feature near or far, the setting sun burned with ribbons of red, pink, and oranges; clouds edged in scarlet-purple defied blue backgrounds, and the majestic white of distant ranges danced in every hue of dress the sunset could conjure up.

Slowly peace and control returned to Rose's heart. She breathed deeply and gathered her wits about her. The tears had dried but the shame of their memory had to be dealt with. She was about to speak up and apologize when Jan stopped the team. He turned and faced her in the seat. The deliberateness of his manner confused her into stammering,

"Mr. Thoresen, I'm very sorry for my behavior . . . I didn't mean . . ."

He shook his head once, decidedly and spoke. "*I* sorry! Not know for (he searched for the word) river?"

She acknowledged this and he continued.

"Mrs. Brünlee, vas Mr. Brünlee Christian?"

Rose was surprised into just nodding.

"Mrs. Brünlee, ven trust Jesus, not gone alvays, now only." There was encouragement in his tone and an earnestness in his expression made her look him full in the face. His eyes were open down to his soul. "I tell you trut', little woman, God *never* gone, alvays vit you. As Christian brot'er I promise you, God vill help."

A flood of gratitude welled up in Rose. She wanted to thank him, express it some way, but he "chirruped" to the horses, and neither of them spoke going home.

Deep in thought, Rose turned over the events of the afternoon and, yes, even her changing impressions of this man, Jan Thoresen. For he was far deeper than she had imagined—how had she once thought him rather bland and unemotional, an old, worn-out farmer and Amalie's dutiful but indifferent husband?

Rose shook her head. None of that seemed to fit anymore. How different everything and everyone seemed from her first impressions that spring a year ago!

In front of her house he helped her down and escorted her to the front door. The Baron made a fuss there, fawning on her and nearly overturning her, threatening low in his throat at Jan. She patted him and attempted to quell his exertions, but he was too wound up to be placated.

"Down!" Thunder rolled in Jan's voice, and Baron dropped to the floor of the porch like he'd been shot.

"Gud dog," Jan said in his normally serene tone. His address to Rose though, while as polite as always, seemed rather spiritless. "And denk you, Mrs. Brünlee. Ride vas ver nice."

He opened the door, holding it for her and closing it firmly after she passed through. In the house Rose stood where she was until the sound of the horses and buggy faded into the evening.

Chapter 27

The sunrise on Sigrün's wedding day was like a bridal pageant itself, all white-gold and blushing, walking in sacred procession over the far hills and throwing its bridal flowers to the waiting congregation.

Enthralled, Rose watched the spectacle from the front steps. Baron was content to stay quietly at her side as long as her slender hand rested on his head or scratched his ears. At last she stood up sighing with contentment. There was work to do, and it was to be a joyous chore; she had the honor of supplying the wedding roses!

How Amalie had exclaimed her delight when Rose had told her on Sunday last that the now opening blossoms were to be her wedding gifts to Sigrün and Harold. Harold had thanked her too, but Rose's real reward was Sigrün's beatific smile of pleasure. Maybe Sigrün would never speak aloud to her, but their friendship of spirits spoke a deeper language than uttered words.

Now, sharp shears in well-gloved hand, she went first to the climber roses on the south side of the porch and carefully chose and clipped the longest tendrils with the sweetest blooms. True, there were not many yet because the weather was still cool, but here in RiverBend, where roses were still rare, they would be twice admired. The two tea rose bushes, one bearing sunset gold blooms, the other graced with buds and full-blown, deep red flowers, yielded eight lovely stems altogether.

"Beautiful! Enough for a bouquet and for Sigrün's hair. The others will be for the altar." She admired their brilliant colors and lush fragrance.

She wrapped the cuttings in tissue and set them in a long box carefully lined with ice before getting to the rest of her chores. Rose rushed through milking Snowfoot and caring for Prince so she would have time to bake her contributions to the wedding feast.

Finally she was able to bathe and dress. With great care she removed the protective paper from her garment, revealing a deep, dusty rose-colored muslin dress, sprigged with cream and trimmed all over with priceless ivory lace sewn upon layers of ruffles and gathers.

It had been so long since Rose had really "dressed" up, more than a year of mourning and dressing to work, that the sight took her breath away. Into her hair she twisted a long, thin, burgundy velveteen ribbon until there was a flush of color throughout her ash-blonde coil that reflected on her pale cheeks.

Rose hurried to get her things to the buggy, pausing to collect her guitar at the last minute as she recalled the dancing at Sally Gardiner's wedding and her desire to be allowed to play with the fiddlers.

At last Rose's buggy pulled into the Thoresens' yard behind the McKennies' wagon. McKennie children spilled from the back of their wagon to join the children frolicking around the side yard.

So many friends, neighbors, and family are here, Rose marveled. Warm greetings came to her ears and Fiona's hug was exuberant.

"I belong here! I'm a part of all this now," Rose rejoiced. "And so many here are part of God's family—my family, the one God gave me to bring healing to my heart."

The happiness in her flowed in and out as she helped ready the "chapel." Thoresens' enormous barn had been swept and was now being decorated. Neighbors hung evergreen boughs from distant hills twined with sweet peas and lined up sweet scented bales of hay before the "altar." Colorful cloths and rugs transformed the bales into benches, and Rose twisted and tied the strands of climber roses to the altar legs and laid one fragrant branch across the snowy linen cloth where the bride and groom would make their vows.

It was not going to be a stylish eastern wedding, yet Rose had higher expectations from this union than many a fashionable wedding she'd attended back home.

Amalie bustled forward to inspect the preparations, her kind face flushed with joy and excitement. Rose saw, too, how much work Amalie had been doing and stepped up to hug her and urge her to sit down a minute.

"Karl! Little Karl!"

Karl approached shyly at her bidding, standing over her.

"Karl, do get Mor a cold glass of water, please. Takk takk."

Karl grinned at Rose's use of the smattering of Riksmaalshe had picked up from Uli. Amalie sat obediently until he returned. She drank the long glass of well water while Rose stayed with her and patted her plump, brown hand.

"Don't worry, Amalie. Everything is perfect, really."

Nodding, she seemed to relax a little, but something else played on her face.

Oh, Rose commiserated. *She's hurting for losing Sigrün.* Rose patted Amalie's hand again and said brightly, "Harold is a wonderful man. God is good to Sigrün, don't you think?"

Sighing, Amalie agreed, although she struggled for the words in English.

"Ja, Gott is gud. I denk him, sure."

An hour later the crowd of friends and family stood by their "benches" as Jan and Sigrün walked solemnly to the altar where Harold and Pastor Medford waited. How fine and true Sigrün looked! Jan, appearing very genteel in his dark suit, proudly led her forward. He caught Rose's eye, and she smiled encouragingly.

Holding her look, he kept his eyes on her, and as inscrutable as ever, there was something else, too, a kind of firmness or resolve. She dropped her eyes at last, not knowing what to think, and they passed her by. The wedding began. The vows were exchanged solemnly with Sigrün nodding at the proper moments and the blessing pronounced.

Next came the feast, far bigger and more splendid than Sally Gardiner's, Rose observed. Two enormous hams, a roasted goose, several chickens, plates of Smørbrod (open-faced Norwegian sandwiches), baked potatoes, baked beans, new greens, several varieties of cheeses, fresh bread and corn bread, every kind of pie and pastry, pickles, stewed fruits, relishes, and jams and jellies loaded the tables.

Søren and his friend Ivan strode forward with kegs of apple cider, icy cold from sitting for days in the Thoresen icehouse. Cheers and toasts were offered, while Sigrün and Harold sat in chairs on a little platform surrounded by boughs and ribbons, both blushing and smiling as everyone wished them well and piled their gifts at their feet.

The feasting wouldn't stop all day. An empty spot on a table was quickly refilled and then the dancing started, too. Rose remembered her guitar and slipped out to fetch it from her buggy. As she turned to go back, Jan was there. He looked as "grand" as she'd ever known him, she thought, his broadcloth suit showing off well his erect carriage and strong shoulders.

"I carry for you," he stated. She allowed him to and thanked him.

"I vant do," he replied succinctly.

The dancing was well organized and getting underway as they returned to the barn. Rose made to take her guitar from Jan and join the three musicians, but Jan held the case firmly and shook his head once.

"Please, ve dance first?"

"Oh, Mr. Thoresen, no, no, thank you. I don't, I mean I haven't danced in a long time. Thank you, no." Rose reached out for her guitar again, only this time Jan held it away and smiled broadly.

"No. Ve dance now, please."

Never had she seen him smile like that! Was he making a tease with her?

"Mr. Thoresen! I really don't think . . ."

"No talk—dance." Without waiting for her answer, he set the guitar beside the wall and possessed himself of her hand, leading her out to dance. Rose felt her face grow red as Jan took charge and they went whirling across the floor. The young men vigorously leading their partners made way before them and, when the music stopped, Jan called loudly for another.

Rose was flagging, out of breath, but he seemed tireless. Around and around the room they flew until at last the song stopped and Rose collapsed laughing on a bale now pushed up against the barn wall.

Søren called his father at that moment. He left her fanning her burning face with a "Scuse, please."

Rose's breath was coming in short gasps, and she was happy to just sit. What had come over the man! Across the room, Jan was giving instructions for something to Søren, Ivan, and Karl, and she heard him call a hearty welcome to a latecomer. Well, she conceded, it *was* a special occasion, and even staid individuals would unbend a little at a wedding.

She made talk with the folks sitting near her, and as she recovered her wind, got up and moved about, sharing the festive mood with everyone. The dancing went on, the food was in constant supply, the day perfect.

Just after chatting with Berta Schmidt, she felt a heavy hand on her arm and turned to find Mark Grader standing at her elbow. He must have arrived after the ceremony, and his breath had the unmistakable smell of tobacco mixed with alcohol. He was, however, cleaned and dressed for a party. Tossing his slick, black-haired head back, he grinned and demanded a dance of her. Rose demurred politely, but his hand did not leave her arm.

"You danced with old Thoresen. A young buck like me'd be better than an old Norski like him any day." His words were loud and several heads turned their way. Berta looked nervously around for her husband.

"Please, Mr. Grader, if you don't mind . . ."

"Don't mind if I do!" he answered rudely and, taking her other arm, pulled her with him to the center of the barn floor. The music was just beginning, slow and sweet, and his arm went about her familiarly so that she was much too close to him to be comfortable or decorous. Rose was so embarrassed and angry that she tried to pull away but his grip on her waist was determined. He leaned his face into hers, smiling wickedly.

"You're a pert thing even if they do say you're five years older than I be. And a widow woman has to be on the lookout for a good man to take care of her. I'm a man. I could take care of you fine— real fine." His smile widened, and he drew her closer.

Rose's senses reeled. With all her heart she wanted away from this horrid man! *Dear God,* she prayed desperately, *please help me! Deliver me from this without a humiliating scene, please, dear God!* Abruptly they stopped dancing. When she opened her eyes, Mark Grader was glowering. Close beside and behind him stood Jan, Søren, and Ivan.

"Oh, thank you, Lord!" she breathed.

"What you want, Thoresen?" Mark barked out. "You're interruptin' our dance."

Rose tried again to extricate herself, but his grip was like steel.

"'Scuse, Mr. Grader," Jan said mildly, "Ve need talk now. Ver important. Out dere." His hand indicated outside. Søren's eyes narrowed; Ivan grinned in anticipation.

"I'm busy. Now get out of my way." Grader's hand made to push Jan aside, and suddenly he found his arm twisted hard behind his back. Jan held it there while staring fixedly into Grader's eyes.

"Out dere, please," he repeated softly. Grader's hold on Rose relaxed, and Søren and Ivan hustled him out. Rose found herself dancing very properly with Jan. The whole scene had been so discreet that only one or two people glanced knowingly at the retreating backs of Søren, Ivan, and Mark Grader.

"Better, ja?"

Rose looked up into the genuine friendliness of his query and nodded. Tears threatened to spill from her eyes. Jan shook his head once and clucked his tongue, then spun her gently across the floor. There was a soft smile on his face the rest of the dance, but when the music ended, he deposited her with Fiona McKennie and, bowing, left them.

The uncomfortable incident was soon dismissed from Rose's mind as the singing began. Old Mr. Clark called out the tunes, and the group picked them up. Song after song was rendered with gusto and soon individuals were being brought forward to sing solos, mostly ballads with choruses to join in on. Then a courting song was sung for Sigrün and Harold's benefit amid much good-natured laughter.

Fiona McKennie spoke up, "Perhaps Mrs. Brownlee would favor us with a song? Her guitar is right here."

Eagerly the request was seconded and Rose stepped forward to oblige. She'd sung for many entertainments in private gatherings around her city. It was a very lady-like accomplishment, and she felt no qualms as she picked up her guitar. A sudden inspiration came to her and with a gleam in her eye she addressed herself to the bride and groom.

"I'd like to sing a verse to a tune Uli taught me just recently. I only know the one verse, but it is for you, Harold and Sigrün." Smiling prettily with an air of teasing, she strummed the first chord:

> *Der star ein friar uti garden*
> *Mor Lilla, hau, hau*
> *Der star ein friar uti garden*
> *Mor Lilla, hau, hau*
>
> *Kor mange pengar have han,*
> *Du mi dottre Dalia?*
> *Kor mange pengar have han,*
> *Du mi dottre Dalia?*

The Norwegian and Swedish folk roared with laughter and Sigrün threw a linen napkin lying in her lap over her face to hide her blushes. Those who couldn't understand the words could laugh at the results, and soon everyone had an understanding of "the gentleman suitor standing in the yard while his beloved's mother wanted to know how much money he was willing to pay for her daughter."

This would have brought down the house, except that Jan Thoresen stepped up and announced he would sing the last song. His unexpected offer met with a burst of applause, so he bowed and began, also in Norwegian, to sing to Sigrün and Harold. His voice was strong and true, not cultured, but he sang with pleasure and the song gave pleasure back. Harold took Sigrün's hand and looked deep in her eyes as Jan sang. The eternal story of love was there to be read by anyone with eyes to see.

How wonderful that they have a love for God that will hold their love together, Rose mused.

The ballad went into a second verse, and Rose realized Jan was looking at her now as he sang. She couldn't understand the words, but he seemed to be singing each line to her.

Nervously, Rose glanced around. Although many other guests were ignorant of the words also or were watching the bride and groom, Amalie stood staring at Jan with a puzzled expression. Søren, in the back with Ivan and the other young men, raised his eyebrows and looked first from Jan to Rose and back again.

Quickly Rose sat down where Jan's gaze couldn't find her. What an up and down day! She decided she was tired from the long span of activity and was ready to go home as soon as the wedding party left.

The bride and groom were now escorted to their wagon. Willing hands carried all the gifts for them and piled them in. Cooking utensils, linens, blankets, crockery, and preserves: all thoughtful and necessary for beginning life together. Then Sigrün kissed her mother, each brother, Uli, Søren, Jan and, once again, a tearful Amalie. Together Sigrün and Harold drove away into the great adventure of their lives.

Waving and calling good-byes, everyone saw them off, then busied themselves with cleaning up. All traces of the wedding were removed, for the "bossies" would have to come into their barn for milking soon.

Empty dishes, blankets, rugs, and children were gathered. Rose helped Grace Davies with her children; the baby wailed to be fed while the two toddlers were overly tired and alternated whimpering and screaming for their naps.

After the crowd thinned, Rose sought out Amalie to bid her goodbye. The poor woman was weary-looking, and even her smile had a droop so Rose hugged her while pouring out praises and compliments on the bride, the ceremony, and the day in general.

"Ja," Amalie responded in satisfaction, and added a great deal more Rose didn't understand but agreed with heartily. Unexpectedly, Amalie looked deep into Rose's face for a moment, then muttered something and kissed Rose tenderly on the cheek.

"Oh, Amalie!" Rose was surprised and touched.

Amalie just shook her head and sighed as Rose went to her buggy. Jan, Søren, and Ivan were moving bales of hay out of the barn. They'd all changed from their finery to normal farm clothes.

As Rose stacked her things on the floor of the buggy, Jan left off moving bales and came to help her finish, then handed her up to the seat. Søren and Ivan had stopped work, too, and were watching; Søren's expression was studiously blank; Ivan stood grinning like a cat in the cream. Politely, Rose coughed. What *was* everyone staring at today?

"It was a lovely wedding, Mr. Thoresen," she remarked, anxious to get away. "Simply 'grand'!"

"Ja." That same resolute glint was in his eye, and he nodded knowingly. "Next vun better, too, ja? God-dag, Mrs. Brünlee."

She drove away wondering what he meant by that. Søren hadn't asked Meg yet, she was sure. Fiona would have told her! Since Prince was in high spirits and anxious to be home, she gave her attention to her driving and soon forgot the puzzling parts of the wonderful day.

Chapter 28

A week after the glorious weather of Sigrün and Harold's wedding, heavy spring rains rolled into the region. Thunderheads piled up, black and towering along the sky's edge, waiting for some precise moment to rush headlong into each other.

The resulting lightning and thunderstorms were deafening; to Rose it sounded *and* felt as though the heavens were cracking apart. No gentle showers, these! Torrents and sheets of water inundated the area, threatening to wash away the nursling crops.

The creek separating Brownlee and Thoresen land swelled to ridiculous proportions overnight, washing into the lower parts of Rose's yard, covering some portions of Jan and Søren's closest corn field, and swamping the small bridge.

For three nights followed by three dark days Rose never left her house except to tend Prince and Snowfoot in their stalls. There they were dry and warm, and she provided their feed and water, but each foray soaked her to the bone.

The Baron made the trip with her and regularly marched his sentry around the house. The remaining time was spent companionably inside. Rose worked diligently on mending, needlework, Bible study, anything to draw her attention from the stupefying drizzle of rain. Dejected and bored, Baron lay across the closed doorway.

The third evening, Rose was daydreaming idly before the open fire in her stove, untouched knitting in her lap. The Baron raised his splotched head, listening. Not noticing, Rose roused herself to make dinner. The dog stalked about the cabin as if trying to get a bearing on something, stopping and listening, moving from front door to back.

He lay down frustrated, then catching some other sound with his ear, raised up as if attempting to identify it. Rose noted his agitation at last and wearily ordered him to lie back down.

Reluctantly he did so. Rose was stirring a slice of ham sizzling in the skillet and cutting cold boiled potatoes to fry alongside it. Without warning, Baron sprang to a window, viciously barking and scrabbling at the panes.

"Baron! Bad boy!" Rose shouted. One lacy curtain had a tear in it from his nails. She hauled him to the door by his collar and forced him to lie down. To her amazement, he growled menacingly at her.

"Why, Baron! Shame on you. This unending rain is making us both grouchy." She stroked his head and long ears soothingly. "Be a good boy; I'll fix you a nice bit to eat."

The dog merely put his face on his paws and growled low in his throat.

Instead of going all the way to the pump to fetch water, Rose had set her buckets on the back steps to catch the plenteous rainwater. She went to the door now to bring in one of the pails for coffee. No sooner had she placed her hand on the door latch than the Baron was between her and the door, snarling threateningly, holding her from going out into the pantry.

Rose took her "stick" from the wall, unused for several months now and, pulling him by the collar while smacking his haunches with the switch, returned him to the front threshold.

"Stay!" she commanded in anger. "Both of our tolerances are wearing thin." This last she said to herself.

Rose closed the doorway into the pantry and walked the few feet to the back door, lifting the latch. Unexpectedly it swung out and powerful hands grabbed her, pushing her back, twisting her arms behind her.

She shrieked in terror and an open hand slapped her full in the face, silencing her.

"None o' that, lady," an ugly voice rasped. "We're goin' in there and you are gonna keep that mutt under control, or I will shoot him—do ya get me?"

Stunned, Rose nodded. By the pantry door they paused again.

"Now, you do what you need to do to get him out here where we can keep him locked up!"

The Baron was howling and clawing at the door in a frenzy. Rose opened it a crack and tried to order him back, but he ignored her, redoubling his efforts to get at the two men.

"Little brother, I'll git behind her and push her into the house. You run out the back, but close the door. When he follows you, we'll have him trapped in this room. Come around to the front, and I'll let you in."

It was accomplished with remarkable ease. The Baron barked and thrashed in frustration and anger inside the pantry while the man holding Rose in his vise-like grip opened the front door to let his partner in.

Dripping and breathless, he stepped in and shook the rain off his hat.

"Hel-looo, Miss Rose!" he greeted her sarcastically.

It was Mark Grader. He shrugged off his leather cape, streaming water onto her floor, and stepped up to the stove. The other man released Rose and latched the door, also dropping his wet overcoat on the floor and sidling up to the fire.

"By the by, Mrs. Brownlee," Mark continued grinning, "meet my big brother, Orville."

"Shuddup!" The other man shot back, cursing under his breath.

Rose sank down wearily on a dining chair. Orville Grader. Sent to prison for hurting a man so badly that he would never walk again. His sentence was fifteen years, so that must mean . . .

Mark continued leering. "Yup. This here storm came in plenty handy. After we killed the prison's work-gang boss and took off, they couldn't track us three inches in this rain, so we lost 'em right away."

"Yes, Ma'am, mighty handy—'cept Orville's horse slid down a creek bank and broke his danged leg. We were just north of here, headed west when I thought of you. Actually," he leered, "I've thought a *lot* 'bout you these last few months, all alone out here. Seems to me a rich lady like you all by yourself is just askin' for company."

He eased up to where she was sitting, still in shock, and began to toy with a strand of her hair. "Yes, and I thought 'bout you a lot since that weddin'."

His eyes narrowed with hate. "Them Norskies think they throwed me out good, but here I am—and here you are. Here you are . . ."

His fingers stroked her neck, just above her collar. Rose jerked her head away, and he laughed, walking back to the stove. His brother glowered at him.

"You stupid fool! The only thing we want here is her horse. Soon as we get dry, we take enough food and the horse and git." His dark features were hardened with anger, hate, and fear.

Rose felt sick. Prince! Gentle, old Prince, her friend! He wouldn't last more than a day or so driven by these hounded men.

He would fall and die, somewhere out there in the cold rain . . . Rose prayed silently, "Oh, Lord! I call on you to help me! Please help us!"

Orville spoke to her harshly. "Git us something to eat. Make it hot and plenty."

A crack of lightning lit the cabin followed immediately by the thunderclap. Mechanically, Rose went about cutting up more ham and potatoes, dropping them into the skillet and thinking vaguely how long ago starting dinner seemed, how safe her life had seemed. She was under no illusions as to Mark Grader's intentions toward her, and she shuddered in fear.

The potatoes browned slowly in the bubbling ham juice. As she stirred them, certain words began to play in her mind, arranging themselves into phrases, lines. For a time they didn't make sense, didn't penetrate her fear. Slowly though, she realized the same lines were repeating themselves, and she took notice.

> *. . . Because thou hast made the Lord,*
> *which is my refuge, even the most High, thy habitation,*
> *There shall no evil befall thee,*
> *neither shall any plague come near thy dwelling.*
> *For he shall give his angels charge over thee*
> *to keep thee in all thy ways.*
> *. . . He shall call upon me, and I will answer him:*
> *I will be with him in trouble;*
> *I will deliver him and honour him . . .*

Rose could almost remember reading that Psalm, but had she memorized it? She didn't think so. Silently, with her back to the two men, she mouthed the words. Trust in God's ability to rescue her began to grow quietly in her heart.

"What should I do, Lord?" she queried.

The ham and potatoes were done and the coffee was perking, sending out its aroma. Rose served the food and set empty cups in front of the hungry, desperate men. They were both eating ravenously, all their attention on their food.

"Get the coffee, woman!" Orville demanded. Mark looked deliberately from her to her bed and back and smirked wickedly.

Rose tried to keep her face impassive even as another stab of fear turned her cold. She went back to the stove and picked up the pot. Stealing a glance at the two men devouring her ham and potatoes she paused, trembling.

"Lord?" While she stalled at the stove trying to gather her wits, more words played through her thoughts like quicksilver.

> *Blessed be the Lord my strength,*
> *which teacheth my hands to war,*
> *and my fingers to fight.*

"Oh!" Rose spoke aloud.

"Quit mutterin' to yerself and get over here with that coffee!" Orville roared.

Warm peace flowed through her. "Sorry," Rose smiled confidently. She removed the lid to the pot and, calmly and deliberately, *threw the bubbling contents over both of them*!

Howling in pain and rage they staggered up from the table, but Rose had thrown open the pantry door and released Baron. As she fled out the back, Baron's ferocious attack was producing shrieks and oaths. Straight to the stable she sped, slipping in the mud and streaming rain to Prince's stall door.

"Out, Prince!" she urged. "Go! Get out of here!" She flailed his haunches with her open hands, but he stood there bewildered, refusing to leave without her.

"Go on! I can't save you if you don't go! Get!"

Still he stayed near the stable, sidestepping in confusion at her frenzy.

The furor in the house came to an end abruptly as a single gunshot coupled with a yelp of pain struck a blow to Rose's heart. She stood still in the dark, pouring rain to hear what would happen next.

Vile cursing from both of the men filled the night air before Orville's voice spat out, "Throw that mutt's carcass out the door and take care of me! My God, my throat is bleeding—hurry!"

The sound of Baron's heavy body hitting the steps was followed by footsteps slapping through the soggy yard toward the stable.

"He's going to find me!" Rose panicked. Leaving Prince, she crept around the stable, keeping the sound of footsteps on the opposite side. Mark Grader swore when he found the loose horse. He led him back into his stall and, glancing at Rose's tools, picked up a board, nails, and hammer. Outside he closed the stable door and nailed it shut, fortifying it by adding the board securely tacked across it.

"Hey, Miss Rose!" he called in acrid tones, "Yer horse is nailed in tight. And you know there's no way you kin git across that creek to Thoresens'. Try it! They'll find yer bloated body in the river if you do. Nobody else is close enough to help you, and there's nowhere to git out of the rain. You can count on my coming out here to find you if you try to shelter anywhere around here, so do the sensible thing. That dog of yorn tore up my brother pretty bad. You come in the house without causin' us any more trouble and take care of him. When we can git out of here, we'll leave you peaceful like."

Rose gave no answer.

"I'll not dicker with you, lady! Git in the house or freeze outside in the rain. Makes no never-mind to me." He waited a minute more and stalked angrily back to his brother.

As he went by, Rose crept the other way around the stable. She examined the stable door and shook it vainly.

"Oh, God! What have I done?" she moaned. Jan had made the door solid and heavy. Even if she could get it open somehow, she could be trapped if Mark came out unexpectedly. Her body shook with cold and she wondered stupidly where to go. Casting about the yard, she considered tramping the three miles to McKennies. Would she lose her way in the dark?

She stumbled through muddy grass and brush toward the rise and walked by the overgrown soddy. The soddy! He wouldn't know it was there! Could she get the door open? It hadn't been opened since Brian had shown it to her and Fiona nearly a year ago.

She felt in the mud and grass, searching for the entrance until her fingers found the rotting boards. Surprising her, the door moved after she pulled on it only a few times.

"The rain must have washed some of the grass and dirt away," she rationalized.

Pulling the door closed after she crept in, she felt her way into the black, musty hole. It was dark, dusty, and moldy smelling. She sank down on the dry dirt floor in gratitude.

She may have slept—she couldn't tell how long if she did, but Rose was shivering with cold. Hours dragged by while she huddled to get warmth in her soaking wet dress.

From time to time the recollection of the gunshot and Baron's yip of pain drew fresh tears, and she wondered if her hiding place would be visible when daylight came. But she was safe, safe for now. Baron had hurt Orville, badly, Mark had said. And given his life in payment.

"What if they stay because he is too hurt to ride," Rose hoped for Prince's sake. But then she would be forced to stay in hiding without food or heat. Worse yet, they might find her. What would they do to her for her part in their troubles? No one could know she was in need. No one would come to help.

She dozed. She awakened and prayed. She recited the scripture verses that had meant so much to her in the house. Her bones began to ache from cold, and a different sort of drowsiness tried to steal over her; she struggled and fought its deadly seduction.

"Lord, only *you* can help me; I trust you with my very life."

Wearily she stood up and tried to walk the distance from side to side to keep awake. Five times, ten times; she was growing numb. She rested. She forced herself to walk again. Walk. Walk. Walk. She rested. Walked. She sank down onto the dirt floor again and consciousness seeped away . . .

A draft of fresh air blew over her face. Someone touched her cold, cold cheek and picked up her hand.

"Brian! Brian McKennie! Here—she is here!"

Effortlessly she was lifted up, and the voice kept talking—to her—she imagined, but what was it saying? The words didn't make sense; they were strange, foreign . . .

Cold. Was she in the icy river again? No, James and the children were in the river. Where was she?

"Rose! Little Rose!" The voice called her urgently.

"Help me," she moaned. "Don't let me fall in the river . . ."

"Nei, Rose, I not let you fall," he murmured gently and held her close so his warmth would comfort her.

Then capable hands carried her through the bright light into the house. Fiona and Meg McKennie worked together to peel the cold, wet clothing from her body and put her in bed, where gradually life began to flow back into her chilled body.

Next morning Rose awoke to find Vera and Jacob Medford sitting near her.

"Ah! You're awake at last," Vera smiled.

"Yes." Rose frowned. "How did I get here?"

"The Thoresens and McKennies found you in the old soddy. Jacob and I have been watching you since this morning; Fiona and Meg were too tired to stay any longer but wouldn't go until we 'booted' them out."

She leaned over and covered Rose's hand with the quilt.

"You need to stay warm, Rose. And now I must get you some hot food and drink. Jacob will stay with you."

She got up, and Jacob moved to her chair and patted Rose's shoulder in a friendly manner.

"Mark Grader was here and his brother Orville," Rose fretted.

"We know, Rose. We know all about it now."

"Where are they? How did you know I needed help?"

"We didn't. Thoresens found out first. When they saw that Baron was shot up they—"

"Baron! What do you mean, Pastor? Tell me!" Rose pulled anxiously at his hand, and he held it tightly.

"Baron swam the creek and went to Thoresens'. I forgot you didn't know that."

"Do you mean he's not dead?" Rose was sobbing.

"Hey! Don't do that, Rose! Vera will hang me out to dry if she sees you doing that! No, he's not dead. Amalie patched him up even before they found you. You have to try to stop this, or I'll be in big trouble. Do you want to hear the rest?"

She nodded, tears of joy and relief dripping down her cheeks.

"Like I said, good old Baron swam across the creek (you can't even take a wagon over it still!) and, even though it must have taken him half the night, he crawled to Thoresens' where just before daybreak he set up a howl and a commotion that brought out the whole house."

Pastor Medford warmed to the tale. "I hear that Jan Thoresen was fit to be tied when he saw Baron was shot. He, Søren, and Karl forded the creek on their bays (I'm still not sure how they got across!), then they sent Karl on to fetch Brian McKennie. Mark Grader never even heard them coming when they broke in."

"He didn't put up a fight either and was already tied up when Brian and Karl got there. Grader kept saying he didn't know where you were—that you'd run out the night before, and he hadn't been able to find you. Brian and Jan searched the yard, the pasture, the ridge; they rode the fields between here and McKennies' back and forth, Karl and Søren helping them."

He sighed. "I guess you never really know what is going on inside someone until they are under pressure. Grader suggested that maybe you had tried to cross the creek on foot. Brian says Jan made like he was going to break Mark in half—and I think he could, you know. Scared Grader good! Just in case, Søren and little Karl rode down the creek apiece. That's when Brian remembered the soddy. Well, Jan got there first and ripped the door clean off. You were there, all right. Cold to the core."

Rose was quiet, looking out the window at the now blue sky and mounting sunshine. Thinking.

"And Orville Grader?" she asked finally.

Jacob coughed.

"Dead?"

He nodded soberly. "It seems the Baron gave as good as he got. Mark Grader didn't know how to stop the bleeding. It was pretty bad and, well, too bad for helping."

Rose stayed in bed that day, but got up the next. No sickness or fever developed from her exposure, so she dismissed with love and thanks the women who had taken turns being with her. When the creek went down several days later, Amalie and Uli brought Baron home in their wagon, Søren driving.

In her happiness to have Baron home, she hugged Søren, who blushed with embarrassment. All the Thoresens came to visit that week, doing the chores, caring and fussing over her.

All save Mr. Thoresen.

When Rose asked Uli how he was she answered vaguely, "Onkel is working. He's working lots right now, I think. He didn't even come in for lunch yesterday. But mostly he was walking in the cornfield. I saw him."

She looked at Rose, puzzled, but Rose shrugged her shoulders and didn't venture a reply.

Chapter 29

Everywhere Rose looked, across the neighboring fields, out onto the prairie, and her own back yard for that matter, all told her that the tumultuous spring was over; summer had at last arrived.

The precious, newborn green of the prairie grass was turning gold, the precursor to just plain brown. Even the water from the days of near-torrential rainfall had dried up. Corn that for weeks had been tender was shooting up quickly in the blazing sun.

Yes, it was warm! Her shrubs and garden required watering every day now. She fetched her two pails, (good old friends) and went to the pump.

Two buckets full would water her climber roses. They would bloom all season and then from the new canes they grew during the summer, give a second burst of color before winter. Two buckets more for the trumpet vine off the end of the porch, and the geranium pots on the bottom step were next.

She hummed to herself, thinking about the hoeing to be done when her watering was done. At least watering the green garden was easy.

As she straightened up from the geraniums, two men were walking through the Thoresens' cornfields—Søren and Jan—coming to her house. For the last several weeks Rose had not even had opportunity to speak to Jan. He had seemed strangely distant and unavailable.

The two men drew near, both reserved, and perhaps Søren was a bit uncomfortable when he said "Hello"? Jan was his normal self: deep, disquieting blue eyes that added no clues to his expressionless, steady gaze.

Neither one of them offered a reason for their visit, so Rose invited them in and put on a pot of coffee. She found herself carrying the brunt of the conversation because Jan merely sat, with his arms folded, and Søren, looking more distressed as the coffee perked, would only answer her questions "yes" or "no," saying little else.

"Amalie is fine?"

"Yes."

"Has anyone seen Harold and Sigrün recently?"

Søren muttered unintelligibly and nodded.

(A new tack) "The corn is growing well?"

"Yes." (sigh)

"How about those calves in your pasture? Aren't they getting big?"

No answer.

"I sometimes watch them in the morning. They are so frisky . . ."

Rose's heart began to quicken. She tried to keep up the facade, but was something terribly wrong? Her hands shook as she took down her lovely cups and saucers and set them on the table. She was afraid to ask or say anything further.

Søren just stared miserably at his feet.

Jan was looking at her, intent, unreadable.

Nervously, Rose licked her lips, set out the cream and sugar, and poured the coffee. No one moved, no one said a word. Rose glanced from Søren to Jan. Jan was still watching, silent. She put the pot on the stove and pulled her chair up to the table, sitting down.

Finally, Jan sugared his coffee as usual, no cream. When he finished stirring it he spoke to his son. Søren sat up straight and ran his hand through his hair in distraction.

"Like Tom," thought Rose and smiled fondly.

Søren's smile in return looked like his stomach hurt, and Rose shot him a quizzical look.

"Ah, Mrs. Brownlee, I ah . . ." His eyes pleaded with his father, but he received no look of relenting. Jan spoke to him again, and sipped his coffee. So far he was the only one even touching his beverage!

"Mrs. Brownlee," Søren began again, "I am here as my father's, ah, spokesperson. He wants to talk to you and is making me, I mean *using* me to translate." He sighed again. "I'm sorry—this isn't very comfortable for me, but, well anyway . . . you understand."

Rose's eyes widened. She didn't understand at all!

Jan spoke again; Søren sat up straight and repeated formally:

"From now on, please disregard me. I'll be saying what my father says, and you may answer him through me."

Perplexed, Rose nodded.

"Mrs. Brownlee, (this is my father speaking), the first time I saw you in church, I realized you were different from other women I knew. You had a hunger for God on your face. You were searching for him with all your heart."

All her heart? He had *seen* that? Startled, Rose turned to Søren, but he was fidgeting with his hands, embarrassed. She shifted her gaze to Jan. Their eyes locked, and he spoke directly to her, Søren translating.

"You were also grieving. I knew that because I, too, have grieved for loved ones. I saw it in you right away, and I prayed for you."

Prayed for her? Was there no end to the understanding of this man, to his depth? Rose was humbled.

"When we came to work on your house I saw you had character, determination, and a dream. You worked hard for your aspirations. You wanted to be the whole woman God created you to be, and I admired you for that. I tried to help you any way I could. I wanted to be your friend."

Jan paused. Søren paused. Rose waited.

"Are we friends?" he asked.

"Why, yes. Yes, of course," Rose stammered.

"Gud," Jan replied without waiting for Søren, then he continued, and Søren translated.

"Mrs. Brownlee, I have been alone for a long time now. The Bible says it's not good for a man (Søren choked in absolute mortification as he repeated these words to her) to be alone. I think it's not good for a woman either."

Rose sat up in astonishment. And there it was again! That determined glint she had seen at Sigrün's wedding.

"Once before I tried to speak of what is in my heart, the day at the river. But I blundered and you were still hurting and couldn't hear. Then when we couldn't find you the morning Baron came to us for help, I knew, I knew then that we must come to an understanding. I am your friend, but now (Søren stumbled over his words here), now I want to have you as my most precious friend. I must know if you could find that possible."

Unflinching, Jan's gaze held hers, and several minutes passed.

Rose's thoughts were awhirl. He'd not led her to think of him in that way . . . or had he? He'd always held himself so aloof, so, just so *friendly*. Yes, so *darned* friendly.

She frowned and looked away. This wasn't right—shouldn't a man declare his . . . intentions . . . to a woman himself? Poor Søren! She sighed. Yet how was a man to do so and tell her all, everything in his heart when language was such a barrier?

She frowned again. But how hard is it to learn the word "love"?

Rose shook herself into action.

"Søren. Would you please leave us? And thank you."

She didn't look at him. His job had been difficult enough.

When the door closed behind Søren's relieved back, Rose got up and went to the stove. Her coffee was cold. She lifted down another cup and filled it with fresh coffee, then she seated herself and stirred cream into it. Without looking toward Jan or saying anything she quietly sipped it. Minutes passed; her coffee was gone. Still she sat, waiting.

"Rose," softly.

Rose! The 'r' rolled lightly on his tongue the same way it had when he'd found her in the soddy. Her heart lurched a little. With difficulty she controlled her feelings and glanced up. His gaze was still intense, but guarded. Yes, still guarded! She looked back to her hands folded around her cup. The silence lengthened.

"Rose."

She could not look up again. A tear dropped onto the tablecloth. Another hung on her cheek.

His large, rough hand moved slowly toward her face and oh! so tenderly touched the tiny droplet.

"I luf you, Rose."

Ah, plainly said at last and surely written on his face? The strong features relaxed their vigilance; his blue, blue eyes at last echoed his heart. Rose and Jan stared, heart to heart.

Do I give myself to this man? Rose asked herself. *This man who has cared for me and been a friend on a deeper level than any I have ever had? Yes, I value his regard and companionship more than I have allowed myself to feel. Lord, is this the reason you brought me here, to this place?*

Jan pushed back his chair and stood to his feet, hand outstretched. She hesitated. What about the difference in their ages? His tall frame filled the room and denied his age.

"Rose. Vill you come . . . to me?"

She touched his offered hand, and he drew her up to himself, into his embrace, stroking her cheek, her hair, saying from his soul so many things she didn't understand but could feel. Her face was against the rough flannel of his shirt, and she felt his heart quickening with joy.

She looked up; he bent down to her.

"I will," she whispered.

He kissed her, tentatively, and again, surely, sealing their commitment. With Jan holding her small hand in his so-very-big one, they stepped outside and sat together on her front steps.

"Rose."

"Yes, Jan?" The first time to ever call him that!

He kissed her hand and held it close.

"My Rose."

"Yes, Jan." What contentment!

"I vill learn. To speak."

"Yes. I will learn, too."

"Speak Riksmaal?"

"Ja." (Giggle.)

"Ah! Rose?"

"Yes, Jan?"

"Am old man."

"Yes, Jan." What pain!

"I take care. Alvays."

Rose didn't understand. He waved his hand toward the fields and pastures across the creek.

"Mine. Yours too."

Oh! Yes, he would provide for her even if the ends of their lives did not come out evenly. He held her hand to his face, a sun and wind burned face. It didn't seem old to her now. It seemed . . . dear and noble.

"Rose."

"Yes, Jan?"

He was silent, so she searched for his question in his eyes—oh, she could read them now!

"Yes, I do. I love you, Jan."

Once more, sweetly and tenderly, he kissed her, then put her hand back in her lap.

"Vill next wedding be best, ja?"

Rose finally understood, and they laughed together, sharing the little memory that had puzzled Rose. As they tried, they found they could express one way or another what was uppermost in their hearts.

"You like live here?" he asked.

Rose surveyed her little domain, her yard, garden, tiny house.

"What about your farm? Amalie and the children?"

Soberly he considered. "New life now, t'ink." He scanned his property and home. "Close, can valk. Søren marry too. One year, two year. Bring bride home."

"Jan?"

"Ja, little Rose?"

"When . . . ?"

"Ah!" He grew mischievous, something Rose had only seen in unguarded moments with his brother's children.

"You like big man, me?" Chuckling at her discomfiture, he put his arms around her to draw her to him, then as quickly removed them. He was serious again.

"Rose."

"Yes, Jan?"

"Not vait much." There was longing in his look.

"No."

Chapter 30

Sleep was elusive that night. Rose tossed and turned until the early hours of the morning and, when she awakened, the sun was just melting the dew off the ground as she stared with longing across the fields to the house in the trees.

Would she see him today? Would he come?

Before noon Thoresens' buggy rattled down her lane into the yard. Beside Jan rode Uli, who jumped down, ran to Rose, and threw her sturdy little arms about Rose's waist in joy.

"Oh, Mrs. Brownlee," she whispered. "Onkel told me!"

"What did he tell you?" Rose whispered back.

"He told me that you are going to be *my* Aunt Rose. Is that right? Are you?"

Jan was standing back, listening to Uli's question and waiting.

Smiling at Jan, she answered Uli, "Yes, that's right. I'm going to be your Aunt Rose."

Wide was the smile he returned to her. He was dressed in his suit, hat in hand. His blonde hair, usually covered, contrasted vividly with his deeply tanned face.

"Uli," he called and gestured toward the buggy.

Clapping her hand over her mouth she skipped to the buggy, scampering back with an armful of pansies bundled up in a clean cotton cloth. Rich in fragrance, they were deep, silky purples and reds, glowing yellows and blues. Grinning, she handed them to Rose.

"For me, Uli?"

"They are from Onkel—he cut them himself this morning for you. He says you love flowers."

Rose stole a look at him again. "Yes, he is right; I do."

"Uli," he called again, "Go, take Snøfot play, takk."

"Yes, Onkel!" Uli ran obediently away.

Now he came and took her hand, kissing it tenderly. He held it and drew from his pocket something shining, golden, and blue. Jan slipped the ring on her finger and kissed her fingers again.

"My Rose!" he murmured.

The circlet set with sapphires sparkled in the light.

"It is beautiful, Jan."

He led her to the porch where they sat down together.

He still held her hand possessively.

"You come today?" he asked.

"Where are we going?"

"Come dinner—see fam'ly."

"Have you told them yet?"

His mouth creased into a slow smile. "Not tell—vit vords."

"Oh! Do you think they guess?"

"Søren, ja, Amalie . . ." He shrugged by the missing word. "Ve tell all fam'ly . . . both."

"Together."

"Ja," he smiled. "Toget'er."

"I should change my dress first."

He examined her and nodded. "Wear for me, please, dress from Sigrün's vedding?"

She agreed. "Jan, does Søren approve of us . . . does he like the idea?"

"Ja. He ver happy." Suddenly he grinned. "But not like be fat'er's . . ." frowning, he searched for a word. "Not like talk for fat'er," he chuckled as he concluded.

"No, I don't suppose so. I wonder, will he take you with him when he proposes to Meg?"

Jan astonished Rose by roaring with laughter. She had hardly ever heard him laugh out loud. It pleased her. Reluctantly, she went inside and changed, taking especial care in her toilet before declaring herself ready. When she stepped back outside, Jan was still seated on the step, and Baron lay beside him, head in Jan's lap.

"*Ve er venner,*" Jan explained. "Friends."

"He must love you now because you saved me that day." Sitting beside them she went on. "I never thanked you for that, Jan. I do thank you, you know."

"Ah, Rose." He pointed to his heart. "God bring you to me, make live, not die. I t'ank him I find you dat day. I luf you, little woman."

Arm in arm they strolled to the buggy, Jan calling for Uli, and they set out for his farm. Søren heard the buggy coming and was there to meet them.

Helping Rose down he said softly, "I wanted to be the first to say 'welcome to the family'." He kissed her cheek, a little awkwardly, but sincerely.

"Søren, that means so much. Thank you." She kissed him back, making him grin crookedly.

At the kitchen door Amalie stood. For once she didn't say anything. There was an anxious, unspoken question in her eyes. The family gathered and sat down to eat, and Jan blessed the meal. Then before the food was served, he stood up and called their attention.

The boys—Karl, with his hands on the biscuits, and Arnie and Kjell, both with serving spoons uplifted—looked up, surprised; Uli had a smug little grin plastered on her face.

"Fam'ly," Jan began, "haf happy news today. Soon," he glanced at Rose, "Mrs. Brünlee and I marry. She be mine vife." His blue eyes danced. "She be Aunt Rose for you."

Karl and Arnie were astounded, but Kjell let out a whoop and Uli clapped her hands in jubilation. Amalie pressed a satisfied and teary face against Rose's cheek while all three of the younger boys and Uli clamored for details until Jan spoke at length in Norwegian, answering the children's questions. Too excited to eat much while they discussed and planned, the food grew cold until Amalie insisted they eat or go hungry during the afternoon's work.

Chapter 31

Sunday, Rose greeted Meg and Fiona warmly, not saying anything out of the ordinary. Jan had buttonholed Pastor Medford and, out of the corner of her eye, she watched as he, in his normal mild manner, informed Jacob of the news. Pastor Medford's expression became in turn amazed and elated. Enthusiastically he pumped Jan's hand up and down while Jan remained nonplussed. Rose had to hide a giggle when Vera remarked,

"What can Jacob be so excited about? He's practically taking that man's arm off."

Considering Jan's stocky frame, Rose didn't think it likely!

Service began as usual with Rose sitting next to Amalie as she frequently did, only instead of a line of children between them and Jan, he took his rightful place beside her. She thrilled at his obvious (to her) satisfaction and glanced around. No one seemed the wiser. Even Harold and Sigrün just in front of them hadn't noticed. Only the four smirking faces next to Jan might give it away. She put a warning finger to her lips and they tried to restrain themselves.

At the close of his sermon, Jacob paused. When he had the congregation's notice he again shook his head in bemusement.

"Folks, I've been asked to make an announcement. There's going to be another wedding shortly."

Now he had their attention! Speculative glances considered Søren, Ivan, several of the other young men and women.

"Hrmm! Since I've only just been informed myself, I know you'll be as surprised and certainly as delighted as I am. Folks, I am happy to announce the upcoming marriage of Mrs. Rose Brownlee and Mr. Jan Thoresen!"

Amidst the burst of amazed congratulations, Sigrün turned in joyous tears and embraced Rose.

In her ear Rose heard a soft whisper, "Oh, Rose, you will make Onkel so happy!"

"What did you say?" Rose grasped Sigrün's shoulders. "Sigrün! You talked!"

A silence fell. In embarrassment, Sigrün shifted from one foot to the other. Everyone was watching, breathless.

"I'm so happy, Rose," she whispered again. "For you, for Onkel."

A roar of approval went around the congregation; Amalie and Sigrün clung to each other, weeping, while Harold pounded Søren on the back. The joy of their announcement was swallowed up in a greater event—a healed heart.

Every day after their engagement was announced, Jan would visit Rose. Sometimes in his work clothes, he would bring a lunch and they would picnic, talking and planning contentedly before he went back to the fields. Mostly though, he came of an evening, driving the buggy, in his dress clothes, and bearing a gift or some other sign of affection, courting her with all the "trimmings" of that time-honored institution. And always, Uli was with him.

Rose finally understood that from the very start, Jan's undeclared love had caused him to protect her reputation, never allowing appearances to give feed or fuel for evil talk.

On these evenings Jan would bring his Bibles, English and Norwegian, and they would spend happy hours sharing through verses. Jan was indefatigably tough on himself in the pursuit of English, and pushed himself to improve.

It was Jan who suggested that her house needed an addition and then drew up plans for a large bedroom to be built off the back of her present parlor-bedroom. When she approved of the idea, he went to work, bringing his tools in the evenings and laboring two or three hours before returning home. Rose was concerned that the summer farm work coupled with this extra was "too much" and said so. He laughed at her fears.

"I build for us; makes strong ever' day. Ven done, we marry."

Rose blushed like a girl over his motivation and loved him dearly. About his farm, his obligations to Amalie and the children they talked and prayed, too. Apparently Jan spent time with Søren and Amalie discussing it, for in a few days he told her,

"Dis year I vork vit Søren, Karl, Arnie, and Kjell. Next year I gif my farm to Søren. Karl, Arnie, and Kjell haf fat'er's part and become men for Amalie."

"But what will you do next year?"

"Ah." Taking her by the hand he led her toward the rise behind the house, playfully pulling her to run until she was breathless and giggling. Up the hill they trudged until they stood on the brow. Behind them in the hollow nestled Rose's little "farm" with the stream separating it from three hundred twenty acres of Thoresen land. But Jan's intent gaze swept over the fallow ground before them—Rose's fields, untouched for years.

"I farm dis," he stated calmly. The light of challenge gleamed in his eye, and he put his arm around Rose, drawing her close by his side.

She snuggled against his chest, reveling in the strength, the security. Stroking her hair he observed kindly, "Is hard life, Rose, for farmer's vife."

She smiled up into his face. "You know I'll try my best. And I'll eat gjetost the rest of my life just for you!"

"So! Still vant marry me?"

"Very much, Jan."

"Ven? Please say."

Rose thought for a minute. "On a Sunday, after church. Not a big wedding, like Sigrün's, just simple with all of our friends and family."

"And your fam'ly?"

She made a crooked smile. "I really don't think it would be possible."

He grunted noncommittally, "Sunday ven?"

"Three weeks?"

He agreed, folding her in his arms, kissing her firmly, seriously. "Ja, can vait."

The next evening Søren came with Jan and worked on the house. Together they finished the siding and Søren approved.

"Seems like old times, huh?" he teased. "There will be plenty of room for both of you when this is ready. In the fall we'll build a barn. A real one," he chuckled. "Then Father will bring some cows over for you."

By the end of the week it was finished.

"Vould like all house paint, now?" Jan inquired.

An image of next spring's flowering shrubs and trees against a shining, white house floated up before Rose.

"White? With green trim?"

"Ja. Do, two days."

Jan must have turned that day into a holiday, for after morning chores, the whole Thoresen family trooped over to paint. Amalie was as excited as Rose, chattering nonstop as she unpacked a lunch feast for them all. The primer coat went on before noon and needed to dry a few hours so the boys and Uli shed their shoes and socks and went wading in the creek.

Jan took Søren up the hill to discuss crops for the unplowed acres while Rose and Amalie made coffee and laid out the lunch. While the coffee was perking Rose showed Amalie the new room. It still smelled deliciously of fresh lumber. The walls and floors needed to be sanded and oiled so it was entirely empty, but Jan was going to get to that soon. He'd improved the pantry too, rebuilding the shelves, and replacing the flooring.

In fact, Rose realized that her house was as much Jan's as hers. She couldn't admire or brag on him more.

After lunch, the crew began to paint. Amalie, Rose, and Uli worked together on the lower half. Uli labored steadily, collecting little smears on her nose and chin.

Baron sniffed her work and came away looking much the same, to their amusement. Fondly Jan ruffled Uli's hair, and Rose felt a pang: the only father Uli had ever known would be leaving her. How glad Rose was that they would only be across the cornfields and creek from her. Steadily they worked.

"Halloo!" a feminine voice called. Søren jumped down from his ladder. It was Meg, riding one of the McKennie horses.

"Miss Rose, I'm deliverin' a telegram to ye. Mr. Bailey was bringin' it to me for he was knowin' I'd be goin' home tonight."

Concerned, Rose took the paper and opened it.

Arrive RiverBend for wedding approximately July 15.
Tom, Abigail, Jamie"

"Oh, Jan! Jan! They're coming! Tom and Abby and Jamie—they'll be here for our wedding! Oh, isn't it wonderful?"

"Ja, is gud. Make you ver happy?"

"Oh, it's just too good to be true, isn't it? I never expected Tom to decide to leave his business or . . . " A puzzled expression crossed her face. "But Jan, how did they know when the wedding was? We only decided last week and . . ."

A suspicious thought occurred to her. "Jan, how did they know?"

He raised his eyebrows innocently.

"Kjell! Come here, please, Kjell." The boy came forward obediently. "Kjell, did Onkel send a wire last week when you were in town?"

Kjell opened his mouth to answer, but Jan ran to him, threw him over his shoulder, and carried him off, tickling him unmercifully.

"That man!" Rose expostulated to Amalie and Søren. "Do you know, I'm sure he wired Tom and Abby to come!"

"Aren't you glad?" Søren grinned.

"Why, you must have been in on it!"

"Ja, ve all," Amalie returned demurely, and she and Søren laughed at Rose's discomfiture.

The Thursday evening before the wedding, Jan took Rose to town in his wagon. The sun had just set, leaving the sky awash with red, purple, and gold as the train steamed into the station. Mr. Bailey and the conductor began to unload freight while Rose anxiously searched for her brother and his family.

A few minutes later, grinning and hair disheveled as usual, Tom stepped down and waved. He turned and helped Abigail, who had Jamie in her arms, and Rose waited impatiently to hug them all. Tired and grimy from the long trip, they were nevertheless as happy as Rose was, who alternately laughed and cried over them.

Baby Jamie waved his hands and crowed amidst the confusion. Suddenly Rose remembered Jan. He was standing off a bit, hat in hand. That steady, scrutinizing look was on his face as he waited patiently.

"Tom, Abigail," Rose said proudly, "I would like you to meet Mr. Jan Thoresen, my fiancé. Jan, this is my brother Thomas, Abigail his wife, and little James."

A moment of discomfort passed as the two men took the other's measure. Jan spoke first as they shook hands.

"I am ver pleased to make your acquaintance, Mr. Blake," he said mildly.

Rose knew he must have worked out the sentence in advance.

Tom answered, a little patronizing, "A pleasure to meet you, sir. And I hope you are aware of what a great girl you are about to marry."

"Tom!" Abby remonstrated. She reached to shake Jan's hand, but Jan did not release Tom's and answered seriously.

"Am getting best vife in vorl'. Ve so glad you come. Make Rose ver happy."

A little shamed by Jan's graciousness, Tom gave in and nodded. Rose had chosen him and chosen well.

Little James was in Rose's arms, and she showed him to Jan. Jamie fixed his wide brown eyes on the big man who merely stared back steadily. After a few moments, Jan reached out for him, and

Jamie came willingly, grabbing for Jan's tie and jabbering to him. Exchanging approving looks, Tom and Abby went about collecting their luggage.

Twilight, stretching the prairie out limitlessly in the rich afterglow of sunset, descended on them as they drove to Rose's home. Abby exclaimed at its beauty.

"It's big," Tom marveled. "It seems almost endless. I can see so far!"

"Tomorrow I will show you around," Rose promised.

Tom and Abby stayed with Rose until Saturday afternoon. She drove them out in the country where seeing could speak louder than any description, and they in turn helped her with her chores and gardening. Jamie fell in love with Snowfoot and played with her ears and collar as often as the little goat would hold still for it. Snowfoot also completely fascinated Jamie when she ate the larger part of Jamie's straw hat. Baron remained safely aloof from the little guy who hadn't mastered walking yet, but kept close watch on him whenever he was outside as if he understood that Jamie needed supervision.

The visitors tasted fresh goat's milk and cheese (Tom and Abby both marveled at Rose's quick milking skill), enjoyed a Norwegian dinner with Thoresens', and had tea with the McKennie clan. The two days passed rapidly. Saturday evening Rose drove them to Mrs. Owens' where they would spend the rest of their visit.

The next day was Sunday, Rose and Jan's wedding day.

At the close of service, Jan took Rose by the arm and, standing before Pastor Medford and the congregation, they said their wedding vows.

Jan was calm; he repeated each line flawlessly. Rose's voice trembled and caught until Jan pressed her hand in reassurance. Stronger and sure, she finished. He bent low and kissed her, briefly, gently.

Family and friends crowded around them laughing, hugging, shaking Jan's hand, and kissing the bride. During this time Jan kept Rose's hand possessively in his, and she smiled at his steadfast "I don't care; I'm not letting go" expression when he returned her look.

They were ushered outside where tables laden with food awaited the whole company. It was a modest spread compared to Sigrün's wedding, but with plenty for all to enjoy themselves and eat their fill.

For about an hour they visited with their friends and received all the well-wishing they could ask for. Still Jan held Rose's hand, even when Uli, realizing Onkel wouldn't be coming home, clutched morosely at his leg. He boosted her up and held her, big girl that she was, with one arm and tickled her cheek with his rough chin. As he set her down he pointed to Rose's brother across the yard. He was in deep conversation with Jacob while Abigail and Vera were obviously discussing babies.

"Pastor and Tom gud friends today."

"Yes. Tom said he and Abby would spend the next few days with the Medfords seeing some of the country. If I know Pastor, Tom will be hearing all about the Lord, and we may see a new man emerge. I'm praying so."

"Ja, dat is gud. Ve go now?"

"Now?"

"Ja, if you please."

Rose glanced around. There was no reason not to, except for the little quiver in her stomach.

"All right."

Leaving her for the first time that day, he strode to the grove of trees where Prince was hitched to the buggy. In just a minute he returned, driving right into the yard where she stood. No one misunderstood his intention; he was taking his bride away. The crowd gathered around, kissing and hugging Rose goodbye.

Through the ladies pressing her, Tom made his way to Rose and whispered, "He's a fine gentleman, Rose. I wish you great joy." He took her arm and helped her into the buggy, and Jan and Rose drove away.

Outside town on the country road, the air was still and warm. Prince trotted briskly, for he knew this was the way home to his cool pasture. For the first few miles they relaxed in the quietness of the drive. Then Jan's arm went about her waist drawing her closer to him. He gently caressed her arm; she leaned her head on his shoulder.

At home they separated, Jan to the stable where he took care of Prince and moved Snowfoot's tether. Rose was in the house, first changing into a cool cotton dress, then trying to decide what needed doing. She ended up making coffee. When Jan came in they both felt a little self-conscious. Rose realized they'd never been alone in the house together except the day she had sent Søren home. Jan's bags were still by the door where he had left them in the morning as he arrived to drive her to church. He picked them up.

"I take care of clothes?"

Rose nodded. It was much too early for dinner; still, she began to peel potatoes anyway. In the new bedroom she heard the sounds of drawers opening and closing, Jan sitting on the bed causing the board to squeak. She had a pan of potatoes boiling merrily when he came out, changed from his suit into fresh work clothes. His empty bags he carried up to the loft.

"Need vater?" he asked when he came down.

"I think we have plenty for now, thank you."

Nodding, he roamed through the parlor, examining the books on the shelves, finally settling in her rocker in the kitchen. Baron settled beside the chair, content.

"Would you like some coffee?"

"Ja, takk takk."

She brought it to him, sugared just as he liked it.

He sipped it appreciatively.

"We'll have cold chicken and mashed potatoes with gravy tonight for supper if that suits you," she offered. "There's dry apple pie, too, made fresh yesterday."

He made approving sounds through another sip.

Rose went back to the stove to find something to do.

"Rose."

She stirred the bubbling pot and answered without turning around.

"Yes?"

"Come sit wit' me?"

He pulled her gently onto his lap and they rocked, just a little, back and forth. His arms were folded over her gently.

"My Rose like?"

"Umm-hmm." It was nice, just resting on his chest, feeling his whiskery cheek rasp against her hair and sniffing the clean, now familiar smell of his skin. They rocked together, the moment lengthening into a comfortable spell.

"Life ver long," Jan reflected. "Like prairie road. Go far, past can see?"

"Yes, I suppose so."

"It gud, know God go wit', all down long road. 'Round bend in road sometime is hurt, some bad t'ing. When years go by, I come to t'ink all love passed to me. No vife for me ever 'gain. Den, at next turn in road, I fin' you, little Rose."

He kissed the top of her head before going on. "Haf love you, Rose, for all time you here."

"Have you, Jan?" Rose turned so she could see his eyes, and he kissed her forehead.

"Ja, dear one. Now, today, you my own. No more lonely heart. Never leave Rose by self all vinter to cry and get thin."

She gladly lifted her face up for him to kiss again.

Chapter 32

Winter's first big blizzard stormed out of the north and blasted around their house. Jan bundled up and fought the flurry of blinding snow out to their new barn to do the chores while Baron broke trail just in front of him, barking and leaning into the wind. Besides Prince and Snowfoot, Jan's wagon team and two cows now occupied the barn and depended on Jan for their food, water, and milking.

Rose had learned how to make big, hearty breakfasts: hot cereal, eggs, bacon and ham, biscuits, butter, jam, milk and coffee were waiting for Jan when he stumbled into the pantry and shook off the snow and ice. He warmed a moment by the stove before they sat down to eat of their bounty. Sipping his second cup of coffee, Jan paused before bringing out the big Bible. He insisted on reading in English every morning to improve his pronunciation, and today he began:

> *Da vilderness and da solitary place shall be glad for dem;*
> *and da desert shall rejoi', and blossom as da rose.*
> *It shall blossom abundantly,*
> *and rejoi' even wid joy and singing:*
> *da glory of Lebanon shall be giv' unto it,*
> *da excellency of Carmel and Sharon,*
> *dey shall see da glory of da Lord,*
> *and da excellency of our Gott.*
> *And da ransom' of da Lord shall return,*
> *and come to Zion wid songs*
> *and everlasting joy upon der heads:*
> *dey shall obtain joy and gladness,*
> *and sorrow and sighing shall flee 'way.*

When he closed the book Rose laid her hand on his.
"Jan."
"Vat ist, little Rose?"
"I'm going to have a baby."
The slow smile that overspread his face brought tears to her eyes.
"Are you, little Rose?" His blue, blue eyes deepened. "Den ve are most blessed, ja?"

Name Pronunciation Guide

Amalie	Ah´-ma-lee
Gjetost	Yay-toost
Jan	Yahn
Kjell	Chell
Sigrün	Sig´-run
Søren	Soor-ren
Thoresen	Tor´-eh-sen
Uli	Yoo-lee

About the Author

Vikki Kestell is a writer and Bible teacher. She holds a Ph.D. in Organizational Learning and Instructional Technologies from the University of New Mexico and has more than 20 years of experience as a program manager and writing/communication professional in government, academia, semiconductor manufacturing, nonprofit organizations, and health care.

Dr. Kestell belongs to Tramway Community Church in Albuquerque, New Mexico, where she teaches an evening Bible study for working women. She and her husband Conrad Smith make their home in Albuquerque. Visit her website, **www.vikkikestell.com,** or on **Facebook** at www.facebook.com/TheWritingOfVikkiKestell.